The Little People and the MagDhuibhfinn[i] Earth Worm

GW00685606

A novel by

H M Barlin

ISBN: 978-1-7393612-0-4

First Edition

---

[i] Though it is spelled in an almost unreadable way – unless you're Irish – it is pronounced m'guffin.

DEDICATION

This story is about people who are othered. It is for all those past present and, undoubtedly, future lives turned upside down or destroyed by those who feel they are entitled to a bigger slice of the cake. It is for people whose religion, race, culture, language, caste, status, class, ethnicity, origins, skin colour, body or bone structure, hair type, sexual orientation, gender, abilities or disabilities are different from the 'normal' people who surround and – often – persecute them.

Specifically, it is for the First People, the First Nations, the aboriginal populations of the world.

For they have suffered most at the hands of the greedy and rapacious individuals – giants only in their own minds – amongst whom they are forced to live.

Contents

ABOUT THE AUTHOR

H M Barlin was born in South Africa and lived there until 1991. Years of growing up under the Apartheid regime were a lesson in how easy it is to assume privilege - but also in how to spot when others are doing it: education by immersion, if you will. In response he became a teacher and applied to teach Black children in the townships. However, those who had assumed the rulership of the country decided that an expensively-trained teacher should not be "wasted" on Black students.

After moving to the United Kingdom to participate in 'the greatest experiment ever made' – the European Union – he continued teaching English literature in Secondary schools. His interest soon refocused on his love of linguistics which became his main teaching focus and has strongly influenced the current novel's play with language.

This book was written after Brexit.

Chapter 1 |Xi!xu‡qe Arrives

It was going to rain. He could smell it, feel it on his skin, hear it, taste it. And the rain would come in the form of a storm born of a deep low that had brewed out in the eastern north Atlantic. He knew that, too. A child of the elements, |Xi!xu‡qe[i] felt weather in the marrow of his bones.

Across the aisle from him, a little girl huddling against her mother's side had no idea of any of this. Her eyes were glued, wide and wondering on the ugly, hairy little boy opposite her with his messy bits of chin-hair and a face like a prune! All his clothes were a kind of dirty brown…and he had no shoes on! The mother had kept her gaze tactfully averted except for the occasional involuntary, sidelong slide of her eyes. When questioned later, she would swear that the *creature* that had frightened her daughter was unlike any human being she had ever seen, that he seemed to read their thoughts. Like the Yoda character in that Star Wars movie: alien, menacing and impossibly old. And he wore a kind of animal skin cloak that was odd even in the multicultural world they lived in!

"Animal skin! Imagine!" she exclaimed to the policeman, looking around at the other passengers, dressed in 'normal' tee shirts and jeans, or tracksuits; there was a man in a sports jacket, a bit odd, but as she noticed more she became aware of a burqa clad woman beside a man in sort of pyjamas –

---

[i] Just say 'Kiku'. Nearly everyone else does. For the bold, there are notes on pronunciation at the end.

salwar-something, she thought – and a girl in a multicoloured sari, and even a tall man in a kilt. Weird. Still, the leather cloak-thing seemed to her unnecessarily outré. Eventually, the unwavering stare of the child got on |Xi!xu‡qe's nerves, which were already frazzled by the penetrating subsonic hum of the Holyhead-Dun Laoghaire ferry's engines. Although no one else was aware of it, the elephant-like rumble was well within |Xi!xu‡qe's audible range, and was a most unpleasant colour, besides. It made him think of river water after the hippopotamus had passed. It was nearly time, anyway. Gradually, out of the thrum of the ship's engines, a higher whine emerged, much higher than the ship's noise. Incredibly, the Giants around him seemed oblivious to that, too.

|Xi!xu‡qe knew what it was and what it meant, and whom. Only Magnus Kleynmans would approach the ferry in a helicopter. Even in a retrostabilised one. Especially in the teeth of the oncoming storm that the Giants must certainly have located and plotted. Kleynmans! The bloody man had been tracking |Xi!xu‡qe since he'd slipped across the border in Nabapeep, in the North Western Cape. His Sān Council Secret Service counterpart in the Griqua area, an agent - a rather fetching young woman, he'd thought to himself – called Krotoa, had briefed him about the B.O.S.S.[ii] operative, supplying a picture.

The helicopter whine was getting louder. He could even see the ears of the Giants attuning themselves to it, the tiny adjustments that Giants were, unbelievably, completely unaware of. He put the shiny wooden head of his knobkierrie[iii] into his armpit so it looked like a crutch and

---

[ii] Bureaux of States' Security. An umbrella security system cobbled together out of the old agencies. It is not always a harmonious federation.

[iii] A traditional fighting stick, common in Southern Africa. His would be about 90cm long surmounted by a ball of about 8cm in diameter and carved of solid ironwood.

hobbled away. Slipping into the toilet, |Xi!xu‡qe looked at his wristwatch. There was an hour to go before they docked in Dun Laoghaire. Obviously, Kleynmans would arrive on board well before that. A search would easily locate the Pygmy agent.

Washing his hands, he looked at himself in the mirror: in the service of deception, the scrappy beard could be shaved off, but the ravines around the nutmeg eyes hidden deep behind lower lids, the mahogany skin, exaggerated by long exposure to the desert sun.... There was no easy way of passing himself off as a Giant child. Not to someone looking for him. It had been done but usually with the help of the specialists at HQ. And there was his knobkierrie. Well, he used that as a crutch. It was a little short so he had to bend over – pitifully, he hoped – but |Xi!xu‡qe had to admit that it didn't look much like a crutch, especially the aluminium and grey plastic devices they made nowadays. He huddled over it, pasting a look of harmless innocence on his face.

It was going to come to a fight, then. Better to take it to them outside. Abandoning all other thoughts, he jerked the door open and hobbled out into the corridor. The stairway to the upper deck was almost directly opposite him. Up it and to the right was a door marked 'Crew Only'. It led to the upper outside deck, an earlier recce had revealed. Negotiating the stairs was a fraught business. Every two or three steps a Giant would lean down and offer help to the poor, disabled little boy. |Xi!xu‡qe smiled sweetly and assured them that he was used to it.

On the other side of the 'Crew Only' door was a metal staircase: down to the car decks, up to the crew quarters and onto the main navigation deck. The helipad was there. He pulled his kaross tightly around his shoulders. Experienced though he was in extreme weather, |Xi!xu‡qe was surprised by the vehemence of the wind when he stepped through the door. Clinging to the door handle, shoulder-high to him, he hopped over the raised threshold. To his left was a ladder with a chain strung across it. It led to the helipad. Above his head, he heard voices. They were preparing for the chopper's arrival. The smell of storm rain was strong now. With every gust, |Xi!xu‡qe grew less sure of his hastily made plan to stow away on the helicopter. Hiding on the ferry was beginning to feel like much the safer option.

Suddenly, it was on him, its stabilizer thrusters screaming, the vast clatter of its supersonic rotors slashing at the air. He huddled against the bulkhead; the helicopter was coming from the other side of the ship but, if the wind blew the bloody thing past its landing point, they would be looking directly down at him. Then the racket stabilised and began to diminish: it had landed.

Above the growing whistle of the wind, |Xi!xu‡qe could hear the voices of the men as they disembarked and greeted each other.

"Kleynmans, Ceptun. Think you for allowing me on board, men. Ah believe you've been briefed?" |Xi!xu‡qe couldn't mistake the flat vowels and rolled 'r's of the South African.

"Never heard of anything like it! Nothing this exciting ever happens on ferries!" The captain's voice was amused. He was having trouble taking all this seriously. "A little boy, they said you were looking for…"

"He might look like one, Captain, but he's not, I assure you." Kleynmans' voice was lower, threatening, "Kliklukli is a highly trained and lethal agent." |Xi!xu‡qe winced at the mangling of his name. Typical of Giant arrogance not to bother to learn how to say the name of an adversary.

"Well, alright." To his credit, the Captain sounded rather dubious. "We've had a look at the passenger list and there are no unaccompanied minors. My Purser here checked on that personally. Now you said that this deadly agent," the Captain was practically giggling, "was dark-skinned, wrinkled, carrying a club and about four and half feet tall. Right?"

"He would be passing himself off as a child but the club – knobkierrie – would be difficult to hide."

"As it happens, one of the crew saw a child rather like that but he was crippled – said he was unbelievably ugly – wondered what the parents might look like –"

"That'll be him. Ugly little brutes, bushmen."

On the deck below them, |Xi!xu‡qe was beginning to feel a bit insulted. In the picture Krotoa had given him, Kleynmans had a sunburnt, fleshy, slack-cheeked face with the nose of a hippopotamus and the wattles of a guinea fowl. Who was he calling ugly!

"He's down on the lower passenger deck…," another man, perhaps the Purser, said.

"Good. Corporal, take two men and fetch him. Keep your weapons concealed. Don't want to start a panic."

"I say," the Captain began to protest, "I can't say I like the thought of armed men among my passengers. He's tiny, you say. Surely three strapping soldier-types can handle him?"

"No chances, Captain. You've got no idea what this little bliksem[iv] can do. Go, corporal."

|Xi!xu‡qe tensed. There were two ladders to the deck above. He had chosen the one on the windward side, gambling on their choosing the one on the leeward side because it was more protected from the weather. Giants were lazy and hated discomfort of any kind. He was right, they doubled down the other side. Above, the Captain and the Purser quizzed Kleynmans while they waited. The B.O.S.S. agent was giving away nothing in the face of the sailors' curiosity.

At last, there was a clattering and the stamp of a boots on the metal deck. The soldiers were obviously Army rather than Marines, who would move more quietly.

[iv] Afrikaans: an exclamation expressive of surprise, shock, displeasure, etc.

"Nowhere to be seen, Sir," said the Corporal in a South African accent, "although a couple of people did say they have seen a little crippled boy going up the stairs from the lower deck…"

"Up? He'll be heading to crew areas to hide…"

"Impossible. The crew we questioned said their quarters are locked." The corporal at least was beginning to sound more confident.

"Yislaaik! Troep! You're starting to look rather green around the gills!" Kleynmans suddenly remarked, apparently to another of the landlubbers in his command. |Xi!xu‡qe heard a clatter of boots as the soldier bolted for the taffrail, heaving. Kleynmans' voice was more amused than alarmed, "Are you feeling a bit seasick?"

Suddenly a face appeared over the chain rail, looking down directly at |Xi!xu‡qe. The miserable eyes of the soldier grew round. He tried to get words out: "Heurgh!" was all he managed before the vomit stopped his mouth. Before the yellow stream reached the Sān operative, he was up the stairs. Grabbing the rail at the top in his left hand, he pivoted through the air, the kierrie singing in his right. There was a sharp click of wood on bone and the bewildered private crumpled. The other soldier dropped almost before he could move. The corporal was next, caught on the backswing with a sound like a driven golf ball. Glancing blows, all. Not death-blows.

All hell broke loose as the rain intensified. Sudden sheets obliterated the vision of the sailors, who were running up the ladder to the helipad, shouting. Instinctively, Kleynmans ducked a scything blow from the kierrie.

The captain was cringing back against the bulkhead in terror. To him it seemed the very wind had become a banshee, the rain a weapon.

"Quick," shrieked Kleynmans, all thought of his mission obliterated by the instinct for self-preservation, "on the chopper. Get us out of here!" he shouted at the pilot.

Among the Giants, he alone knew that he and a few civvie sailors would be no match for the Sān agent. Hell! He hadn't actually even seen the little bugger yet!

Within seconds, the machine's doors were sealed. Within minutes, its electric motors and turbo stabilisers were whining and screaming with the strain of lifting the machine into the storm-torn sky. As they lifted off the scene of chaos below, Kleynmans hoped the soldiers would be alright. There had been no chance of getting them on board. The ship's medic would look after them. If they were still alive. He knew that the head of a knobkierrie swung by a trained fighter like the Sān agent could reach nearly 200 kilometres an hour, generating nearly 1200 Newtons of force. Like having a 120-kilogram man stomp on your head with one heel! Odd then, he thought, that their skulls were not smashed in. "Get us back to Dún Laoghaire," he ordered, pronouncing the port's name 'loggery'. |Xi!xu‡qe's wasn't the only name he'd failed to master. "We'll try to catch him there."

But he didn't hold out much hope.

Not a metre behind him, in a storage locker that was accessed by an external hatch, the tiny form of the Sān agent clicked the latch shut and folded into the cramped space. The end of the journey would be uncomfortable but he was as good as there.

Chapter 2 MacBhreithiún and the Council

MacBhreithiún[i], Shadow Prime Minister of the shadow government of Pygmies, sang a little ditty as he made his way through the tall, early autumn grass. Now and then, he stopped to smell a daisy – a futile task but one for which he had no need to bend down, being little more than a metre tall. Besides, he rather relished the green, vegetable scent of them: it reminded him of artichokes with lemon butter. He had never seen a real artichoke but that hadn't stopped him obsessing over what he'd seen on TV. He was looking forward to passing the fuchsia bush he had spotted from the top of the cnoc[ii]. It was just over one of those annoying Giant fences.

When he reached the bottom of the hill, he stopped to smell the few flowers that were hanging through the wire strands of the fence. The tantalizingly edible scent of its red flowers made his tummy rumble. Light-headed with joy and coveting the mass of flowers on the other side of the fence, he bounded over the metal strands – straight onto a slope that he'd quite forgotten. Clutching wildly at the fuchsia branches, he narrowly avoided rolling onto the road at exactly the moment a huge, roaring steel behemoth raced past. Cursing, he scrabbled into the thicket of stems to avoid

---

[i] Pronounced 'MacBrown'
[ii] hill

8

being seen. But the car did not even slow down. Good. Being seen by a Giant always resulted in a furore and could result in the Council closing an area for months. Years, if a particularly obsessive Giant believed the sighting and camped out. Mind you, the recent tendency of such myth merchants to use trail camera traps had provided the Leprechauns with hours of fun.

"Fathaigh damanta salach!"[iii] MacBhreithiún cursed, "fouling the world with their revolting technologies." The bloody things had become even more dangerous since electric engines had stopped them belching toxic sound-clouds and stinking fumes. Craning his neck and looking over his left shoulder, he examined his seat. There was a new grass stain on his good new, wine-coloured trousers. "Bloody hell! And just as I'm after going to meet a VIP from the Security!". Mind you, it was a not unpleasing colour. Even matched the dark green of his coat, he thought. But this wasn't the time. He called down a particularly rich curse on the driver of the motor car. MacBhreithiún gazed ruefully at the profusion of deep red bells on the Deora Dé[iv] - tasty they looked sure, but his appetite had dissipated. Businesslike, now, the Elder rammed his formal hat – only slightly creased from being kept in his pocket – onto his red locks, looked left, then right, then left again (he always got that wrong) and flitted across the grey road, disappearing into the tall green grass of the Home Field.

"Who would that be coming in the long grass? Mac!" cried ÓCléirigh, leaping out of his chair, a huge grin spreading across his round face when an Taoiseach[v] appeared. "Cinnte[vi] I never thought to see you again after the

---

iii Dirty damned Giants
iv 'Tears of God'
v The Irish Prime Minister. A Little People title. Originally.
vi Sure

samhraidh céilí [vii]!"

"Why not, in God's name?" growled MacBhreithiún, "It was only a bloody dance. Bit of a party, maybe."

"Well, sure yer seemed a little unsteady like when yer left. And yer didn't show up at home for three weeks, Roisin said. Though she didn't seem particular peeved, mind you. No, not her, she didn't."

"Why don't you mind your own business, Clerk, and make sure the meeting room's ready?" MacBhreithiún was invariably infuriated within only a few moments of being in the company of the old – well, not really old: he just seemed so – pedant. ÓCléirigh behaved as though he was the recipient of 10,000 years of Leprechaun wisdom, whereas MacBhreithiún knew that the man's name and rank dated from the arrival of the Christian Giants, less than a thousand years before.

"Cinnte…"

"And stop using the Gaelic words you don't know the proper meaning of. You're causing the Elders to turn in their graves!"

But if ÓCléirigh heard him, he gave no indication. "… the list of delegates is at the place den chathaoirleach[viii]. Most are already here but the VIP has not yet arrived."

"What? I thought he'd been safely delivered to the Council's safe house?"

"Oh, he is already at the teach sábháilte…"

"English, dimwit! How many of the delegates speak Gaelic?"

"Ah, yes. That's true that is and a good point. I mean, he just hasn't arrived from there, yet." The clerk looked at his watch, which looked the size of an alarm clock on his wrist, "Though I think I might see him coming now."

[vii] The word is pronounced /kaylee/, should you ever be in Ireland. This one was the summer ceilidh.

[viii] of the chairman

10

Of course he could not see him, because |Xi!xu‡qe was still three fields away with his guard of Pygmy agents. Like many Pygmies, ÓCléirigh had been born with a degree of synesthesia. In his case, he saw sound as colour. Being untrained, though, he often confused which of the senses he was using. And, to be fair to the little functionary, MacBhreithiún could just hear the voices of the advance guard as they scouted the route ahead of the escort. Mr – Mr – whatshisname was an important guest.

"We've half an hour yet. I'll go on into the chamber, now. Assemble the others. We should discuss what we know about this man." The Chairman stomped off.

When the delegates were all seated at the curved tables, MacBhreithiún called them to order. Speaking English in deference to the Pygmies from mainland Europe, Scandinavia and Central Europe, he laid out the problem as quickly as he could.

"It's like this," he began, "this man has been sent by the Southern African branch of the SCSS – Sān Council Secret Service, for those of you who don't, well, aren't, well, erm English speaking – because Grand Council lines of communication appear to have been compromised. The failure of the Chinese, Japanese, Micronesian and North and South American delegates to attend the Nature forum has been traced to a very simple cause:…."

"Yes, we know," came the heavily accented but unmistakeably irritated voice of the Zlydzen[ix], "they didn't get invitations."

"…that is correct, Arsenei. In so far as it goes." MacBhreithiún paused massively. The chatter round the table – until then a soothing mauve colour – dropped to furtive violet. "The Security Council decided not to make it known that they had indeed all been invited – only, well…their invitations were for a date two weeks later than

---

[ix] Wikipedia is the source of much Pygmy folklore.

the actual date of the summit."

There was a silence.

"My heavens!" said the Welsh Bwca[x], the Cornish Bucca and the Scots Brunaidh simultaneously.

The Danish Nisse, Swedish Tomtenisse and the Norwegian Tomte uttered exclamations of surprise, or oaths (they alone knew which). Marjatta, a Finnish Tonttu, one of the Executives at the High Table, visibly blanched beneath her makeup.

Artyom the Domovoj broke in, "You are telling us that someone *altered* data of secret transmission on a secure-line?"

"Precisely," the Chairman said. The level of the clamour rose to shade of bilious green.

"That is not technical failure. That is enemy action,", the Domovoj announced.

"Someone has hacked our system, that is all. This has happened before – the Giants can be cunning..." an immaculately dressed, black-haired Pygmy said with a shrug.

"Hang on, Taotao Mo'na Inina[xi]." As Chairman, MacBhreithiún knew that the woman from Saipan expected a full title, "when we found out, we sent others, using other secured lines. All were altered – to your region *and the others*."

"Erm...er...why," Locryn stuttered into the silence that followed, "Didn't we just use Wavel to check? I thought that was secure...or whatever."

"Fair point, you might say," answered ÓCléirigh massively, "but there were attachments: the agenda, and a position paper, that were too big for Wavel..."

"So zom perrson," the Finnish Tonttu interrupted, then

---

[x] http://www.mythcreatures.co.uk/ is an interesting and informative site to visit.

[xi] 'ancient people'

paused to think, "Somebody *not* at soorrrce of emails must have do it. Because only to the easterrn departments: Asia, the Amerrigas. Everyone in the European departments get gorrrect date. Gommunication system is organized in deparrtments for exactly this reason of secoorrity. That points to the Eastern Department, then, because all vestern deparrtment get gorrect eenforrmation."

The Bwca (who thought of himself as something of a Pygmy historian) chimed in, "What's worse, much worse, is that the Pygmy communities in the Americas also got the wrong data. For they have been part of the Eastern Department – the Far East – since ancient times, before the Giants discovered America and decided to call it 'west'. This suggests that someone with Pygmy Council clearance did it, because the Giants think of America as west, not east."

"What?" Hugh the Brunaidh, looked confused.

Marjatta rolled her eyes and explained, in her Finnish accent: "Look: Giant would not teenk of Amerrriga as east. Eef Giant had sabotaged communication, message would have been rrreceived in *Beegmy Farrr East* by Memegwisi, Nimerrrigar, even Trrraugo. All of deese Beegmies arrre in west *forrr Giant*. Eet was not rrreceived by dem. Derrrefore, whoever sabotage email was teengking like Beegmy, not Giant."

"Thank you," ÓCléirigh broke into the shocked silence that followed her explanation. "To sum up, someone who knew that the Far East – the Americans – would also be affected is the saboteur. Because the Americans are important contributors in the climate emergency in terms of contributing CO_2 *and* bringing solutions to the table. Somebody wanted them OUT!"

The chamber erupted in a writhing rainbow of outraged noise.

"...that excludes a Giant...." ÓCléirigh, trying to establish reason in the chaos he had largely stoked, failed miserably.

"Councillors," called MacBhreithiún, banging the table in front of him, "you are all correct. I think we can conclude that the Eastern office is compromised. Now, because of the close historical links between some of the Western office –" he carefully directed his glance away from the Russian Domovoj, "- and the Americans, it has been decided to draft in a neutral agent from the Southern African department. In the name of caution. His name is –" The chairman glanced down at the sheaf of paper in front of him and his eyes widened – "tlip – klik – kluk – what the hell? For God's sake, ÓCléirigh put this up on the screen.

When the name came up on the interactive screen, there was a collective gasp. And then all the delegates of the Grand Council were trying hilariously to outdo each other pronouncing it:

ǀXiǃxuǂqe

Chapter 3 Kleynmans Reports

Agent Magnus Kleynmans stood in the darkened room facing screens and dials and all sorts of whatnot, as he would have dismissed it if asked. Coming from a Voortrekker heritage, fighters, frontiersmen and farmers, he claimed to have little patience with technology as a way of doing things. Certainly his bedraggled suit jacket and creased white shirt, open at the neck, supported his claim of rustic simplicity. Beside him was the suave figure of Peregrine Falcon, the B.O.S.S. Western Europe Security director. Kleynmans was impressed by the presence of the director. Secretly, though, he was even more impressed by the electronics that surrounded him.

A loose federation of world security services, the Bureaux of States' Security (B.O.S.S.) had money and an impressive surveillance and communication system. Chairmanship rotated amongst member states. Its physical centre was this theatre: HECTIc[i], as they called the room they were now standing in, allowed communication with any of the national security bureaux. It also housed sophisticated mobile phone and satellite tracking systems. The hub of the Secure World Network, it was rumoured to have enough

---

[i] Headquarters Electronic Communications and Tactics Information chamber

computing power to analyse more data than currently existed in the world.

At that moment, they were all focused on the giant screen in the front of the room.

The arrival of Kleynmans at the SIS building, the European HQ in London, had not been comfortable. News of the farce on the ferry had reached the director. Peregrine Falcon had immediately called a meeting. Kleynmans was dragged into HECTIc and his boss, Balthazar Bartholomeus Bootha, the Sub-Saharan (Southern Africa) Head of Station, was called up. He answered the video call from his home with a large piece of boerewors sausage in one hand and a can of Castle lager in the other.

"Ja?" was his opening. He clearly expected a subordinate. When he saw Falcon's suit and tie, he dropped the sausage and beer. "Sorry, Sir, didn't expect you on a beautiful day like this."

"Idiot!" hissed Falcon, "I'm in London, 6000 miles away. It's raining here, you numbskull! We're not having barbecues!"

"Not a barbecue, Sir. A braai. Nasty things, barbecues…those pink sausages you have put factor 50 on to cook…"

"Bootha!"

"Sorry, Meneer… umm, Sir! But they burn too quickly!"

The interview had gone downhill from there, irrevocably ruining the day for the Sub-Saharan (Southern Africa) HoS. A short exchange about recent events revealed that Bootha knew less than any of them about Kleynmans' quarry. The roasting that followed was interrupted when the screen split and the Secretary General of the UN appeared asking the same questions just as indignantly. The meeting ended in confusion, recriminations and threats. The European director cut the link and turned to the African agent.

"What the hell happened on the ferry, Kleynmans?"

"ǀXi!xuǂqe is a much more wily" – 'wahly' he said but took care to pronounce the San agent's name perfectly. He knew it would floor the director and he needed time – "opponent than what you might think, Sir." Specifically, he needed time to try and work out why ǀXi!xuǂqe merited so much attention at such high levels.

"This Chiclu...Kliklu....Tikootay..." Kleynmans left Falcon struggling then, magnanimously, rescued him: "We just call him Kiku, Sir, and in answer to your question: Ah took three marines to the ferry to ceptcha the operative because there was no – NO. ZE-ERO. – urgency in my mission. In fact, Ah had been told to just track him, originally. Whoever said to 'pick him up', as per the encrypted order...ja, well, no, obviously thought that he would be easy to arrest."

The director blanched then blushed violently and turned to the screen to hide his reaction. To Kleynmans, it was immediately obvious where the order had originated.

Sensing an advantage, Kleynmans continued quickly, "And Ah ended up with concussed marines in intensive care," he countered, "and there's a shipful of terrified sailors and mystified ship's officers, *all civilians*, who hev already spread their version of the story halfway round the world."

"Who does the Sān work for?" A voice from behind Kleynmans said in an American accent. Turning, he realised that there were two other figures in the gloomy recess of the HECTIc. Unable to make out their faces, he turned back to Falcon.

"Answer the question, Special Agent Kleynmans," the figure said. There was a threat in his voice that told Kleynmans that these were serious people and that the director was not about to save him.

"He is en agent of the Grend Council of Pygmy Peoples, Sir. Specifically, he is an officer in Sen Council Secret Service."

"He's an LP?" said the First Dark Figure

"A what?" said Kleynmans.

The First Dark Figure sighed. "LP, Kleynmans: Liddle People, or Perrson, in his case. The Sān are not the only Pygmies. It's hard to know how many there are worldwide but worldwide they are. Their Grand Council sounds like a government but it is completely decentralised, with no physical seat. As far as we know, it represents other races of very small people – Pygmies is a blanket term they call themselves. We're not sure how powerful they arre. For thousands of years, we've lived separately from them. They have avoided us since the 6th century BCE because, so the story goes, we won a war against them that precipitated hundreds of years of hostilities between us and them. We – thad is, normal people – long believed that they'd been erradicaded by our forebears. Wrongly, as it turned out in the '50s when we stumbled on one of their bases in Arizona. Area 51. You may have heard of it."

"You mean the aliens are ectually tokoloshes[ii]? But the tokoloshi is just a story!" "'Pygmy' is just another name

---

[ii] In certain Bantu cultures, a 'mythical' water spirit about 120 cm high who is said to steal the life of people as they slept in their huts. It is now understood that such people died of the carbon monoxide build-up of from their fires. Obviously, Pygmies had nothing to do with it but the Southern African PPSS adopted the title as a designation equivalent to the mythical '007' designation.

for Bushmen, isn't it? Shorly, the SCSS is only local, Bushmen fahting for their lend...?" Kleynmans mumbled. Surprise had made him forget his accent; and he was flabbergasted: Bootha had told him, his training had been clear...surely such little beings.... "End wha is it such a prroblem? Surely they can't be thet dange –" he remembered the attack on the ferry. If |Xi!xu‡qe was just one example of a 'Pygmy' agent.... Slowly the truth started to dawn on him.

The other figure broke in. She was an English woman by her voice, well-spoken: "Intelligence suggests that the LPs are co-operating to plan a big event. We want to know what it is and he's our only real lead. Knowing why he is travelling might enable us to prepare countermeasures." The speaker looked at her companion. "For as long as we have known about them, they have stayed carefully in the shadows. They haven't bothered us even though they have clearly developed some fairly sophisticated technology. And stolen a lot from us. Of course, we kept their existence secret so as not to start a panic. Or some kind of vigilante war. You know what people are like," she paused to let them imagine the scenario. "Equally, we can't let them band together, centralise. Apart from the fact that it would be impossible to conceal their existence, a summit of Pygmy peoples could be problematic for the human race: they're living in the midst of us, in our forests and parklands..."

"Problematic? Disastrous, my people think," the American sounded grim. "We have liddle idea what they know about our security and...everything else.... They may be planning to overrun us for all we know. Probably are."

"Well, we have no reason to expect an attack. We've never taken them as a serious threat before," said the woman, reasonably. "They've never presented any difficulty."

"Or not to expect one, an attack. Otherwise why did they steal our technology? Why are they suddenly sending agents across the world?"

"*An* agent. Maybe. We don't know," said the well-spoken English woman. "Anyway, that's why your mission was to capture him once he reached British waters."

Head still reeling as he tried to assimilate this whole new world, Kleynmans struggled to regain objectivity. "Wot hes he said? Wha was he coming? What was so important thet he would maim mah men?"

The HoS took over: "We don't know. We haven't caught him."

"But he was on the boat. He hed no escape. He must hev been there when the fairy docked!"

"He wasn't. We quarantined the ferry – some story about a new Covid variant – and searched it from top to bottom. Took two platoons 8 hours. Not a thing. But we found where he went."

"Wheh?" But Kleynmans was no fool. He had already guessed what had happened.

"Forensics found DNA consistent with LP in the storage locker of your helicopter."

"Clever little bugger. The atteck was a feint. A dawversion." There was a brief silence.

"Exactly. Anyway," the Second Dark Figure stood up and walked into the light, "we need to know what he's doing here. What the LP are up to. I'm Lady Ward-Back, NSA. by the way."

"The Bruttish NSA?" Kleynmans asked, pointlessly, who else?

"Yes. And this is Jeff Heinzforth, Europe Bureau Chief, CIA."

"CIA?" Kleynmans was floundering. Two of the best funded and most powerful security outfits in the world. And the most ruthless.

"What's he – they – doing here?" Kleynmans stuttered turning to Peregrine Falcon and trying to calculate the magnitude of the job he had botched. "Wait! *You* sent me to follow him, didn't you? I dunno wha. Ah'm just surveillance. I didn't even know about Little People. I was just following orders."

"Whose orders?" For some reason, Kleynmans suddenly found the American's pronunciation of the 'r's in 'orders' more irritating than |Xi!xuǂqe' clicks.

"They came through mah boss, Balthazar Bootha. Encrrupted, he said."

"Did he tell you where they came from? Or how they knew this…Kiku…was coming?"

"No. Just wheh he would cross into Sa'th Efrica."

Everyone turned to Falcon. "And I just received an HQ encrypt that he was to be arrested on the ferry," said the European chief.

"So, gentlemen," Lady Ward-Back spoke for the first time, "two orders were received by two B.O.S.S. HoS's concerning the same mission. A mission we know practically nothing about." She sounded like a teacher explaining to particularly slow pupils. "But we do know the GCPP has been trying to force our compliance with the Paris Climate Accord. The Sec Gen said as much behind the scenes at the UN: 'A summit of their own could influence our governments. Perhaps drag into the light our reluctance to move on fossil fuel extraction' *she* said." The NSA Director added her own insight: "They might very well be right, given our carbon output."

"So, the little s.o.b. is a messenger between branches of the GCPP – the southern branch…and who? We need that message!" An insight from Heinzforth.

"S.O.B.?" Lady Ward-Back looked disgusted at the archaic initialism.

"Sorry," said Heinzforth, his voice dripping insincerity.

Kleynmans cut in, "I big yaw pawden, Ma'am…"

"What?" interjected Heinzforth.

"Obviously, something is going on that requires personal contact rather than electronic," the South African continued, focusing on his accent. "The…er…LPs are in trouble! They're trying to organise something – maybe the climate thing – and they've got a mole. You say we're trying to prevent this gathering – summit – whatever you call it. And someone seems to think this is our only chance: stop Kiku, we stop the summit, or whatever. Only we don't know where all the information comes from. We don't know why we're chasing this little oke, or even how we know about him."

"'Oke'?" Lady Ward-Back looked perplexed. But the Shadowy Figures and the B.O.S.S. European Head of Station looked at each other. Who? That was the question. It was all decidedly peculiar. Was someone trying to help them? A Little People traitor? Why not just contact them direct? Or was it one of their own?

Why had there been no warning beyond the bogus – were they bogus? – orders to stop the Sub-Saharan Pygmy?

Chapter 4 |Xi!xu‡qe's Mission

"Wha' in the naime of Nodens uz tha'!" shrieked the Brownie, Hugh, in his thick Glaswegian accent.

"Mein Gott! Hieroglyphics?" Thebault the Kobold had his head in his hands. The Bwca, Afallon, and his cousin, Locryn the Bucca, were rolling on the floor laughing.

"Who ever see name like that?" asked the Domovyk, Heorhiy.

The door at the back of the round assembly room slammed open and a cohort of Goblin and Gnome guards marched in, halted, inward-wheeled and stood to attention. Through the ranks, the bemused looking Sān walked into the room.

"Good day. My name is |Xi!xu‡qe," said the Pygmy. He stood about 30 centimetres taller than most of the delegates.

There was pandemonium. Afallon and Locryn screamed, "A Giant!" and dived under the nearest table, banging their heads together.

Hugh's eyes widened, "Help ma boab! You say…wha'?" was all he could get out.

Thebault and Heorhiy broke into a central European Slavic patois that sounded suspiciously like a stream of imprecations.

MacBhreithiún was momentarily spellbound but, recognising the potential for insult, recovered quickly. Personal insults about height were universally regarded by the Pygmy peoples as beyond the pale and could lead to whole cultures not talking to each other for generations.

"Ladies, gentlemen, what on earth do you think you're doing? He's one of us, see? This is… Kikuke?"

"|Xi!xu‡qe," clicked the agent, marching up to the table and standing in front of the screen that bore his name. He picked up the attendance list and stylus and wrote on the interactive surface:

Домовик
Zlydzen
Нарбут
Hugh
Afallon

By the time he had finished, the room was almost silent. "Please explain to me," he said, "how you pronounce these words."

The delegates looked sheepishly at each other.

"You can call me 'Kiku' to make it easier on your simple tongues." |Xi!xu‡qe, henceforth Kiku, smiled angelically.

"And on that note, tea!" announced the chairman.

|Xi!xu‡qe looked at him in amazement. Clearly, 'tea!' was another of many cultural hurdles to be cleared.

"Just say MacBrown," said MacBhreithiún, steering |Xi!xu‡qe towards the table by his elbow. "And, by the way, why did you not have my name up there? It's no easier to say."

"I would not insult my superiors by questioning their manners," replied the Sān.

Catching |Xi!xu‡qe's hint at his own superiority, MacBrown clapped him on the shoulder, "I've a notion we're going to get along famously."

Over tea, |Xi!xu‡qe asked MacBhreithiún to explain some of the rules for pronouncing the names of other delegates.

"Call me, Mac," began the chairman, "and by the way, like, I'm a Clurichaun, coming as I do from the South. And

24

my name is Owen, spelled E-o-i-n, in fact. But don't let all these shenanigans with names bother you, you know. It's all regional. Take Afallon. He's from Wales or thereabouts and they took on the very early Breton version of a Celtic language. Same as the Cornish, don't you know? Now they, the Cornish that would be, call themselves Bucca, spelled B-U-C-C-A and so does Afallon but he spells it in the old Welsh way B-W-C-A. Do you get it now?"

|Xi!xu‡qe's head was spinning. "I can write several languages and speak more but I have never encountered this before. You say the Bucca is Avaggglon…. That's like Afrikaans."

"Hang on a mo, there. You don't have to be tearing out your tonsils saying that. It's a soft 'g' like you're letting the air gently caress the back of your throat. And he's a Bwca, not a Bucca."

"What? Those words sound the same. Exactly!"

"Ah, that may be," admonished MacBhreithiún the Clurichaun, "when you say them. But they're very different creatures and don't let them hear you mix them up or it's shirty they'll get."

|Xi!xu‡qe wasn't buying any of that: "Now you're just trying to sound like Yoda!"

The look on Brown's face could only be described as rueful. "To tell you the truth, it's Yoda was made to sound like us. Though they only picked one bit of grammar, being American and Giants *and* unaware of the range of regional epistructural variation." By the end of this utterance, his shoulders were hunched dejectedly and his voice sounded angry. "Giants. Ignorant." he muttered. "And I don't suppose *his* green colour and small size are accidental…there's them thinkin' everyone's a leprechaun, and green with it…. Parochial!" Clearly the matter was a painful one that had been frequently dissected. "But that's Giants for you: take it over, rip the guts out of it and crow about what you've made. Ah, well. Anyway, we'd better get on with this meeting. No time to dwell, and all that."

|Xi!xu‡qe decided he wouldn't try to pursue the issue. In fact, he thought, he would never raise the language thing again. It hurt too much – and evidently not only his own head, either...

The conference went on for the rest of the morning and well into the afternoon. In the end, they had decided that Marjatta was correct in her assessment: someone in the Eastern Department was stopping the messages of the Grand Council from reaching the Eastern Region. They discussed why this might be happening for some time but it always came back to the same thing: who would want to prevent a meeting of Pygmy representatives if not the Giants? And who would want specifically to keep major polluters like China, the USA, Brazil, Argentina and Venezuela *out* of the loop?

"Most likely, then, the Giants are at the root of it," Peyton the Brownie suggested, "given that the planet summit is about ways of mitigating the climate change caused by Giant economic activity. They have powerful groups – lobbyists, they call them – whose work it is to influence politicians. Obviously, no politician needs a lobbyist to get them to do the right thing, the thing that is beneficial to everyone, the thing they've been elected to do: protect the world! Many retired Giant politicians are paid to influence their governments; often, they even do so in contradiction to what they stood for while in power themselves!"

Torbjorn the Tomtenisse was inclined to agree. "They have been logging Swedish forests for decades and the whole land has become warmer. They do not notice it but we do. Now the snow settles later and melts sooner. The Giants do not see what is does to the young animals, either." His eyes filled with tears.

Thebault the Kobold, who was a systems analyst by trade, muttered something about the permafrost then put up a piece of code on the screen from his laptop. "I am importing a routine which I wrote that draws together and compares the GC outgoing messages," he explained in his precise English. The screen was suddenly awash with thousands of messages flashing up. "Here is the electronic traffic between Pygmies – or Pygmy computers, anyway. Let us narrow that down to the period of the summit announcement." A flurry of typing. The majority of the messages disappeared. "Now let us select only those that mention the climate summit." More typing. "There you are." Kobold sat back.

There was a period of silence as the delegates looked at the screen.

"But they're not all the same. Weren't they all the same? I can see the message we got in Gotland," Disa the Di sma squeaked in his high voice.

"Yes," the Kentish Kloker announced, "but those ones have got different dates – the wrong date!" There was a murmur of confusion.

The Kobold took over again, "Let's separate the GCSS HQ one – that's the template that we were all sent ours from – and all the ones that have a different date from that." This time the typing took a little longer. "Damn!" said the Kobold, "This bloody C++. It was so much easier in COBOL." Though few understood what he was talking about, all murmured agreement. The messages on the screen arranged themselves into two columns.

"The ones on the left are different!" exclaimed Hugh the Brownie.

"…and they're all from the Eastern Region: China, Japan, Malaysia, the Pacific islands, Hawaii…" the Kloker read them off.

"…and the whole of the Americas, North and South: the Mannegishi, the Memegwaans, Jogahoh, Nimerigar, Pombéro, Trauco..." Hugh butted in.

MacBhreithiún stepped up to the podium, "And, of course, these are all the LPs who complained that they had been left out the original summit. And they're not all here, either."

"Effectively, we knew that from because they did not come but it is interestink to see whole confusion resulted from one source," Arsenei the Zlydzen droned in his morose voice, "The question is, who changink message? It cannot have been Giant. How would Giant access messagink system at Eastern Rrregions headquarrrters? He would have stood out like shorrrt thumb." The delegates from the British Isles, who shared a childish sense of humour that they thought was sophisticated, struggled not to burst out laughing. Zlydzens were known to be sensitive, quick tempered and violent, which made them dreadful guests at parties. And dangerous to interrupt. "It must derrforrre be Pygmy vot is against climate summit or acting on behalf of certain Giants. We must find him and…neutrrralise."

None of the delegates liked the way the Zlydzen savoured the last word and all of them had reached the same conclusion long before his verbose analysis but all agreed enthusiastically anyway.

"The question would be – would it not? – who?" the Clurichaun chairman said from the dais.

"Someone cunning and murderous!" shouted the Domovoj.

"An assassin! I vote for Arsenei!" shouted the Tomte. The Zlydzen looked both proud and insulted simultaneously.

"Afallon!" called out Locryn the Bucca, who was rather more admiring of her Bwca cousin than was generally thought proper.

MacBhreithiún held up his hands, "Delegates! Delegates! You are too hasty, I should say. Too hasty by half!" When the hullabaloo had died down, he continued, "That is exactly why Kiku has been called from Southern Africa Region. It is the only region that seems to be both unaffected by the breach and geographically separate enough from the rest of us to be…er…what I mean is…I should like to say….er…"

"Trusted."

The word came from the back of the hall, where the stranger was sitting. The other delegates turned and looked at him in shock. Suggesting a Pygmy was dishonest was the most slanderous libel imaginable – in spite of the fact that most enjoyed or even lived off stealing things from Giants. That was Gathering, and a sport. Cheating or lying was wicked.

"Exactly," said the Clurichaun, defusing the situation. "And what is more, he is a to…tok…assassin!"

"I am a tokoloshe," said |Xi!xu‡qe. Remembering the inept language lecture over tea, his eyes and creased face folded into a smile at MacBhreithiún's difficulty. He looked like a child who has just seen his practical joke work.

"What's that when it's at home," the Cornish Elf challenged petulantly, tossing her head, "and how does it make you more trustworthy than the rest of us?"

"The impi of the tokoloshe requires absolute dedication to the achievement of the aims of the Grand Council of Pygmy Peoples no matter what is required. We are trained in all forms of martial arts, especially the knobkierrie."

"Impi?" several voices called out.

"It is the code of the warrior. In Japan, it is called Bushido."

"You are ninja!" shouted the Domovoj and his Polish cousin, the Domowik, simultaneously.

"No. A tokoloshe," |Xi!xu‡qe replied indignantly, as one might to overenthusiastic children. "Do I *look* like a ninja?" He drew himself to his full height of 132cm and looked down on the Pygmies around him.

There was no further discussion of the matter.

"So what are you going to do?" the Brownie, least intimidated, asked.

"I will take my orders from my elders in the Sān Council Secret Service department. We know that they cannot be part of the breach." The assembled Little People bristled. "It is believed that the leak is associated with GASP – the

29

Combined Security Defence Directorate of the former USSR." He looked in the direction of the Eastern European delegation.

Arsenei the Zlydzen nodded his head knowingly. The Belarussian Zlydzen, the Domovyk and the Domovoj looked nervous.

"We know that there are historic links between the Western European Giant security services and the KGB. Though enemies, they often established links. It is feared that the same philosophy might persist between some branches of GASP and elements of the Pygmy Peoples Secret Service in that region." The Domovoj looked serious and even Heorhiy the Ukrainian looked sheepish. "It's impossible to tell. My operation must necessarily remain covert, therefore."

No one in the room could think of any argument against this. One thing was easy to agree: the Pygmy Summit on Planetary Welfare, as it was formally known, must be reconvened and take place – soon.

The survival of the biosphere demanded it.

Chapter 5 |Xi!xuǂqe's Mission

When |Xi!xuǂqe got back to his room after the obligatory celebration cocktail party, he was musing about the idea that the Pygmy peoples had managed to pick up some of the more agreeable Giant habits, among them cocktails. Goblin cocktails were rather more earthy than he liked but the Pyxie ones made by the Torbjorn, the Swedish agent, were much more to his taste – like blossoms.

All this didn't stop him from noticing the blade of grass on the carpet in front of his door at the safehouse. He had stuck it to the bottom the door handle on leaving for the meeting. It was an old trick, a variation on the strand-of-hair-on-the-doorframe tell. Clearly, someone had been into his room. Standing well back, behind the doorframe, |Xi!xuǂqe turned the handle and nudged the door. It swung open a few inches. Nothing. No explosion. No gun shot. He pushed it harder. It swung open fully.

Still nothing.

The atmosphere tasted grey, neutral. Peeping round the corner, he sipped at the air. Someone had definitely been there. The taste was… Goblin? Listening carefully, he tuned into the air disturbances in the room. Though there was the residual hum of a living being, it had largely died down and was dim. There didn't seem to be anyone – or anything in the room.

But there definitely had been.

Deciding that real danger was unlikely, he nevertheless advanced cautiously into the room. The window was closed, as he had left it. Whoever had entered through the door had probably left by the door, too. And there was that lingering taste, and now the distinct colour, of Goblin. The only Goblins at the meeting had been the Zlydzen, Arsenei, and the PPSS agent, Peyton. Were there others lurking around the Leprechaun HQ? Of course, Eoin MacBhreithiún, 'Mac', himself, the Prime Minister: Leprechaun. An Elf. Surely Mrs Donoghue was too honourable; she had been polite, solicitous, friendly. He thought she was also an Elf, anyway. Not her, he concluded. Нарбут, the other Zlydzen. He pictured the name on the delegate list: Narboot, the Zlydzen pronounced it. Soft-spoken, gentle, he was old and very quiet, even shy: he was no assassin.

So: discount all the Council senior officers. Who was left: the Brownie Peyton? Undoubtedly pretty for a Goblin, who were given to snub, often blunt noses and chins. English Brownies like her were Goblins unlike Scottish Brunaidh or Cornish Bucca, who were Elves. Some distant history thing. She had been very clued up about the climate issue. Her comment about Giant behaviour, though…did that suggest too much knowledge of their activities? That she was too interested in Giant methods? Political? Enough to doubt her? Possibly.

The other Zlydzen, now: many in the Council had called for an assassin and their collective eye had lighted eagerly on Arsenei, who had turned out to be an ill-favoured, dark-browed Goblin in an incongruous green hat with a ridiculous white feather. But it was difficult to see how that marked him as traitorous, and many Pygmies wore hats. |Xi!xu‡qe thought of the pride, poorly masked as modest indignation, in the Goblin's face as they called for him to 'neutralize' the supposed Pygmy traitor. No one else really stuck out as likely to want to break into his room, even though he knew that several council members were also members of the PP secret service network. Some were even active agents.

So, Arsenei was one to be watched, if anyone.

He scouted around the little room. Though it would be difficult to use in the small space, he held his kierrie short. Opening the cupboard, he tensed, stepping back. His clothes. Probably put away by a chamberman, or maid. Dropping to the floor, he looked under the hanging garments. Nothing. Quickly he twisted his body to look under the bed frame. With the butt of his kierrie, he raised the hanging edge of the bedspread. Nothing came at him. He adjusted his eyes to the dark – a useful adaptation retained from evolution in the dark of the rainforests. A ball of fluff blew along the floor, disturbed by the movement of the cover.

Nothing else.

Puzzled, |Xi!xu‡qe turned to the last possible hiding place: the recessed basin in a 'hidden' cupboard. Perfect place for a trap. Standing well aside, he touched the curly gold handle of the door. Nothing. He swung the little door aside and a light flickered on.

Instantly, the Sān agent was in the middle of the room, his kierrie before him defensively. But there was nothing, just the little basin with its ridiculously overdone taps in the shape of gold daisies. Pyxie design, he thought. Pyxies were celebrated for their interior design flair.

Then he noticed it. Leaning against the side of the basin was an envelope. It had a crest: the Grand Council. Gingerly, he lifted it between two fingers. It was just an envelope. Deciding that he must take care to secure the doors of the basin-cupboard in future, he opened the flap. Inside there was a single sheet of paper. In messy writing in the middle of the sheet was a simple message.

Meet me at the main gate at midnight. Mac

Mac? Suddenly it struck him: Eoin MacBhreithiún! Of course: "I'm a Clurichaun, coming as I do from the South." Clurichauns weren't Leprechauns, except culturally. They weren't Elves. They were Goblins! |Xi!xu‡qe cursed himself

33

for a fool. Mistakes, forgetting, inattention could get you killed! He felt like he'd had had a lucky escape.

|Xi!xu‡qe sniffed the air. The moon was high in the sky. The earth was settling peacefully into swathes of indigo and violet. Over the interference of alcohol and cooking, he sensed the lateness of the hour. It must be nearly midnight. He checked his phone. Twenty-five to. Just time to wash up and get rid of the edges of the Pyxie's powerful cocktail.

Twenty minutes later, |Xi!xu‡qe stood in the deep shadow of an oak that must have been old when he was a boy. The sky was clear and the cold nipped silverly at his cheeks. He felt comfortable touching the gnarled bark of the stately old tree. Around him everything was cast in shades of lead, the moon stealing all colour. The Sān Dwarf was only marginally aware of that, though. His training and natural synesthesia meant he could use other senses. The pale green canopy of the oak sang in its clear note of A. It was, he mused as he wondered at the absence of any movement from the direction of the house – where was the Goblin? – the note settled on by western European Giants as the basis for tuning their musical instruments. What was it like, he wondered, to truly know only a fraction of the world? They must have been aware of it, though: the frequency – note – they had chosen could hardly have been accidental. All those eons surrounded by forests of that colour but not hearing its note at all? There must have been some level at which they heard it, sensed in it a natural note to make the centre of their music making. And the sequence of frequencies doubled – 220 Hz, then 440, 880, 1760 – to make the rest of the As on the piano keyboard. And as on the piano keyboard, the British had chosen it to subdivide the imperial mile after the Roman...

A movement rippled the shadows of the blackthorn that grew along the path.

Instantly his senses focused on it. The sound of the dark half-shape, its scent indiscernible, then clear as daylight –

the sharp hot stink of fox[i].

Then the lights went out.

All input from his eyes disappeared as a rough pair of hands covered them.

|Xi!xu‡qe froze.

"Ha Ha! Got you there, my lad!" cried Eoin MacBhreithiún, giggling. It was all the Sān could do not to throw him over his head into the gorse bushes across the way.

"Great Kaggen[2], Eoin! I nearly died of fright! I nearly killed you!"

"It's too nervous you are, Kiku. All this spy business getting to you, is it?"

"Well, you're the one who broke into my room. Can you blame me for being a little edgy?"

"Break in? Me! I've got a key for the rooms. No need to break in."

"Anyway, all this cloak and dagger meeting stuff…don't tell me you brought me out here to drink with you," he said, spying the little silver flask the Clurichaun had drawn from his coat pocket.

"No. No. Not at all. Though, if you fancy a nip, you're welcome," the little man reassured him, proffering the flask.

"Why did you want to see me? Like this?" He gestured around the tree. "And where were you? I had no sense of you at all."

"Why! In the tree, do you not know!" chortled the Goblin giggling with delight. He pointed to the darkest part of the tree. |Xi!xu‡qe reached out. It was a cleft in the trunk, large enough for someone as little as Eoin to fit into. It would have disguised his scent and the A of the oak disguised the note of his presence, too. Second time tonight, thought the agent, his face wrinkling in angry disapproval of himself. There is

---

[i] "The sharp hot stink of fox": for this synesthetic image, I thank Ted Hughes in his poem 'The Thought Fox'

much danger here.

"Anyway, be done with the shenanigans," MacBhreithiún put the flask away and took something else from his pocket. He held out a flat silver bar. The agent took it from him. It was a flat, featureless, shiny steel bar about 4 cm long, solid, with a ring at one end and a black plastic hollow at the other. An oval sticker bore the legend: 1 TB.

"It's a USB key," said the Sān.

"That's right," nodded Eoin, "such as will have a computer program loaded onto it. And, so it has: it's designed to reconfigure the messaging system of the Pygmy central government and override whatever it was as was done to it." The tone of his voice changed, became lower, confidential, "But there's another much more important file: the MagDhuibhfinn Earth Worm. It's the real mission you are here to fulfil. All that stuff about the summit is true enough but, well we could have WhatsApped them, or Waveled them, since the other one's owned by..."

Wavel, owned by a shell company whose overall owner was the NSA, had been set up to replace WhatsApp. It was offered as freeware to the world in the belief that this would make it less provocative of interagency suspicions. Ironically, it had been embraced by a number of other agencies, including the Grand Council of Pygmy Peoples and their security service, the PPSS. When this fact had become apparent, the NSA had been sorely tempted to eavesdrop on their 'allies'. In the end, however, they had resisted the temptation because that would have involved writing backdoors into the code that could have been used against them. Commonsense had prevailed: destroying the integrity of your own messaging service seemed like a stupid thing to do.

"Wait! Wait! Just go back a bit. Maguffin Earthworm?"

"MagDhuibhfinn, Kiku. MagDhuibhfinn. You're in Ireland now. It's pronounced MagDhuibhfinn."

"That's what I said!" In his indignation, |Xi!xu‡qe's voice

went up an octave.

MacBhreithiún gave him a long level look. "Sure. Sure you did. Anyway the Earth Worm – two words – is a Goblin technology. It's a worm." It was |Xi!xu‡qe's turn to stare, long, unwavering and sceptical at his companion, who sighed. "A worm," he said, "is a little program that can be loaded onto a computer where it will make copies of itself and attach them to other internet traffic from that computer. Then the copies will install themselves on the other computers it reaches and the network they're on. We're going to infect all the computers in the world."

Despite himself, it was all |Xi!xu‡qe could do not to hold the silver bar a little further away from his body. He had been taught about computer viruses and worms but nothing like this. "I know what a worm is, Eoin, but this is the maddest bloody thing I've ever heard in my life: sabotage on this scale will create utter chaos. You must see that there's something a teeny bit provocative about infecting all the Giant's computers? The GCPP might understand, just – but not the FBI and the NSA, and GASP, and B.O.S.S. and the Giants and all their governments will be incandescent with rage! There'll be retaliation – not all the Giants are oblivious to our existence. I'm being tracked by a Sub-Saharan B.O.S.S. agent right now." He was aware that he was flipping from one objection to another, that his was not exactly a calm or reasoned objection. But…calm? Reason? In the face of the maddest, most reckless, idiotic…it was the bloody poitin[ii], that's what it was! The GCPP were all drunk…. He paused exhausted, then finished: "And, in any case, the security systems will just catch it and eradicate it."

MacBhreithiún's calm response only seemed to |Xi!xu‡qe more psychotically insane: "Yes, we know about

---

[ii] A particularly vicious Irish moonshine.

Kleynmans. He shouldn't be a problem. But it'll be okay, you know: the MagDhuibhfinn. It's been proofed against any firewall or security software. We've been working on it for years."

"So you're going to bring down the world's computers? You're mad! What do you think the Giants' response will be? I'll tell you, the same as always: they'll blame one another and everyone else and start a war. We'll all be killed, if not as enemy – which we will be if they find out we did it! – then as collateral damage!"

"Relax, Kiku, you're getting well ahead of yourself. The MagDhuibhfinn isn't designed to damage anything. Just…tweak a few things."

There was a pause.

"Like?"

"You know all the smart apparatus the Giants have taken to with such alacrity? Alexa, Google, Hue, Hive, Nest, smart fridges, smart kettles, smart plugs, washing machines, cars? Everybody's making the bloody stuff! But imagine if we could tell all those things to turn the heating down, stop boiling the kettle the minute the bubbles start rather than going on for 20 seconds. Imagine if we could get the freezer to set itself a degree less freezing, the fridge at 6°C instead of 5°? The Giants had the idea themselves in the 00ies or the teenies, or whatever: do you remember the diesel engine particulates test scandal when those manufacturers cheated their engines to run cleaner when the test was going on? What if we could make all car computers set their running parameters to even less polluting levels? If mobile phones closed all apps that used energy when they were no longer being used? Or screens turned off a little faster? And that's not even talking about all the TVs left on standby, the charger plugs left plugged in, national power stations, even! There is almost nothing that couldn't be tweaked to run a bit cleaner, burn a bit dimmer, switch off a bit faster or more often. In other words: use a bit less energy."

|Xi!xu‡qe looked at the little man in his dark green almost-camouflage, tunic. "I see. So little by little, the Giants – "

"– and the Little People, mind! We're fewer, but not much better."

"– would be reducing their carbon footprint without necessarily even knowing it. That's brilliant!" he thought for a moment or two, "Only why not just load the MagDhuibhfinn onto one of your computers, then?"

"Ah, well, that bit was a bit technical for me but, for some reason that I don't understand…. Something about differences between our TCP/IP and theirs. It's why they had to access one of our mainframes to disrupt our communications. It's a deliberate variation we made, apparently, to stop them from hacking us. Apparently, we *could* do it but that would make it instantly traceable. You can imagine…"

"…what would happen if the Worm were traced back to a Pygmy machine! Why not any other Giant machine, though? Of course, it would bring down the wrath of the whole Giant establishment on whichever poor soul owned the machine."

"Exactly," the little Goblin's voice had gone soft, "that's why it needs to come from the most secure – and trusted – machine possible: one of the CIA the FBI or GASP or NSA central servers. If you can get it there and run it, there'll be much less reason for their firewalls and security software to notice and potentially raise the alarm. That's one reason. Another one is that the Giants will never be able to lay the blame at the door of anyone but themselves. That should redirect any suspicion and limit retaliation, especially if it's one of their most powerful!"

|Xi!xu‡qe looked dubious but couldn't think of any further objection.

"And would you look," MacBhreithiún continued, "we've already located the fastest most stonkingly powerful computer on the planet. That's where it will go. That's where it will have the fastest roll-out, making it even less possible to stop it."

"Where's that?"

"Ah, Kiku, would you take care now! Too much too soon. Too much too soon! For the moment, you are only going to the Americas to reconnect their systems with the Pygmy HQ. So let's leave it at this: you must prepare to travel to Canada tomorrow. ÓCléirigh, the buffoon, will supply you with codes, contact details and whatnot. In truth, even I am not allowed to know your destination in advance. It's all compartmentalised. But you'll hear from me. The girls and boys here will be given orders to pass onto you – in code, bloody ÓCléirigh insisted – for each step of your journey. Toronto. That's all I know. All they'll tell me..." The Clurichaun tucked his hands in his pockets and stalked off complaining into the night.

|Xi!xu‡qe was pleased the chairman hadn't been told more: already he had let slip what he did know: Toronto.

Back in his room, |Xi!xu‡qe turned the gleaming silver bar over in his hands. It was a brilliant plan, no doubt.

If that was the plan. If MacBhreithiún had been truthful. |Xi!xu‡qe was tempted to plug it into his tablet. He even went so far as to remove the machine from his leather shoulder bag. But what if? What if what the Clurichaun had told him was true? He might be bringing the wrath of every Giant security agency down on the seat of PP government.

Carefully. He split the seam at the bottom of his bag and inserted the USB. The housewife in the bedside drawer provided a means to sew up the seam.

Chapter 6 Jenny Miler

The next day, |Xi!xu‡qe set out for North America.
Toronto had been chosen, it turned out in his briefing on
the way to the airport, because the Mannegishi inhabited the
Northern Great Plains. It had also been felt that the city's
high population density would lessen the chance of
detection. Besides, the Mannegishi still had some residual
fondness for the British Pygmy clans. And Canada had a
much less aggressive immigration policy than America.
Also, they were seen as more understanding: an
unaccompanied child would be treated sympathetically. But
mostly because there was a long, porous border between the
two and, situated on Lake Ontario, Toronto offered several
points of access to it. Pygmies seldom used official channels
unless using public forms of transport. And disguises.

The Mannegishi, the Memegwesi, and their cousins the
Memegwaans, were among the oldest of the Pygmy peoples
outside Africa. They were fully conscious of their ancient
roots. In fact, |Xi!xu‡qe was advised to use the term 'Far
Eastern' carefully because it was a centuries-old coinage of
the Western European Pygmies who had arbitrarily decided
that their old settlements in the far west of Europe, Ireland
and the British mainland were The West and that everything
else was East.

After all, the impassable ocean – Pygmies weren't great
seafarers – meant you couldn't go any further west.

Naturally, after the flood submerged Doggerland, cutting
the British tribes off, the European Pygmies were forced to

re-colonised the lands back towards the rising sun, along the ancient land routes and into new lands. Any communities they founded were thus 'East'. As far as they were concerned, crossing the land bridge to the Americas was as far east as you could go before you reached another impassable ocean. They had no idea it was the same ocean.

Occupying the largest territory of any Pygmy group, the North Americans still called themselves the 'Little People'. The more generally acceptable modern term 'Pygmy' was used by the Southern Europeans, who rather relished the link to the Greek heroes.

It was decided that |Xi!xu‡qe would fly from Dublin.

The Sān Council Secret Service arranged the trip. After an uneventful journey on which, often dressed as a boy, he was lodged with a sympathetic Giant family of suitable complexion and stature who drove him to the airport and saw him through boarding as an unaccompanied child. The Air Canada staff were charming, polite and concerned. They saw him into his seat. They gave him a colouring book and plied him with soft drinks. |Xi!xu‡qe, who had developed something of taste for Jameson's Irish Whiskey, put up with it. He coloured some of the pictures in because the Giants seemed concerned that, after an hour, he hadn't done any colouring. They were pleased and relieved that he slept through most of the flight. When he awoke, covered in a blue and grey blanket, the plane was approaching Toronto Pearson.

A taxi had been called for him and, as he left the baggage reclaim accompanied by a smiling young air steward in her dark grey uniform, he saw a man with a large sign saying 'Xixuqe'.

"That's me," he said looking up at her and pointing.

"Oh, my goodness! Is that how you spell 'Kiku'? I had no idea. What language is that?"

But |Xi!xu‡qe had disappeared into the crowd with the driver.

Within the hour, he was in a room in the Marriott Fairfield Inn. Its non-descript cream walls, dark wood fittings and nauseous lime-green points were like a playroom, he thought.

Showering, he went over his next move: making contact and getting his onward-bound orders. He decided it would be better to leave his backpack in the room when he went. Its bright colours might attract attention and identify him as a child. It wouldn't do to have a concerned policeman decide he was lost and needed safe-keeping in a police station – a 'precinct' – somewhere. Besides, at least he was out of the reach of Kleynmans here. The B.O.S.S. man was still in Europe. Still in Ireland, for all he knew. There should be no difficulty in getting his new orders.

He had been instructed to meet his contact at Montana's "five minutes down Hurontario", they had said. |Xi!xu‡qe tucked his kierrie into his armpit and hobbled out of the hotel onto - Courtneypark Drive West. Suddenly, he wasn't so sure; he'd thought this was supposed to be Hurontario Street. The traffic whipped past in a steady stream. Disorientated, he turned right and walked. At an intersection, the road seemed to split. One way claimed to be Maritz Drive. The other was signposted Kateson Drive. There was no sign of Hurontario Street. He stood, wondering. As he was about to turn around and walk back past the hotel, a young woman, or girl, touched him on the shoulder. "Are you lost?" she asked gently.

"Yes. Thank you. I'm looking for Montana's?" The raised intonation at the end of the sentence came easily, he'd heard it so often since boarding the plane.

"Oh, yeah, sure. It's that way. You turn right at the junction…" Suddenly she stopped and seemed to appraise him. "I'll tell you what, I'll take you there, eh." This was less a suggestion than a factual statement.

"Oh, that won't be necessary. I seem to have turned the wrong way…"

"Say! You're not from around here! Are you English?" She seemed excited so he didn't correct her. "You here with your folks? And they just left you? Wow! You must be a clever boy for them to trust you like that!"

Somehow, her enthusiasm prevented him from snapping at her. 'Boy? I'm practically as tall as you!' he thought. And he was. Still.

"I'll show you," she said and, physically turning him around, started to walk him back the way he had come, chatting happily. "My name's Jenny. Jenny Miler. Not that you want to know. I live here so I know where Montana's is. It used to be one of my favourite places when I was a kid. Still go there sometimes. You meeting your folks? I must say, my folks wouldn't have let me wonder about Toronto in the evening when I was…. Say, how old are you?"

"Old enough for my parents to trust me not to get lost going from the hotel to this Montana's place." |Xi!xuǂqe looked at her, his eyes crinkled in laughter at himself.

"Right! That didn't work out, eh!" she laughed and continued chatting. He watched her out of the corner of his eyes. She really did look like a child. She looked like Abayomi, the child of his sister. He liked the sound of her voice, too, and let her chat on. At the very least, the way she spoke to him would give passers-by the impression she was 'the adult'. "There it is!" she announced pointing at a garishly over-lit building that looked like it might have come from a cowboy movie. "I better call my mother just to tell her I'll be late tonight. I was supposed to…." Her explanation trailed off as she opened her phone and pressed a speed dial number. He stepped tactfully away so as not to appear to be listening. But there seemed nothing in the call for him to worry about.

She snapped the phone shut and they walked to the front door. She went in with him. "Do you see them?" she said. They both craned their necks. |Xi!xuǂqe in a pretence, she in earnest even though she could not have known what she was looking for.

"Evening!" chirped a waitress in a red and white checked cowboy shirt, "Can I help you?"

"Hi! Yeah. We're expecting to join someone but we can't see them," Jenny answered with an odd sort of confidence. |Xi!xu‡qe had the feeling he'd picked up a 'friend'. Or been picked up?

"Oh, really?" the waitress answered, looking around as if she knew who to look for, "Do you just wanna sit and wait? Maybe they're delayed?"

"Yes," |Xi!xu‡qe took over, decisively, "that will be excellent. Thank you for your assistance, Jenny. I'll just wait for them."

"Ok. But what if they don't come? What if they've got lost? – are they also English? Are you all on holiday? – listen, I'll wait with you? I like talking to you," she added shyly.

It was clear to |Xi!xu‡qe by this time that neither Jenny nor the waitress were going to leave him alone. Choosing, he said, "Ok. Sure. That's fine. We could just sit down for a bit…?" He had no idea what he was going to say when his contact appeared. What if he, or she, was a Pygmy, as was entirely possible? How was he going to get rid of the girl who reminded him of Abayomi? Pleasant though it was to be reminded, so far from home, he must be alone in this.

By the time the food they'd ordered arrived, he had relaxed a little. Jenny turned out to be kind and entertaining. She seemed genuinely concerned about her 'little, lost boy'.

"Do you have their phone number? I could phone them. Or do you have a phone? Should we call the police? Aren't you worried? … I'd better let my mother know."

In fact, |Xi!xu‡qe was more relaxed than he had been since leaving the Kalahari. Somehow, the combination of having nothing to do but wait and the motherly fussing of Jenny made the non-appearance of his contact a blessing. As she spoke to her mother, he sat staring out of the window as the lights of the passing cars slowly flowed together to become a river of homeward bound workers. The drivers were scarcely visible in their cars but reflected light occasionally flashed details onto some of the faces: tired, strained, eager to get home, women, men, dishevelled or office-tidy, a balding head here, red lipstick there, dark-rimmed glasses, a mane of hair, a snub nose...

Suddenly, |Xi!xu‡qe sat bolt upright. Then stood and hurried to the window. He craned his neck, studying the snub-nosed profile in the front seat of the almost stationary saloon. There seemed to be a cerise aura of eager, angry anticipation around the man's head.

"Have they come? Can you see them?" Jenny was at his shoulder.

"Yes. He's come."

In the half dark interior of the car, the profile of Magnus Kleynmans slid slowly out of view, travelling in the direction of the Marriott Fairfield.

Chapter 7 First Contact

"I can't see them. Where are they?" Jenny seemed excited.

ǀXi!xuǂqe was sitting again. He understood now why his contact hadn't come. Maybe he should have realised instead of sitting here prattling with this girl. But what it was he should have realised, he was not sure. The plan had been left deliberately loose. That was a procedural basic in operations when the development of an agent in the field had to be matched to conditions. One order to the next, matching orders to conditions on the ground. The condition now was that Kleynmans had found him. How? No knowing, ǀXi!xuǂqe decided. Follow procedure.

"Jenny, I need to go to the loo – umm, bathroom."

"But what happens if your mom and dad…?"

"They won't." He left her beginning to mouth an objection.

In the cubicle, he dug out his phone. Sure enough, there was no message from his Controller in the Sān Council Secret Service. Could that mean they did not know about Kleynmans? Unless they did and that was why his contact hadn't shown up. Or perhaps, his contact *had* been blown. But even if he had, at least B.O.S.S. didn't know about the rendezvous point: Kleynmans had been headed to the hotel. Should he just sit and wait for the call? How long could he be in the restaurant?

The B.O.S.S. agent would stake out his room and wait for him.

How many others had been in the car? It had not been a taxi, so a driver, Kleynmans and perhaps two in the back. Four in total, probably. As if to reassure himself, he checked the leather bag on his shoulder, touched the base with the USB key sewn into it. Making a decision, he left the bathroom.

Back at the table, he managed to hush Jenny long enough to get her to listen.

"Listen, I'm not what you think I am. First of all, I'm not a child. Wait." She seemed on the verge of laughing. "Here." He freed the identity card from a concealed pocket in his jacket, "It's an ID card for the Service I work for. I was sent here…" But after only a cursory glance, Jenny had turned over the card and was looking at the introduction card he had attached to the back of it.

"This is Cree. Why have you got Cree on it?" if she hadn't been uneasy before, he thought, she was now.

"It's for my contact. The one we we're waiting for. A code," Lame, he thought, she had already recognised the language. She didn't comment. Probably didn't notice the lie. Why should she? "Only he won't come now."

In the end, ǀXi!xuǂqe told her about his mission to contact the Eastern Pygmy Peoples, leaving out the reasons.

"You can't say 'Pygmy'. It's racist!"

"Actually, Jenny, it's the word we use ourselves. See? 'Grand Council of Pygmy Peoples'. We adopted it from ancient Greek, after the destruction of our main trading post – a little town called Troy." She was goggling again. For Pisambaro's sake! Why did he have to explain this now. But he couldn't very well stop. "You may have heard of it. Of course, the Greeks turned it into a myth about their fighting some great and powerful nation. Homer's myth of Troy is that it was some heroic Greek war fought over bad manners. Nonsense. There was no Helen. No Paris. No abduction. They just wanted control over the Asian trade routes. Modern archaeologists – Schliemann to begin with – were

always puzzled about how puny Troy seems to have been…"
ǀXi!xuǂqe's mind slid angrily into the two thousand years of
lies and propaganda that had been used to wipe his race out.
"Anyway, making 'Pygmy' and 'Dwarf' politically incorrect
is another way of cancelling talk about the "Little People":
us – Notice the bias in the name? Same as the First Nations
were called 'Indians': they were something else; didn't
belong in 'America'…even after it was obvious the new
continent wasn't India. Like them we're people, but
impostors. Worse, not real people: *little* people, like
children. Inconsequential. Not to be taken seriously. Still,
some of us use the term interchangeably with 'Pygmy'.
Habit. And avoids confusion. Besides, we're not so small-
minded about names," he finished, shrugging.

He looked into Jenny's face. She seemed to be reeling.
Understandably. Imagine what it must be like to be asked to
recreate your whole view of the world. In a restaurant.

But he was in for a surprise.

"Right," said the little woman, "What do you need from
me?"

"What? How can you…? Why…?"

"Don't worry. I'll tell you when we have time. Right now,
I'm guessing we're in a hurry. Let's just say a whole lot of
my early life makes a lot more sense now than it ever has."

It took him ten minutes to explain that he was expecting
instructions concerning how to proceed. They would
certainly involve his having his passport, which was with his
clothes in the hotel, presumably watched by Kleynmans.
Together, they concocted a plan to get his rucksack from his
room.

"Obviously, you'll be instantly spotted if you go in."
Jenny said.

She was taking it to like a duck to water, ǀXi!xuǂqe
thought. He was amazed but didn't have – wasn't given? –
time to ask questions.

She would pose as a chamber maid. The first order of

business was to get a uniform. "It's evening, though," she said. "Not the time for chamber maids. But their uniforms will be in the basement changing rooms: I know that: I was a chamber maid when I as in college. All big hotels are the same."

Damned if she wasn't enjoying herself! he thought.

The entrance to the parking garage beneath the hotel was the first hurdle. There was one way in. Easy to watch. Doing so was one man, loitering on the ramp. Not for the first time in his career, |Xi!xu≠qe was thankful for the arrogance of the Giants. Jenny walked past the man, got her heel 'stuck' in a pavement grate and struggled helplessly. Of course, the man couldn't resist playing the gallant saviour. But by the time he had rescued her and tried a few of his lines, any suspicion he may have had was gone. She walked in, swaying. Finding the employees' changing room was easy. Most of the lockers weren't even locked.

Within half an hour, Jenny was standing at the employee entrance, knocking.

"Where's your ID card? What are you doing here?" the angry-looking duty housekeeper scolded, emerging from her office.

"I forgot to bring it. I'm from the day shift. They called me in – someone at the front desk. Apparently there's a bit of a situation in the penthouse suite –," Jenny rolled her eyes in mock frustration at the excesses of the wealthy, "–and they're in a hurry for…"

"Ok. Go quickly. Wait!" Jenny froze as the woman turned and went into her office.

"You'll need this if you don't have a passcard." She studied Jenny narrowly. "Do. Not. Forget to bring it back!"

"No, ma'am," said Jenny, curtsying subserviently. Behind her back the woman smiled. Where do they get them, she wondered. Sweet little thing, though. So polite.

Finally in the lift, Jenny pressed the button to the 5th floor, where |Xi!xu≠qe's room was.

As the door opened, a man in darkish clothes turned to look at her. He quickly put his hand into his windcheater. With only a moment's hesitation, Jenny stepped out, looked exaggeratedly at the floor identifier, smiled brightly at him and said, "Silly me! Wrong floor!" stepped back into the lift and pressed 6, 8 and 9. As the doors closed, the man started walking quickly towards her.

She ran out of the lift on the next floor, hitting the door close button as she left, then swiped the passcard to get into the service staircase. As the door closed, she saw the guests' fire escape door open and her pursuer run out, catch the number on the lift indicator and run back into the stairwell. She headed down the stairs.

Back on the fifth floor, she hurried to 511, Kiku's room. Swiping her passcard, saying a quick prayer, she stepped in. Out of the corridor, she leaned against the restroom door and took a breath. Then she went cautiously into the room.

Standing at the foot of the bed, back to her, was a large man. He turned and she was staring into the brick-red, snub-nosed face of a middle-aged man. His eyes narrowed, glittering dangerously.

"Good evening, sir," she said, struggling to steady her voice. This must by Kleynmans. Her mind was going like a rocket. What to do?

"Who are you?" There was something about his accent that reminded her of |Xi!xu‡qe.

"Chamber service, sir. I was sent here by Housekeeping, sir. To make the bed?" As she said this, she looked at the perfectly made bed. The man gestured at it. An interrogation. A threat. "Oh! That's odd, sir. There must be some mistake…"

"Aw you sure about thet?" he sneered, "Or is thus some kahnd of trick?" His eyes narrowed into ravines and the sunburnt plane of his forehead wrinkled.

"A kind of trick?" Jenny looked horrified at the very thought, "Oh, no, sir. I'm sure they've just given me the wrong instruction. Or room?"

"Ok. Well, bugger off!" The rubbery lower lip flapped moistly in dismissal.

"Oh. Erm, they might have just misunderstood the problem." She fussed officiously, "I'd better check the bathroom and the trouser press. That's where most problems happen. Or the window. Or maybe.... My job.... Er, better cover all bases?"

"Wait! Whadda you mean the trouser press?"

"The gentleman who is in this room complained about it yesterday," she said, "Would that be you, sir?"

"No, it bleddy wouldn't," he was beginning to look more and more angry. Suddenly, the slack mouth tightened with suspicion. "Isn't there a boy staying here – a little bleck boy? Isn't thus heez room? Et the desk they told me he was here."

"Oh, no, sir, the man who has this room is a sporting goods salesman. Or he told me he was. Tall, bit of a belly. About your own age, sir, if you don't mind my saying so, sir. Distinguished looking, though, sir. Oh! Oops! Not that I meant that..."

But the paunchy, brick-faced, foul-mouthed man had lost patience: "The wrong bleddy room," he spat, storming out.

It took a moment to find the rucksack behind the trouser press, where |Xi!xu‡qe had said it was.

Avoiding Kleynmans' men, but not wanting to risk bumping into a member of staff, she took the fire stairs down to the ground floor. The rucksack over her shoulder would surely prompt fears of theft. They wouldn't recognise her. Anything could happen.

But this route meant she would have to exit through the front door. She couldn't go through the garage: the housekeeper and the guard there might remember her... but not the rucksack. That meant risking the lobby.

She paused at the exit onto the foyer floor and looked through the reinforced glass pane. Apart from the concierge at the desk across from her, a man loitered at the coffee vending machine.

Steeling herself, she pushed the door open and half trotted towards the desk. The concierge looked at her questioningly. "He forgot his table tennis bats, eh!" she called. The concierge looked puzzled but thought better of delaying her by asking questions. He tilted his head in commiseration.

The man leaning on the coffee vending machine near the door was yards away, watching her. He straightened up, started moving.

Jenny called back over her shoulder, "Back in a second, Gaston!" she called brightly over her shoulder, "He's waiting in a taxi outside!"

And she was past the man and through the door, forcing herself to maintain her half run until she reached the corner.

Behind her, the man had just resumed his position against the vending machine when Kleynmans burst through the fire escape door.

"Who's in 511?" he shouted at Hiram Jeffries, who was standing at the desk wondering who the hell Gaston was.

All hell broke loose as the man in the foyer realised what had just happened.

Chapter 8 On the Run

The adrenalin was kicking in, now. Terrified, Jenny ran as fast as her legs could carry her. Behind, someone was shouting but she couldn't hear what and wasn't stopping to find out. Leaving the hotel, she had heard the fierce, uncouth shout of the man who, she was now certain, was Kleynmans. She ran for a full city block before she dodged, exhausted, into a service alley. Still panting, she peeped around the corner. Nothing seemed to be there. She scanned the few faces on the sidewalk, looked across the traffic at the opposite side of the street. No running men. No pursuit. No Kleynmans.

She felt a hand on her shoulder and her knees buckled beneath her.

Then |Xi!xu‡qe's face was over hers. "It's alright. It's me. You were brilliant but, yislaaik, you can run! It's not easy to look like a cripple and run at the same time!" He laughed, gesturing with his knobkierrie.

Then they were both laughing and she was hugging him. He let her, knowing something of the thrill that comes with survival, the joy of truly living.

"We have to go," she said, finally.

Where would you have us go now, Jenny Miler? thought |Xi!xu‡qe. What did she mean, 'have to go'?

"You've done enough, Jenny Miler," said |Xi!xu‡qe, his hands on her shoulders. "I should never have asked you to become involved. Go home to your family. Be safe. You have the gratitude of the Pygmy nations and I will make sure your name is known."

Jenny looked at him, horrified, "Oh, no! You don't understand," she said, "My mother's family comes from a line of slaves, stolen from the west coast of Africa. I'm one of you."

"Many were stolen, Jenny, and their stories are terrible. But this is a fight that is not yours…"

"But it is," she almost shouted in his face, "they were Little People – Pygmies - too. Mom's ancestors were enslaved in a !Kung-speaking region of Ivory Coast. My grandparents told me stories of the Little People. only, I thought they were a myth in !Kung culture. Kiku, I'm one of you!"

The little agent looked into her eyes and turned away. Maybe that was why…. Someone had told her. It made sense then, how quickly she had accepted in the restaurant that he wasn't a child. Also her eagerness to help. Her size.

And she had recognised the Cree introduction on the back of his ID card. Maybe any Canadian would have, but she had pronounced the click in the word '!Kung'.

"But, Jenny, I must travel to meet the Mannegishi. Over the border, in America. It is full of danger."

"Who are the Mannegishi? My mother told me something about Memegwesi; grandma told stories about when her ancestors lived with the Plains People. Are they the same? Maybe I remember the name wrong. It sounds the same. Besides, I know people. I know Cree people. I know Cree. Why do you have Cree on the back of that card? The Cree are across the border…"

"I know, Jenny, it is where I must go. I was supposed to meet a Cree agent – a sympathiser – in the restaurant. Not my parents. Sorry, I didn't mean to lie…"

"We're a bit past that, wouldn't you say? I just about got myself killed to get your rucksack…"

"It's too dangerous."

"Let me come! I can help!"

ǀXi!xuǂqe looked into the chocolate eyes, so urgent and so young. The little waves of her hair formed the distinct krus – the tight curls that, allowed to grow, would undoubtedly announce her race. It would be like his own sister's. He decided. "Yes. You can help, you are right. I need to meet a Cree agent…"

"A spy? How will you find him?"

"NO. No. No, enough with spies – a travel agent. He's supposed to get me to the Mannegishi on the other side."

"I know an agency. We went to school…. Irrelevant. You're lucky. He's the only Cree travel agent in Toronto, as far as I know. It's in a bit of a dangerous part of the city, though."

ǀXi!xuǂqe looked at her and raised an eyebrow. Somehow, he didn't know how, something had been agreed. He was tempted to tell himself to 'go with the flow' but he despised cliches.

They had been walking as they talked and had reached a place where the run-down buildings and discarded furniture on the pavements – sidewalks, ǀXi!xuǂqe reminded himself – suggested a down-at-the-heel neighbourhood. He noticed especially that the abandoned furniture was truly unusable. In other parts of the inner city, Jenny told him, such furniture still looked usable, often desirable even: easy chairs in unfashionable colours but with no other visible defect, highchairs that seemed there only because they had outgrown their usefulness, or vice versa. This, it seemed, might be where those discards came to die. With a pang, he remembered the tales of the elephants' graveyard his father had told him about a long time ago, a long, long way away.

If the streets looked dilapidated and unsavoury, the alleyway they went down to reach the Cree travel agent looked positively primeval. The rears of buildings loomed over the narrow street – pathway, really – creating inlets, caves and overhangs in which any danger might lurk. Tensed ǀXi!xuǂqe walked slightly ahead of Jenny, who stayed noticeably closer to him. He tensed for action at every shadowed side-cavity.

When it came, though, it was not an ambush.

Four young men stretched across the alley in a cordon in front of them. The tallest of them, slouched contemptuously, sneered down at them a few metres away.

"Na, wanksta, what you doing in this 'hood? You got a red rider fo' us?" he drawled, chewing languidly.

ǀXi!xuǂqe took in the thumb tucked into the jeans pocket, the cocked leg that awkwardly placed weight on the hip. This was no fighter, he thought. Gangster, bully, hooligan, tsotsi[i] perhaps, but no fighter. Even the way he flicked the switchblade open and closed suggested a display intended to intimidate rather than a preparation for action. The little agent felt almost sorry for him.

"We are not here for trouble. We seek only to go to the travel agent." Nevertheless, ǀXi!xuǂqe slowly shifted the bulk of his weight off the knobkierrie in readiness.

"You here, you looking for trouble," the leader scoffed. "Leave the rider with us and you can go. We'll look after her, alright." His three sidekicks sniggered unpleasantly.

ǀXi!xuǂqe sighed and put his backpack down. "You know I cannot do that. Please just let us through and there will be no trouble." As soon as he said it, he knew that he had made things worse. It was stupid to threaten a boy such as this in front of his people. And this tsotsi was primed to go off half cocked.

"You? Trouble? We show you about trouble. Get her, bluds. I'll take the sassy cripple." The three 'boys' moved forward smirking, their eyes on Jenny.

ǀXi!xuǂqe realised there was nothing for it. Unshouldering his 'kierrie and moving fast to the left, he thrust himself sideways at the alley wall, planted his foot on it and launched

---

[i] In South Africa, a township hoodlum, often extremely violent.

himself in and arc over the three attackers' heads. Before his foot had landed on the opposite wall and while his body was still arcing over the ground, the kierrie had swung - tik! tok! - and the two outside boys were falling to the ground. The third was felled by the Pygmy's left heel hitting him in the temple. His last waking thought was that the foot that came at him had no shoe on.

It was as hard as horn, though.

Then |Xi!xu‡qe was standing between the fallen thugs and their leader, who had barely taken a step. Wide-eyed, he looked at |Xi!xu‡qe and then at the knife in his hand. Steadying his gaze, he swung the blade menacingly back into the closed position. It was an amateur mistake of the sort |Xi!xu‡qe had predicted. Before the blade opened again, the agent had sprung into the air, launching a roundhouse kick that caught the kid squarely on the nose. There was a sharp crack, the boy yelped, blood spurted from his face and he staggered back, falling on his backside.

"I have been careful," said the Pygmy to him, calmly, "but now it is time for you to leave." The young thug scrambled to his feet, seemed to realise that he was bleeding heavily, yelped again and sprinted off down the alleyway holding his nose. He left behind his three accomplices and his knife. |Xi!xu‡qe picked up the knife and threw it into a bin. Then he turned to Jenny. "Let us proceed."

She had hardly moved. Her hand was still covering her mouth and her eyes were wide. Slowly, she seemed to see |Xi!xu‡qe and take in the three unconscious boys, the footsteps of the fleeing gang leader. Then she reached out her hand and took |Xi!xu‡qe's. They continued on their way.

The travel agent's wasn't what |Xi!xu‡qe expected. Jenny showed him into a long, darkened room that smelled of smoke. The lighting was reddish and the other colours muted to black. There was an occasional slope-shouldered silhouette at a table in the booths around the walls. It was clearly a bar.

Jenny led him along the length of the bar to a door at the far end and they entered what seemed to be a private office. It was the size of a broom cupboard but a broad, sleek-headed, square-faced figure sat at a tiny desk. He looked up and his cruel face split into a broad, gleaming-toothed smile. "Jen-Jen Miler! Tansi! Tansi, Jen-Jen!" he cried in obvious joy and, squeezing his frame around his tiny desk, took her in his arms. When they had discussed their well-being sufficiently to satisfy Pete, as Jenny called him, she turned to |Xi!xu‡qe. "This is Kiku, Pete. Kiku this is…"

"Peechee. Mountain Lion," the Cree travel agent finished, "This is my given name. Westerners shun the language of the First Nations." He drew himself up, proudly. "I am pleased to make your acquaintance, Kiku, friend of Jenny Miler."

"And I yours, Peechee. I am |Xi!xu‡qe of the Sān. I, too, know that the Europeans do not see the language of our First Nations."

Peechee, Mountain Lion, son of the Cree, looked at |Xi!xu‡qe, pleased. He shaped his mouth to pronounce the San agent's name and stopped. Then he laughed a huge laugh, open as the sky, "Already I like you, Kiku! You are a brother to me." He took the small man's hand in his paw and shook it gravely.

"Peechee, epimpahtayahn[ii], so I must speak quickly for the matter is urgent."

"You speak Cree? I understand: you run, Kiku. Speak your need and I will serve if I can."

"I am sent by the Grand Council of the Pygmy Peoples to make contact with the Mannegishi."

"You are he? I had not thought…but of course. I know of you now. You are to be conducted in secrecy to the Nimerigar."

"That is so. You are the contact of the council? I had

[ii] Literally, 'I am running'. Metaphorically, 'I am in a hurry'.

expected you in the city!"

"I received neither orders nor contact information. I did not even know you had arrived," Peechee protested. "I know only that I am to conduct you in safety to the Pryor Mountains. Maybe there was change..." He paused.

"Change? This is strange." |Xi!xuǂqe interrupted. He thought for a moment. Was this another case of interference? But this Far Eastern agent had not received any message rather than an altered one, like the climate summit invitation. "Forgive my confusion, I did not even know that my journey would be communicated that far in advance. I expected step by step. It is not normal."

"These are not normal times, Agent Kiku. So, it is fortunate Jenny Miler found you and that she knows me. I have heard that there is much concern among the governments of the Little Peoples of the East and here in the Americas."

"You are well informed, Peechee." |Xi!xuǂqe looked at the Cree closely. It was very unusual for so much detail of an agents' onward journey to be communicated down the line. "Who has been in touch with you?"

"Do not be alarmed, Kiku. As I was saying, there has since been communication from the PP Secret Service that a Giant agent called Kleynmans has tracked you through the United Kingdom. I was surprised because I had not expected...erm...I did not look for....er, aah...someone so...and I have this for you." He retrieved a sealed, brown envelope from the desk drawer. Surprised at what seemed a contradiction of operational protocol, |Xi!xuǂqe tore open the flap.

"Do not think of it, Peechee," replied |Xi!xuǂqe, reading. "Indeed, these are onward instructions to Pryor...." He changed the subject, "and yes, I know Kleynmans is here. I, we, have seen him...."

"He nearly caught us!" Jenny chipped in.

"Then we should not delay. We will move as soon as I

have arranged with my man at Deloraine Airport. I will make out tickets. You will travel by train to Rough Rock Portage because they will not expect this and few will observe you. You must fly into the US, though."

"Deloraine?"

"Yes. But you must fly there from a local airport, Rough Rock Portage."

"Why not take a train straight to Deloraine Airport?"

"That journey would take you two days. It is 1,000 miles as the crow flies. And that's across the Great Lakes. 1,200 through Canadian territory."

"I had not appreciated. How long will the train journey to Rough Rock Portage take?"

"No one does. It will take only 9 hours."

Within the hour, they were on the train as it pulled out of Union Station.

Chapter 9 Kleynmans Lays his Plans

Kleynmans was furious. He stood in front of the lifts on the fifth floor, waiting for his agent to come to him. "You bleddy moron!" he shouted as the lift door opened. A lady with immaculately coiffed blue hair stepped out of the lift. Before she could register her outrage, the fire door opened and the remiss agent appeared. Kleynmans ran at him, repeating his greeting. "How did you manage to let him get away?"

"I didn't even see him, Sir," the man whined.

"What you mean? He must hev come past you. He must hev. He didn't come to the room number they gave us. Ah know. Ah was there. So he must hev gone to another room but he hed to come past you!"

"Nobody came past us except a chamber maid. When the Pygmy didn't come I followed her but she disappeared. Went to the 6th floor. Or maybe the 8th. Or 9th."

"You followed a chamber maid? What did you think? What, execkly, was your reasoning? Thet Kiku had disguised himself as a –" Kleynmans stopped dead. "The maid!" he yelped. "After her. get her! She's helping the Pygmy."

He didn't admit that he had been in ǀXi!xuǂqe's room. That he hadn't searched the room. Or that she had tricked him into leaving her there. But he realised that he had let her get whatever the little agent had sent her for. He didn't even admit to himself the possibility that 'she' might have been him!

When the two men came back, Kleynmans was on the phone. They had seen what they thought might be a child disappear round the end of the block. Cursing the enormous Canadian block – why couldn't they be short, like blocks in Jo'burg? – they had given chase but by the time they reached the corner there was nothing to be seen.

They didn't dare to approach their boss but listened to his side of the call.

"No. Nothing. Are you sure he was here?

"Well, so you say but we found nothing.

"Yes, he was booked in.

"Yes, under that name.

"No. He wasn't. He's a clever little bliksem.

"I'm beginning to wonder about this 'information' you're giving me, Sparrow. I mean, how reliable is it?

"How do I know that?

"Ja. Okay, you're risking your neck just talking to me.

"So where next?

"You'll have to spell that. Why can't these people use English?

"Mannegishi. Ja. How?

"Well bleddy find out, man. Where do these Mannegishi live?

"Well that can't be far, if they're still in Canada.

"WHAT? How can it be 1200 miles. How far is that in kilometres?

"2000? Why is this country so big? Wait!" Kleynmans took the phone from his ear and looked thoughtful. Raising it again, he continued, "It will take them long to reach there. Perhaps we can catch them on the way. A train would take what 3, 4 days to get there, right? And there can't be many going.

"Only one line? Great! We just have to watch the station.

"Airports? How many are there?

"Jislaaik, man. What do you mean 'ten or fifteen'?

"Oh. Private ones. How are they getting funds, Sparrow?

And arrangements? Who's making them?

"But you said you are there at the heart of the organization, man. Find out! Yissus[i]! What are we paying you for?

"Who? Spell it. P E E C H E E. I'll try and find him.

"Oh. Okay. That helps. Get me info on where they're going. You have? Where?

"The Pryor Mountains, with a 'y'. Got it. Good work

"Where? AMERICA!

"What? Oh, for God's sake, Sparrow, man, I can't search a mountain range. Narrow it down." He stabbed the screen angrily and thrust the phone into his pocket. "Well?" he glared at the agents.

In answer, they shrugged.

"Come on. We've got one more lead. They're going to the bleddy Pryor Mountains in the US. If they get there we'll never find them. But they have to fly and for that they needed a travel agent and the agent is a Red Indian called Peechee. Stupid bleddy name."

"Boss, you can't say 'Red Indian' anymore," objected the man Kleynmans had shouted at. "They're called the First Nations now. Or by their tribe." He quailed at the filthy look he got in return.

When at last they located the alley down which the Cree travel agent did his business, it was almost midnight. Kleynmans ordered his two agents to go ahead, guns drawn. Halfway down, they stopped, their path blocked by four men.

Catching up, Kleynmans looked at the thugs. They didn't look too certain of themselves.

"Have you boys seen a short, black man, about so high?" he held his hand at waist height. "Might have had a girl with him."

The boys looked at him, their eyes widening. They turned

---

[i] Afrikaans for 'Jesus'. A profanity.

and ran.

"Ja. He's been here!" laughed Kleynmans and gestured his men on.

There were even fewer drinkers in the dark bar when they entered. No one looked up.

"Peechee!" Kleynmans said to the barman, loud enough for the bar to hear.

"Yeah, ain't it?" answered the man.

"Huh? What you talking about?"

"Life. It's just peachy," the barkeeper said, sniggering and gesturing around the hung heads of the two or three drinkers, who hadn't looked up.

"No, you fool. I want to speak to PEECHEE!"

"I ain't your fool, mister," the man said in a low tone. The heads of two of the drinkers were up now and they were looking at the three men at the bar.

Realizing his mistake, the Afrikaans agent backtracked. "Sorry, man. Had a really kak day. Is there a – Cree – travel agent called Peechee here?"

"Back room. Price of entry is a drink." Kleynmans ordered three drinks and paid. They drank before entering.

In the office, there was hardly any room for all of them. Peechee sat looking at them. He knew exactly who these men were from |Xi!xuǂqe's description.

"Good evening, Mr Peechee, we're looking for a small, short, little man who we believe came to see you this afternoon."

Although his face gave no indication, the Cree was deeply concerned. |Xi!xuǂqe had described the men pursuing him in passing. He had not expected them to come here. How had they found the travel agency? How did they know his name?

"Yes. Such a man came here," he answered.

"What did you... ag, can you tell...uh...what you did for him? Where was he headed?"

"Well, this information is not provided for nothing. Just like my travel services." The implications were working themselves out in Peechee's mind. If they knew this much, what more did they know? What could he say without their catching him out in a lie? May as well make some money, though.

"Oh. Fine. Give!" ordered the man who was obviously the leader. One of the others dug into his pockets, looking wounded. He produced a $10 bill.

"You are surely joking, mister," the Cree sneered. Kleynmans looked at the other man, who put four more bills on the tiny desk.

"For that, I can tell you that he was travelling far in Canada." The leader licked his lips. So. He knew that much. He inclined his head and the lackey put another five bills on the desk.

"And that he will travel by train." As a half-truth this was effective. ǀXi!xuǂqe and Jenny would have left by now so the station was clear.

"Oh come on, man! For $100 you can tell us more than that! Where were they going?"

"That I cannot tell you. But I know that their journey is long and the train will take many days. He would not tell me exactly where." Judging by the glitter in the eyes of the leader, Peechee was sure that he had confirmed the last piece of information the man had. What he said next could be as misleading as the travel agent liked. But he waited for more money to land on the table.

"He was obliged to travel through Thunder Bay. I know nothing more."

"Where might he be headed? An airport?"

"Inevitably. Unless he takes a boat."

"A plane, then. What's the nearest airport that he can fly to the Pryor Mountains from?"

"Hard to say but Regina airport is probably the shortest flight."

"How far?"

The Cree made a show of thinking. How far to what? The

airport? The man was an idiot. "About 1,300 miles from here."

"No, man, not from here. I mean from the airport to the Pryor Mountains."

"I don't have all this information in my head, you know," said Peechee. He seemed to be getting annoyed but was laughing inwardly.

"Guess."

"Umm. Say, 400 miles." Had the man not heard of Google Maps?

The South African seemed satisfied and the three men left.

Outside, Kleynmans turned to his henchmen. "Right, so Kiku will take the train to an airport and then fly to the Pryor Mountains: the more I think of it, the more unlikely it seems that he's going to spend days trapped on a train. But, if it's a small airport, which it probably is because he's avoiding us and the Cree wouldn't tell us – he told us that cock and bull about Regina or Vagina or whatever it was to throw us off – they'll have to fly to an airport closer to their destination first. We've got not chance of finding either airport but we do know that he's going to the Pryor Mountains and there are fewer airports near there. We'll have to get permission to enter the US. Then we'll wait for news of them before we go to Pryor. With a bit of luck my contact will know which airport they're flying to.

So, the next morning, he presented himself at the South African embassy. They directed him to the United States Embassy, where he started filling in forms…

Chapter 10 |Xi!xuⱡqe's Story

As the train pulled out of the station, Jenny sat watching the platform of her hometown disappear. She had been to collect clothes from her one bedroomed apartment. She had not been particularly sad about leaving it. This was the sort of thing that she had been waiting for.

Sitting opposite her, |Xi!xuⱡqe looked at the slight figure. The air in the train carriage was electric blue with her excitement. The girl – woman – was small but was obviously an adult. He wondered what her story was. Of course, he thought, they were travelling away from her home and he guessed she had never been so far except on holiday. He checked his phone frequently but there was no further message. It was not surprising. His instructions were to proceed to a meeting with the Nimerigar on the Crow reservation in the Pryor Mountains. His phone battery was nearly flat so he went in search of a plug. When he got back, Jenny Miler was asleep. He sat opposite her and tried to get some rest himself. Nine hours was a long time but they were safe. Kleynmans would never find Peechee. How would he even know what or who to look for? Or where? Even if he did, the Mountain Lion would tell him nothing.

He was awake before she was and sitting looking out onto the great plain and the distant mountains. Again, there was the indication of snow falling – a high pitched whistle that he caught on the edge of his hearing, and a taste of metal. He worried that it might make flying difficult.

"Good morning, Jenny Miler," he smiled at her as she

woke. She stretched, her outflung arms pulling the hem of her dark blue tracksuit up to reveal the bottom of a red image on her white polo shirt. A maple leaf, he suspected.

"Have you been to the dining car?" she said. He admitted that he had not thought of it but realised he was hungry.

Back in the carriage – 'car', he was learning – he looked at her and said, "Jenny, you mentioned that your mother was of slave stock and from the west of Africa. But you are very small in stature."

"Oh, my mum used to tell me that they were from a …er… Pygmy people. She was very small herself. Many of the women in my family were, are, but she always said that I am unusually little even for them. She used to tell me how they lived, her people, before they were taken. It was all just long-ago stories, myths I thought. Are there really still people like my forebears in the world? Why do I not know about them?"

|Xi!xu‡qe looked at her. The sadness of this young Pygmy caught at him: stolen from her roots and transplanted into a foreign world with no knowledge of her people. Really, he thought, she was at the heart of his mission. He found himself musing aloud, explaining to her.

"Because of the rapacious Giants, Pygmies were hunted and almost extinguished from the face of the planet. Giants had bred like rats, overrunning the natural world, destroying its bounty, ploughing up its plains to breed meat, sawing down its forests to make buildings, draining its rivers to flush toilets. And now the whole planet has come to this, teetering on the edge of chaos, its great ocean currents struggling to flow, the heat damming up in huge lakes in the sea and in the air, bringing drought and flood. Soon, the undersea rivers will stop and the deserts spread; species will take over other species' homes and the whales, sharks and dolphins will die out. The great land beasts, too: the elephant, the rhinoceros, the tiger, the mountain lion. And there will be nothing to stem the growth of the antelope herds and then nothing for them to eat and then the Earth will die.

"This is my mission: the Giants have realised finally that their greed is destroying their own habitat, too. They have undertaken to change their ways but their pathetic Paris Climate Accord, their miserable Cop conventions, have proved little more than wind against the fire-storm of the companies that pay the politicians and the Giants' own weakness of will in facing the trial that awaits them. So the Pygmy Council determined a course of its own. Secretly, they made friends with the few Giants who understand – the scientists, the activists, the enlightened few – and they made an agreement of breathtaking boldness. These few, with the help of the Little People, would gather together a convention big and strong enough to sway the will of the majority of Giants. Then the Pygmy peoples – with their great knowledge of and empathy with nature – will be re-introduced to the world and take their place in husbanding the planet back to health. For all to enjoy."

He stopped, caught in the dream.

"Then why are you going to America? Why did you come to Canada? Why are you here?"

"There are forces that stand in our way. Somewhere, someone is disrupting communications between the Pygmy peoples and preventing the far eastern peoples of China, Japan, Polynesia, and the Americas, from attending any of the meetings of the Grand Council. While the actions of some Pygmy peoples have made a difference...."

"What actions? I have heard nothing about action by Little People. Pygmies."

"Often what we do is covert because the Giants believe that anything that inconveniences them must be the action of other Giants even though they know, in the secret corridors of Giant power, of the Little People. For example, the Domovoj blew up several illegal coal-fired power stations in Russia that were remote and so secret only a few Russian Giants knew of them. The Russian security *apparat* – GASP, mainly – are still investigating." |Xi!xu‡qe giggled, obviously tickled pink by the thought, "Of course, with their customary arrogance and consummate ignorance, the Russians had built them in the middle of Domovoj homelands. So they were no secret to the Pygmies...."

"Why do you choose the word Pygmies? The word has been kind of taboo for a while. Surely your people don't accept the word?"

"Well, they do, actually. It is the Giants who tell each other that they should not use the word. It is typical of Giants to pretend to respect groups of people they have 'othered' by deciding, for them, the names they are to be called. In fact, 'Pygmy' is a very ancient word, from Greek..."

"Oh, yes, you said but..."

But |Xi!xu‡qe was not to be headed off. "Yes. So, it was the name of the people east of the great Greek states 1500 years before the Christian Era began, in the time that Homer writes about. The thing is, his great work, The Iliad, is about a war that took place between the Little People of Western Asia and the Giant city states of the southeast of Europe: the Mycenaeans, Minoans, Achaeans, and Levantine peoples. Supposedly, the Lydians were their enemy but, actually, the great trade route to the East was controlled by little people – 'pygmies', or 'short-arms', as the Greek speakers called them – of Troy. Homer, the great poet and terrible historian, simply concealed the fact that Paris and Hector were Pygmies. It wouldn't have looked quite so heroic if Achilles had killed a Hector who was a little over a metre tall, would it? It's typical of Giant history: you start a war and, if you win, you make out that you heroically, justly and altruistically achieved it by dint of your inherent superiority and the favour of the gods.

"After that, the Romans added the Trojan Aeneas – who they forgot to mention was a *Pygmy* warrior – to their other founder-mythologies. As if the foundation myth of Romulus and Remus wasn't enough! The surviving Pygmies of Troy migrated east to meet up with Little Peoples there and also west to Central and Northern Europe. So, you see, for Little People, Pygmies, Europe is the West and the East is China, Mongolia, Malaysia, Japan, Hawaii, Australasia, and the Americas. Because you have been taught Western Giant history and geography, you think the West starts in the middle of the Pacific Ocean. Even the word 'Mediterranean' actually means 'the middle of the world'. Giants even lie about their own lies."

Jenny listened in silence. She was not unduly surprised. None of what she heard from |Xi!xu‡qe was like anything she had learned in school or read in books but so little of it dealt with what had happened to the black peoples of Africa, either. She was used to the idea of history being a story told by those in power. Besides, while her brothers had gone through a period of obsessive interest in dinosaurs, she had been captivated by the stories of Zeus and the other gods, the Greek heroes and the classical civilisations. Her knowledge, though sketchy and imperfect, was like but different from what the kind-faced warrior opposite her was describing. As she listened, she learned of a world that was both like and completely unlike the one she inhabited. With a history in which there were two races of humans: one brash and proud, the other hidden in the midst of the very nature the first race was destroying.

"The Pygmies must be terrified at what we – Giants – are doing to nature," she said when he had finished, "and you must truly hate us for it."

"Not really, though we are afraid. You see, we are aware that we could very easily be like you. In fact, we pinched most of the technology that Giants developed – medical drugs and techniques, electric transport, smartphones, computers, appliances even – they have helped shrink our world, bring us together as Pygmies. We have added our own refinements to many of them… mainly miniaturising them. That's technology Giants have stolen, in turn. Of course, if none of these things had ever been invented, there probably wouldn't be a need for us to use them but life was pretty crude and simple before then. In the Kalahari, we have few of the modern advantages that you have grown up with, and our 'city cousins' are used to. And the cell phone coverage is abysmal!" He rolled his eyes in despair. Jenny giggled at the...well...ordinariness of his complaint, so incongruous in this new world.

"Tell me what it is like in the Kalahari, among the Pygmy people you come from." She snuggled herself into the seat, pulling up her knees and clutching them in her arms.

"It is not a story for young ears."

Jenny looked at him with some annoyance, then her expression became sly. "Are you married? Do you have a partner?"

"I have not heard the stars talking."

"No. I mean..."

"I know what you mean. My mother used to say that you hear the stars talking when you are with the right one. They have not yet talked to me."

"Doesn't that make you sad?" she said, sitting up, "to be all alone."

"In what I do, it is better to be 'all alone' and, besides, there has not been time."

"When will you go back to find your wife? There must be one. Somewhere. In the Kalahari."

"There is little left in the Kalahari. Of my People, anyway."

"Why? Surely there are girls who..."

"Most of my people are gone. The Giants took them. Or killed them." |Xi!xu‡qe looked out of the window but not at the blue, distant, snow-capped mountains. "Once the tribes of my People roamed the whole of the southern lands of Africa. We were of the land and the land was us, too, as were the animals that we hunted.

Our Peoples[i], the !Kung, Jul'hoansi, the |Xam, N|u, ‡Khomani, and Hai|om, Naro, Tsoa, G|ana and the |Gwi[ii] , all, shared the world with each other but we never numbered so many that we had to fight to eat: our land supported us, and we supported the land. We did not demand more than it could give. Our numbers did not grow too many. What for?"

"It sounds beautiful," interjected Jenny, and she did not only mean the rhythm and click of the names. "Like the world should be. But what happened?"

"Giants happened." There was a pause. "The Giants came, first from the north and then from the sea. After that, they took land for their giant cattle to graze on. Their animals tore out the grass so the tubers died and the earth washed away. The rivers bled with the red earth of the land. At first, we lived at peace with them. We moved South and West to the places where their cattle and goats could not live and where they could not grow their crops. But more came and we were in the way. They started to kill us when we objected. Then the white Giants came from the sea. They brought guns. And greed. They hunted us but not like we were animals, to survive; they hunted us for sport. They hunted us to get rid of us. They are still doing it. Even now, the government is trying to move us from the place that was eventually given to us."

"But I don't understand, why do people – the Giants – harm your Peoples?"

"Who knows?" |Xi!xu‡qe shrugged, looking at her for the first time since he had started, "They say we do not use the land well. We dig to find what it will give us. They dig it up to put seeds in it. Then they pour precious water on it and

---

[i] "The **San peoples** (also **Saan**), or **Bushmen**, are members of ... the oldest surviving cultures of Southern Africa, and [their] territories span Botswana, Namibia, Angola, Zambia, Zimbabwe, Lesotho and South Africa." - Wikipedia.

[ii] The extract from the IPA in 'Textual notes' might be helpful here.

wait so they can dig up food – food that is already there. But even so there is enough land for us all if we feed out families rather than try to make more to sell for money. You cannot eat money, only collect it. They say we must dig wells but when the game moves you cannot take a well to follow. So they tell us that we must farm, like them. Or labour on their farms, anyway. But they cannot see that the land is our spirit and the story of our Peoples." It seemed, thought Jenny, that tears hung in his eyes. Or were they in hers? "Giants have done the same everywhere. In North America, they do it to the First Nations even as they call them that. In South America the Aztec, the Inca are extinct. In Australia they do it to the Aboriginal Peoples. In Aotearoa, to the Māori. The Peoples of the Pacific….

"All over the world, they have done it to the Little Peoples." He looked up at her, saw her eyes. "I told you: it is not a story for young ears." And his bronze face crinkled into a smile of fine lines in which his eyes twinkled with a deep-flowing joy. "But tell me about your family."

"Oh, that's a boring story."

"No one's story is boring, Jenny Miler. Each of us has, somewhere in his background, some tragedy or triumph that should be remembered. You are unusually small – for a Giant, I mean. There are many Giants like you. Pygmy geneticists have studied this fact. It seems that not all Pygmies were routinely killed when Giants and little people fought. Especially not the women and children. Many children were pressed into slavery. Many women were taken as wives or concubines. It has always been the way in such…race conflicts. Giants share the DNA of many species of human from Neanderthal peoples to Pygmy peoples. In some, their ancestry is expressed in following generations."

"I hate that – the way people hurt each other. My mother told me that her great grandfather told stories of coming to America and escaping to the north, to Canada. She said that they were slaves taken from the southwest coast of Africa.

Where the Congo is now, she said, though it wasn't before. Till the Belgians came."

"There were many groups from there. The Twa say in their myths that they came from the basin of the Congo River."

"Twa? What a lovely name! Like stars twinkling in the twilight."

"Yes. There were Twa people living alongside my people. Until the European Giants arrived. My mother was Twa. Fishing people."

"Really? You mean we might be related?"

"Indeed, Jenny Miler. Like me, you are a half-height. Though I imagine the relationship is at least 400 years and a thousand kilometres distant: the Twa of the Floating Lands took a long time to get to the Caprivi – Itenge, she might have called it in her stories."

But Jenny's eyes had become misty, "Teach me to say those sounds, the ones in your name." However, a few attempts convinced her that the sounds of her mother English would not tolerate among them the strange clicks of her ancestors. She settled for the familiar: "Still: the Twa of the Floating Lands! How beautiful, eh?" Her eyes twinkled as she watched |Xi!xu‡qe smile at her, his own eyes forming deep basins in the estuaries of soft lines that fed into them, etched by the crescent moon that lit the railcar. "Kiku?..." she hesitated, "I don't mean to be rude but how old are you? I mean, you're obviously not a child! But…"

"Ah, Jenny Miler, Twa of the Floating Lands. Would it surprise you to know that I am 29 years old?"

She looked at him speculatively. She knew his trade but what was it that made this… man… so innocent and yet so knowing of the world? What had made him so old, so cloaked in sadness?

When at last the train pulled into the station, dawn was peeking over the great plain they had crossed.

Waiting on the platform were two people so alike and so

different that Jenny at first took them for father and son – but she was beginning to shed the preconceptions with which she had left Toronto.

"Kiku?" asked the much shorter of the two, "I am Sequoyah Wuttunee, PPS North East department."

Jenny tittered involuntarily at the name, "Sequoia[iii]?" she repeated.

Drawing himself to his full four and half feet, Wuttunee looked witheringly at Jenny and said, "Sequoyah, with a 'y' not an 'i' – it means 'sparrow'!"

"Oh! I'm really very sorry, sir!" Jenny spluttered, realising she had been caught. "I apologise, I didn't mean to be rude."

The taller man stepped forward, laughing: "You're not the first to wonder how he came to be named after the tallest trees on the continent! No doubt his mother had high hopes for him!" He shook with laughter at his joke, which he had clearly made many times before, to judge by Sequoyah Wuttunee's scornful response.

"And my surname means 'porcupine' so you'd better watch out!" the Pygmy bristled at him.

"Anyway," the taller man continued, "I am Piyêsîs. My mother was Cree, like the names of this Pygmy, here," he giggled, not unkindly.

The little man was not amused: "I would be named in my own Mannegishi tongue, if you Giants had not committed genocide on us, as you do on all who are different from you."

The bitterness of this attack was calmed by |Xi!xu‡qe introducing himself by his full name, "Of the Sān Council. I believe we have business, gentlemen."

Sequoyah Wuttunee and Piyêsîs – the Mannegishi Pygmy and the Cree Giant – pulled up short at the implied rebuke of the formal introduction. They took a step back and their demeanour changed immediately to one of utmost respect.

[iii] Jenny is imagining the giant redwoods of the Sierra Nevada.

"Forgive me," wheedled Wuttunee, "this buffoon…"

"A little matter of an aircraft to Laurel Airport, in the Pryors, I believe?" |Xi!xuǂqe's question carried so much menace that the other men leapt forward and grabbed his and Jenny's bags, like porters.

"This way, sir…er, madam," said Piyêsîs.

Chapter 11 Yunwi Tsunsdi

The flight from the little airstrip at Rough Rock Portage to Deloraine Airport had been a little bumpy, but mercifully short. Not much was said but the prickly exchanges between the jocular Piyêsîs and his ill-tempered partner suggested a history, thought |Xi!xuǂqe. Or maybe it was simply Wuttunee's resentment of his name. There could be no doubt that his parents – who must have been Pygmy, after all – had made a spectacular mistake in naming their son Sequoyah[i]. It was a traditional Cherokee name. Perhaps they had been thinking of the giant trees' longevity or sturdiness…. Whatever their intention, his surname – Wuttunee – undoubtedly hit the mark: his character certainly was spiky.[ii]

"Billings Logan Airport, Montana?" said the pilot as they clambered into the old twin-engined Beechcraft.

"That's right," Piyêsîs answered.

"I thought you said, Laurel Airport?" |Xi!xuǂqe asked,

---

[i] Actually, a fellow called George Gist, of whom more later.

[ii] In fact, |Xi!xuǂqe is only partially right: 'Wuttunee' is Cree; 'Sequoyah' is Cherokee and has nothing to do with the tree. The Cree and the Cherokee inhabit lands quite far apart but the Pygmies who shared territory around and among them were often of one People, the Memegwesi. When they adopted the languages of Giants, therefore, groups often took different languages. Sadly, in the process, many Pygmy languages were lost. The same happened to the |Xam – a San group that lived in on the Namibia/South Africa border. This kind of influence goes both ways: the clicks in Nguni languages like Zulu and Xhosa are borrowed from San languages.

suspicious.

Piyêsîs turned to |Xi!xuǂqe, "I was told to book two flights, Boss, a charter to Laurel Airport, with Cape Air, and this one to Billings. A misdirection, you see." He explained. |Xi!xuǂqe's face relaxed. It made sense. And the passive voice suggested a competent guiding hand, too.

"Some asshole's idea of a cunning plan," snorted Wuttunee. Although he had been badly frightened to learn that the Sān agent was not actually disabled and that his odd-looking crutch was in fact a war club, he had quickly recovered his cantankerous attitude. Worse, he had become positively obnoxious when Piyêsîs had refused to stop en route to the airport. "It's not fair, asshole," he had fumed, "Billings is much further than Laurel. I gotta pee!" But the Cree Giant had refused.

Sitting next to Jenny on the flight, |Xi!xuǂqe remarked on the distress of the Mannegishi. "They are a famously dishonest people. The Cree Giants had great trouble with them on the Oregon Trail in the 18th century. Some put the subsequent destruction of the Plains peoples down to them. Mannegishi double-dealing earned the 'American' First Nations, both Giants and Pygmies, a reputation they did not deserve. Of course the White Giants exploited that for all they were worth in order to demonise the original inhabitants and annex their territories."

"Yes, I learnt that in history," said Jenny, who was beginning to suspect that |Xi!xuǂqe was a bit of a pedant…and a lot of a talker! "but what's that got to do with Wuttunee?"

"Probably nothing, stereotypes being what they are. But it might be worth keeping an eye on him," he said to her as the plane dropped and levelled into its approach run.

Billings Logan wasn't what you would call a bustling international airport though it clearly served a reasonably affluent clientele. Shortly after landing, Piyêsîs (who Jenny had taken to calling Pi, spelled π, she explained gleefully) insisted Wuttunee go to the toilet – given the Pyxie's claim of desperation.

"But I found some horsetail in a planter in the hall. I'll be fine now," he had whined, adding for good measure that "stupid Giants" know nothing about what they plant. "It's good for easing the bladder, you know?"

"Go!" ordered the Sān. When the Pyxie had left them, he turned to Piyêsîs, "I'm having my doubts about Sequoyah. His behaviour is erratic. You know him well. What do you think?" |Xi!xuǂqe asked, running his palm over the smooth head of the kierrie.

Piyêsîs watched the movement and shuddered inwardly. "Perhaps we should not divulge too much." He explained in a low voice, "Billings was actually closer than Laurel. This is the land of his people; I would have expected him to know that. Also, he is Pyxie and would know that the plant he used would not help, but worsen his condition. Also, I did not see him stop or take anything from a planter. He would have had to put down his bag."

Not for the first time, |Xi!xuǂqe was impressed by the Cree.

Jenny ran up to them, bright eyed with excitement. "What shall we do now?"

"Now, we live life," answered the Cree, smiling. "Our transport is tomorrow morning, I am informed, so I have made reservations at a hotel just outside the city."

So, thought the Sān, the guiding hand shows itself again. Whoever they were. Pryor Mountain? "Good. What's it called?" |Xi!xuǂqe asked, thinking how fast the Cree moved. Too fast?

"We'll get a cab. I'll get us there, don't' worry."

"What's it called?" |Xi!xuǂqe's voice was flat and level, leaving Piyêsîs in no doubt that an answer was expected.

"Oh, er, the Kelly Inn Hotel[3]. We'll eat at a restaurant near it tonight – the Old Cracker Barrel," he added glancing nervously at |Xi!xuǂqe, "then go into Billings. Or we could go straight to the Pictograph Cave State Park!"

"The Pictograph Cave State Park? What's there, Pi? Is it a geometry museum?" Jenny looked seriously innocent.

"It's got some rock art in it that's over 2,000 years old!" Piyêsîs enthused. |Xi!xuǂqe struggled not to roll his eyes (only 2,000?) but was interested despite himself. He thought about the Tsodilo Hills[iii4], the eland, the lion. Maybe he would find links between his ancestors and the people of this land.

"Let's go there!" enthused Jenny, hanging on |Xi!xuǂqe's arm like a child.

"We are not here for sight-seeing, Jenny. I have a task to fulfil, a duty to carry out."

"But you have to be in the Pryor Mountains, or whatever, to do it and you can't go there now, can you?"

"It is true, what you say. I do not know how to get there. Piyêsîs?"

"I do not have forward instructions from here. It is a covert location. We have only the information about the transport tomorrow morning," the Cree replied, suddenly all military correctness.

"I see you, Piyêsîs," |Xi!xuǂqe's eyes disappeared in a smile, "You think I do not see your pride. So, if we do not know how we are to proceed, it seems we are in Billings for the night. The rock art *is* interesting."

But the trip was disappointing to the others, though Jenny was fascinated by the animals and "fat people".

Only |Xi!xuǂqe truly understood that what he was looking at was the lived and living experience of the First People of the Plains. "Clearly European Giants," he said, "judging by the clothes they're wearing." What he meant was that these paintings were recent but, like the 100,000-year-old

---

[iii] Tsodillo Hills in Botswana has provided shelter for humans for over 100,000 years. It is a site of great religious significance to the San and bares rock art thought to be up to 40,000 years old.

paintings of Tsodilo, they were the story of the people who still lived in this place.[5]

Sequoyah Wuttunee complained constantly about the walk: "And when are we supposed to go to the Pryor Mountains? Where is the HQ? How are we getting there?" he whined. Pi fobbed him off with vague promises.

Afterwards, they had dinner, took a taxi – ǀXi!xuǂqe still couldn't bring himself to call it a cab – to the hotel and settled in.

When they met up in the foyer – 'lobby' – it was clear that they had very different expectations of the evening. From her tiny hold-all, Jenny seemed to have conjured a jade green blouse with pink flowers around the hem and a fashionable pair of blue leggings. The Sān, who had ditched his trainers for the sake of comfort – no one ever actually noticed, anyway – felt rather underdressed in his jeans and khaki tee shirt, until he found that what passed for casual clothing in Billings seemed to be cargo pants and tee shirts in military colours. The others didn't seem to have changed, although they looked rather tidier.

Egged on by Jenny and Wuttunee, the group went to see what downtown Billings had to offer. They walked around the wide streets looking into shops until the light started to fade and the streetlights came on.

"Let's go there!" Jenny pointed at a brightly lit façade, "Daisy Dukes Saloon and Dance Hall! I wanna dance!" Grabbing ǀXi!xuǂqe by the elbow, she all but dragged the reluctant Sān agent through the doors. The other followed, the Cree interested, the Mannegishi exaggeratedly reluctant.

The evening did not go well. While Piyêsîs and Jenny could prove they were of an age to order alcoholic drinks, the barman wouldn't serve Sequoyah and refused ǀXi!xuǂqe's passport as proof of age. The two sat with rainbow-coloured drinks of ice – 'virgin slushies' the barman called them – and watched the others dance to the band. Then a White Giant ruffled Sequoyah's hair, "Cute kid!" he shouted at Jenny, then turned to his three friends and laughed. Several Black Giants looked on uncomfortably, shuffling their feet. Sequoyah, it is true, looked like a child in his denim dungarees.

The Sān had had enough, "We have a long journey tomorrow and much to do." He insisted they return to the hotel,

"Yeah!" hooted the obnoxious Giant, "Your other little boy needs his beauty sleep! I mean, he REALLY needs his beauty sleep!" and his friends laughed riotously.

"You great chucklehead!" shouted Jenny, losing her cool. "What's the matter? Too scared to pick on someone your own size? Skeet!"

If the lout couldn't understand her insults, he certainly understood her intent and started toward her menacingly. Before he had taken a second step, |Xi!xuǂqe was between them. His kierrie was still in his armpit but Jenny had seen what he could do. "Kiku, no! it's ok. We'll just go now."

"What's it 'mommy'? Need your crippled little kid to protect you? Why doncha you buy him some shoes, at least? Deadbeat!" the man sneered. His friends flanked him now, as if they meant to attack en masse. |Xi!xuǂqe was dimly aware of the Black Giants edging away. Wuttunee the porcupine and the Cree Giant looked uncertain, as if fighting the urge to flee.

But he had had enough. Treated like a child, insulted and then threatened by this ignorant Giant, the memories of home and his ancestors alive in his mind, he swung into action. Without removing his kierrie, he pivoted on the weapon, his feet scything at crotch height. The right-hand attacker crumpled to the floor but, before the agent landed, his reverse pivot caught the man on the left hard in the crotch.

Sequoyah's eyes were wide and Piyêsîs' jaw dropped. Suddenly the outcome of the fight looked less than certain.

The third Giant clenched his teeth and advanced menacingly. But the four had turned and run for the exit, evading a bouncer advancing on the site of the fallen men.

Then they were outside on the pavement – sidewalk – running. And laughing. Inside, laughter and screams mixed. The angry curses of the bouncer followed them down the road.

"They'll call the police! We'll be arrested! Then what will become of your 'mission'?" Wuttunee whined when they finally stopped, panting in a park.

"And say what?" Piyêsîs half gasped, half laughed, "that two little boys and a girl beat up three men? Who's going to believe that? And do you think that loser's going to want to advertise that he was beaten up by a 'crippled little kid' with no shoes? I don't think so."

It was a short cab ride back to the hotel.

Pi was wrong, though. The next morning, the local TV news had reports of a "vicious and unprovoked assault" on the son of the Billings mayor. Flying in the face of statements from several, mostly Black witnesses clearly blaming the White Giants as the provocateurs, and amid a storm of White indignation, the police had mounted a manhunt.

"I told you, Pi, you peabrain!" gloated Wuttunee, "Now, you've jeopardised Kiku's mission."

He seemed rather less than worried about this but |Xi!xu‡qe looked worried, Jenny thought, though it was hard to tell which of the lines on his face were laugh lines and which were worry ones.

Pi was reassuring. "Don't worry, Kiku. It's already sorted out, anyway. A Nimerigar agent contacted me. They're coming to fetch us from Sweet Haven."

"Good. It is time to leave this place. Is it far, this town? Sweet Haven?"

"No. No. It's a shop. Sells sweets. A few blocks from here.

"What?" said Sequoyah, "that can't be right. A sweet shop?"

"Where else would two little boys and their mother and father look more natural?" giggled the Cree, obviously enjoying the opportunity to mock his partner.

To the Mannegishi's disappointment – the shop was brightly coloured and the sweets enticing – their contact was already waiting to collect them in a big yellow school bus, its doors open to reveal the driver's seat and the pedals built up for the diminutive driver, who wore an enormous black Mohican and a scowl that accused the world. He impatiently slapped the huge steering wheel – the bus had to look 'normal' from the outside – "Come! Move! Hurry! Danger!"

And the rest of the crew looked nothing like the four had expected. Outlandishly dressed in bright colours and booted in Doc Martens, they looked like the cast of 'Gremlins' had stolen a school bus and were posing as school children. They turned out not to be Nimerigar at all. Instead, a diminutive figure in children's combat fatigues stood at the top of the vehicle's steps, beckoned them aboard, issuing commands in English punctuated by a strange language.

"They're Yunwi Tsunsdi[iv6]!" ǀXi!xuǂqe exclaimed, "They're elves and they're speaking Cherokee! I've never heard it spoken! It's supposed to be almost extinct as a language among Giants." He addressed them in a flowing ribbon of sound. There erupted among them a rapid and clearly excited discussion. Then the man who had called them into the bus, obviously the leader, hushed the others and spoke to ǀXi!xuǂqe.

"You are able speak Tsalagi Gawonihisdi[v]?" he asked in

[iv] "Yunwi Tsunsdi are benevolent creatures who frequently help humans in Cherokee stories, but they have magical powers and are said to harshly punish people who are disrespectful or aggressive towards them."

[v] The name of the Cherokee language

Cherokee[7]. The Sān translated for his companions.

"I have long wished to be able to speak Tsalagi," he replied more haltingly. Turning to his companions, he translated, explaining: "It's nearly all verbs so it's really alive, and action-packed and fast to speak." He turned back to the leader, continuing in English, "Allow me to introduce my travelling companions. This is Jenny Miler, she is Canadian, her Cree friends got us this far, and Piyêsîs here is Cree. And this is Sequoyah Wuttunee of the Mannegishi. Obviously, he is a Pygmy like us."

At the mention of Wuttunee's first name, the Yunwi Tsunsdi erupted in an excited cacophony.

"He is named after the father of our language!" exulted the leader. "Sequoyah gave us our writing[vi] and made us learned!"

A burst of discussion ensued, none of which Sequoyah Wuttunee understood.

When they had boarded the bus and the excitement had died down, the Yunwi Tsunsdi leader and the Sān fell to discussing the journey at the back of the bus. Jenny and Piyêsîs, who were still the worse for wear after the night before, slept in the front. Excluded from the discussion at the back, Sequoyah sat, arms folded, alternatively glowering resentfully and glowing with pride, as he watched the ribbon of the Yellowstone River unspool as the Pryor Mountains grew out of the plane.

[vi] "**Sequoyah**...also known as **George Gist** or **George Guess**) (c.1770–August 1843) …. In 1821, he completed his independent creation of the Cherokee syllabary, making reading and writing in Cherokee possible." https://en.wikipedia.org/wiki/Sequoyah.

Chapter 12 Kleynmans in Pursuit

Kleynmans was livid.

Armed with visas for himself and his assistant, Fanie van der Merwe, he had arranged a charter flight on a small, rickety plane that had landed him in Billings Logan airport. It had been a miserable flight and as soon as his plane had touched down, he dismissed the pilot with ill-disguised anger.

Then he received a Wavel message from his informant, Sparrow. His quarry had flown to another airport – Laurel Airport. Only down the road. But not this one!

"Ag, no, man!" he shouted at the phone as Fanie stood looking purposefully at the ground, "You said Billing, or whatever this place is! Now you say Laurel? You must be the most useless bleddie double agent...

"No. No. Sorry, man. It was just a kak flight. I'll go there. They've definitely got a flight there, ja?

"When?

"Yesterday or today? Ok. Keep me informed." He snapped the phone shut, wondering why he had such a fancy thing with its big screen when Sparrow never allowed video calling. Anyone would think he's got something to hide, thought Kleynmans bitterly. And that annoying high voice! Like a drill. Typical of these Little People.

Eventually they took an eye-wateringly expensive taxi to Laurel airport, only 30 minutes away.

Never mind: the moment he saw it, he realised he might be on the right track. Under a sky like a taut canvas that stretched from horizon to horizon lay a collection of low buildings. They were no more than big huts, he thought. "Yissus! It's like the Karoo, hey," he exclaimed, nodding knowingly. "Ja, if I was hiding, this is where I'd come to as well."

"I hope so, Boss, the taxi's just driven away!" And, indeed, the yellow cab was disappearing down the road. For a moment, Kleynmans considered running after it but then realised he had the company's number on his phone.

The two men walked quickly to the nearest building that looked like a terminal lounge. It was locked. After trying several more buildings – all locked – Kleynmans and Fanie were running. Fanie could have sworn he heard what sounded like a sob from his boss.

Finally, they found an open door. The interior was dim, musty smelling and apparently empty.

"Hello?" they shouted, opening small doors into empty offices.

Finally, Fanie shouted, "Here! Boss! Over here!"

Almost prone in a swivel chair, his feet on a desk that was empty but for the sauce-smeared boxes of a takeaway meal, was an unshaven man looking supremely uninterested.

"Listen, oke[i], did a flight arrive here last night or early this morning? Maybe yesterday?"

---

[i] Opaque South African expression from Afrikaans 'ou', literally meaning 'old' but in the sense of 'old friend'. An abbreviation of the diminutive 'outjie' ('little old') which is spelled 'okie' in English, it's supposed to be friendly. The American almost certainly hears 'Okie', an insulting reference to migrant labourers in his dialect. Told you it was opaque, as is most dialectal language outside its social context.

"Hey, man. Where's the fire? Ain't you got no manners?" The airport manager, for such he was, stood and calmly straightened out his crumpled uniform. "Good day to you, sir. What can I do for you?"

"Bliksem," cursed Kleynmans under his breath, "Ja. Good morning, my good man," Behind him, Fanie almost burst out laughing, "I wonder whether you could be so kind…ag, man…did a plane land here with two very little people, one a dark-skinned man – boy…anyway, small – and a girl? There might have been someone else with them."

"Whoa! You're asking me whether I've seen anyone like that arrive at Laurel?" The man was smirking now, clearly enjoying his power.

"Yes! Small man, more like a boy. Carrying a stick, like a crutch, with a round ball on the head…"

"This kid has a ball on his head? Dude, that is weeeeiiiiird! Is the ball, like, attached? Growing out of his head or…"

"No, man, the ball is at the end of the stick…"

"And the stick's on his head. Even weirder!"

"No, no, no. No. Just… have you seen two people who look like children. I think the girl is also quite dark skinned. The…guy…is about 140 centimetres tall and the girl might be smaller. I think. We only saw her…. Ag, have you seen them?" Magnus Kleynmans was almost pleading.

"Say, whaaat? 140 centimetres? What's that, some English thing?"

"No, men, it's about 4 foot 8 tall. And the girl's also about thet. Short, men. RRReeely shawt!" Magnus Kleynmans always had difficulty maintaining his 'official' English accent under pressure.

"Dude, this is small airport. Not much happens here and if anyone had landed this morning, I'd know: I've been

90

on duty since yesterday evening." He looked at his watch. "My relief's late and I ain't had no breakfast, neither!"

"Yes, yes! I'm very sorry about that but has anyone like that landed here?"

"I already told you, man!"

"Bedonner! Are you on drugs? Why can't you answer a simple question?"

Laconically, the man, who was enjoying himself more than ever, held out his hand. A universal gesture. Kleynmans turned to his assistant, "Fanie!" he snapped clicking his fingers.

When the price had been settled and the money paid, the man stood up. "As I said, nothing ever happens around here. If it did, I'd know about it. The most interesting thing that's happened was a fight at Daisy's in Billings. Some weird shit going down there. Aliens, they said. But nothing…"

He never got a chance to finish the sentence. Kleynmans was out of the door, dialling the cab company for an eye-wateringly expensive ride back the way he had just come.

In the cab, he assessed Sparrow's effectiveness as a traitor. His judgment was not flattering.

Fortunately, there was no traffic and no delay on the return journey. The only other vehicle they passed was going the other way, out of Billings. It was a big yellow bus with 'SCHOOL' on the destination plate.

Sitting in the front seat of the taxi, Fanie noticed that it was full of children behaving badly. "Tupical 'merrican kids," he muttered to himself, "no dussipline or rrespect!" The bus seemed to be being driven by what seemed a very small person. Or a gremlin, like in that old film! Or maybe the kids had hijacked it! He chuckled at how fitting that would be.

But he thought better of sharing his amusement with his boss, who was quietly fuming in the back seat.

Chapter 13 The Great Pryor Mountain Powwow

Twenty minutes after they had left, ǀXi!xuǂqe returned to sit down next to Jenny in the front seat, giving her a half smile as she turned sleepily to him. "So, we got away without Kleynmans finding us. The Yunwi Tsunsdi say he flew into Billings early this morning. There's been no sign of him since, though."

"Maybe we're safe, then," Jenny whispered. Glancing up at him, she continued, "But how does he know where we're going all the time? Do you think Sequoyah Wuttunee is spying on us? Telling him where we're going?"

"Perhaps but I'd be surprised. I can't believe Piyêsîs wouldn't know and I definitely can't imagine Pi as part of a spy ring – or circle." He smiled at his own joke. "Anyway, that's the reason we're not telling him where we're going. After that thing about going to the loo and Billings Airport and everything…a bit suspicious. But, you know, that's not the real question that's bothering me."

"Really? What then?"

"The thing is," ǀXi!xuǂqe stroked his thin beard, "why is Kleynmans always late? Suppose Wuttunee – or someone else – *is* telling him where we're going, why isn't he there to meet us when we get there? I mean, think about it: we spent nearly 18 hours just sitting around in Billings and he didn't show up at all."

"We weren't sitting around. We went to that park. And the nightclub, bar thing. Perhaps he just missed us there."

"Well, not sitting around maybe but let's face it, we made enough of a ruckus all around that place…and there were hardly any other tourists at the park. We would have been easy to spot and…deal with. And then we stayed in the hotel without any sort of guard or other precautions. Operating procedure requires that, in situations like that, we stay away from obvious places…"

"…that seems wrong," Jenny cut in. "Surely the obvious places, like ones full of other people, are the last places they would look just because they're so obvious?"

The agent looked at the young woman beside him: "You know, I'm not sure I like what this whole business is doing to you. Perhaps you should go straight back to Toronto and live your normal life."

"Normal? Boring, is what it was. No thank you!"

"Well," he mused looking at her and then out of the window at the distant mountains, "if there is such a thing as innocence and if you were innocent in the beginning, you're losing it hand over fist. The way you think about these spycraft, things way out of your experience, seems far more skilled than can be good for a nice little – erm – girl from Toronto."

Jenny punched him on the arm. "'nice little girl'! Watch out, mister!"

"What was it you said you did again?" he joked clutching his arm.

She looked at him. "Are you questioning me? I didn't tell you what I do. For your information, I'm a student. Was.

And this is much more interesting than that could ever be. And you *are*: you're cross-questioning me, or interrogating me, or whatever you and your kind call it!" To his surprise, she seemed about to cry.

"Jenny, Jenny, slow down. I'm not trying to hurt you or anything. And it's not that I don't trust you but, see it from my point of view: I'm having a bit of a problem in a foreign city; I'm being pursued by a skilled and dangerous agent. Suddenly, a young woman," |Xi!xu‡qe had to make a mental swerve to avoid the trap of calling her a girl again, "comes up to me and offers to give me directions. The next thing I know, I'm breaking into a hotel with her, she's taking me to her friend – who turns out to be my contact – and arranging for me to fly into the US illegally. I mean, how would it look if some – man – stopped you in the street and did all these things?"

For a moment she looked at him and he was afraid that she really would burst into tears.

Her response was altogether pragmatic, though: "I am Jenny Miler. I'm a student at the University of Toronto. I am studying Social Work MSW. I am in my second year. I am studying on a full scholarship because my mother has – had – multiple sclerosis and is – was – unable to support me. I work part time at…" She stopped as |Xi!xu‡qe put his hand over hers.

"I believe you, Jenny Miler…" Again, he was surprised by her response.

"Oh, yeah? And why do you? 'Cos I'm a harmless little girl and couldn't possibly be a scary agent like you? Because you like me and you're not a very professional agent? Because you think you'll get rid of me before I do any real harm?"

"No. None of those."

"What then?"

"A mixture of things. The first is that I was lost when you came across me. You could not possibly have known where I would be to meet me like that. Obviously, I had told no one where I was going. Only my handler knew – and my contact and I were supposed to set up the meeting with Peechee at the restaurant. Finally, Kleynmans was heading to my hotel, not Montana's."

"Unless I was hanging around the hotel on Kleynmans' orders!" She looked straight into his face.

"And then you helped me escape him? No. I believe you, Jenny, and I believed you then. Instinct, I suppose. After a while you just get to know when someone is lying to you. Besides," he laughed, suddenly conscious of sounding patronising, "your story about just dropping your life in Toronto and your university course and all that.... Well, people don't do things like that; no secret agency would put an operative into the field with such a ridiculous cover story: it's full of holes, it's much too easy to check, and it invites mistrust.... Sorry! I didn't mean...! I meant...."

But she was laughing at him now. Her brown eyes seemed to dance below the twin sweep of her eyebrows. For the first time, |Xi!xu‡qe noticed how, in the sunlight from the bus window, her face glowed golden and how her lips twisted slightly at the corner when she pursed them and smiled at the same time. He smiled back at her.

For the second time, they had somehow come to an agreement on something without actually agreeing on it.

"It's up ahead!" shouted the driver from his raised seat. The Yunwi Tsunsdi crowded forward. So did Piyêsîs, who had woken up groaning. Ahead of them, a small town appeared. "That's Bridger. From there it's only 20 or so miles to the base. But we're in Crow territory, now. Friendly country!"

Everyone cheered except Wuttunee: "What the hell? You said we were there but there's still 20 miles to go? What's the matter with you people?" He returned to his mobile phone. Jenny and |Xi!xu‡qe looked at him and at each other. Piyêsîs' brow was furrowed, too. He looked at his own phone and took it across to |Xi!xu‡qe: there was no signal. The Sān checked his: no signal. What was Sequoyah doing on his phone? It was Jenny who gave them the answer:

"Maybe it's not what he's doing. Maybe it's what he can't do. Or he could be playing solitaire!" But none of them could imagine the Mannegishi playing a game.

It was nearly an hour before the bus drew up at a large building with corrugated roofing and a dilapidated veranda on which a few old Giant men in sweat-stained vests sat smoking. They were dark-skinned and seemed half asleep. They paid little attention as |Xi!xu‡qe, Jenny, Piyêsîs, Sequoyah and the Yunwi Tsunsdi went through the front door. Inside was a hatch with a shrivelled old woman standing at it.

"What can I getcha?" she rasped at them. Jenny looked at Piyêsîs, who looked at |Xi!xu‡qe. The Yunwi Tsunsdi leader, whose name turned out to be Frank, shouted, "Twenty-two cokes, cold, to go."

The old women looked at him and smiled, "Through the door. Third light switch."

The group found themselves in a dusty room, apparently a storeroom for abandoned school desks. Under Frank's direction they all crowded onto the only clear piece of floor there was.

He pressed the third light switch as instructed.

The room began to grow taller and most of the desks rose above their heads. After a moment of confusion, they realised they were in a lift. The rest of the desks made up the wall of the lift. Steadily, they sank into the ground. Within minutes, the lift drew to halt and they were standing beside a train of open railway cars made of gleaming metal. When they were all on board, the train hummed electrically off into a tunnel, to emerge minutes later into a 'station' very like the one they had just left. This time there was no lift. Instead, they were met by an armed guard who led them through a short tunnel to a wide, brightly lit room with Pygmies sitting at rows of tables. Wuttunee's eyes were like saucers.

"It's a mess hall," said Piyêsîs. "There must be dozens of people here."

"Over a hundred, actually. Welcome to New Arrow Shot Into Rock, Pryor Mountain HQ of the GCPP. This is the Secret Service section." The speaker was an officer wearing the most extravagant uniform |Xi!xuⱡqe had seen since serving on the security detail for a South American dictator's funeral.

"I'm General Daniel Ahchuchhwahauhhatohapit, One Who Has Stars For A Blanket, of the Awwakkulé[i]."

Despite his claim to be a war chief of the Crow people, the Apsáalooke, the General was clearly a Pygmy: to top out his copiously bemedaled military uniform, he wore a magnificent headdress of intricate geometric beadwork from which rose a crown of tall feathers, white, black and white

---

[i] The Crow name of the Nimerigar of the Pryor Mountains. They were amazingly strong and ferocious. The alliance between the Apsáalooke Crow Giants and the Awwakkulé Little People, referred to by the General, resulted in other tribes being extremely wary of making war on the Crow.

again, springing from red, beaded quills. From his temples hung white lengths of fur with black tips and from within the crown golden spirals of horse mane fell. Although the whole ensemble stood 20cm high, it reached only ǀXi!xuǂqe's height and not quite to Piyêsîs' shoulders.

Clearly, they were in the presence of a man of pride, dignity and distinction.

"Call me Danny!" he said, grinning at them all.

The next hour was taken up with settling all the Yunwi into dormitories and feeding them – which clearly turned out to be a rather more demanding task than the General's staff had anticipated.

ǀXi!xuǂqe, Jenny and Piyêsîs took dinner with the General, who regaled them with tales of the Awwakkulé and their rocky relationship with the Crow people.

"We used to be really nasty to the Apsáalooke. They tell myths about us being violent and bad tempered and destructive," he giggled conspiratorially then became thoughtful, "Gradually, we relented and our two peoples normalised the relationship. They stopped fearing us and hunting us and we have lived in peace for many centuries. We even began to speak their language. They are an honourable nation, in fact, and when the other Giants came, the white ones, they faithfully concealed our existence. As they have done for many generations now." The General giggled, "The myths are still told but their children are now taught that *those* Awwakkulé are just a story to throw others off our scent. This is the secret of what the white Giants think is 'spiritual depth' in the Crows' eyes: it is mockery!"

Suddenly, his expression became grim, "The White Giants are vicious, though. Mind you, they have not *all* been White for a long time; it would be more honest to call them ashbaaihïi - immigrants. It's interesting," he broke off, "the word 'ashbaaihée' means 'stranger' in Crow but it is an Awwakkulé word meaning 'immigrant' that *we* applied to the *Apsáalooke* when *they* arrived here." He sighed, "The world goes round."

"Nevertheless," he said finishing his story, "it is hard to come to agreement with them over anything. We help the Crow retain their ancestral lands against the greed of the immigrant Giants as much as we are able. Many among them work with us in our operations for the Pygmy council."

It was close to midnight before they went to their rooms, hungry for sleep.

Chapter 14 Into the Net

It didn't go well.

Almost before any of them had managed to get their heads down (Piyêsîs had to curl into a foetal position on the tiny bed), there was a piercing scream.

As if fired from a popgun, |Xi!xu‡qe was off the bed. He hit the floor halfway to the door, kierrie at the ready. Then he was out and down the hall to Jenny's room. She was standing outside her door, big-eyed, pale and trembling with fright. The Pygmy agent thrust her aside and readied for battle.

Inside the room was a spider the size of a dinner plate. It stood, forelegs raised threateningly, poised to spring, fangs menacingly spread.

"Kiku! What…What is it?" Jenny gibbered.

"A spider!" was all |Xi!xu‡qe could manage. The thing was ankle high to him. It would be almost calf high to a true Pygmy, some of whom had arrived. The first Yvwi Usdi[i] on the scene was backing away.

Swirling his kierrie in arcs before him, |Xi!xu‡qe prepared to attack.

"Stop! Stop!" came the almost childlike voice of an Awwakkulé Dwarf, "It's alright. It won't hurt. It's frightened!" He stood at the door, making a soothing

---

[i] Singular form of 'Yunwi Tsunsdi'.

101

cheupsing sound, as if calling a pet. Slowly the great beast seemed to uncoil. "He's a Goliath tarantula," explained the Awwakkulé, "They usually live in South American rainforests. I can't imagine what he's doing here…"

"He? How do you know it's a 'he'?" asked Jenny.

"You want to check?" the Pygmy asked, cocking his head and smiling. Slowly, he walked closer to the creature, keeping in front of it. It seemed quite relaxed now. "Come on, Kiwisünce!" he cooed. The beast made a hesitant motion towards him.

"Kiwisünce!?" |Xi!xu‡qe scoffed. "Now, it has a name!"

"Why not," said the Awwakulé defensively, "But Kiwisünce means 'little child'. They're quite popular pets among Giants' children, I believe. Not so much among Pygmies."

"And why's that?"

"They have a neurotoxin. Like a wasp sting for a Giant but a little more dangerous for a Pygmy." By this time, the animal had started to inch towards the Awwakulé, who had half turned and was clicking his fingers like a child calling a Labrador puppy to follow. The scene was almost domestic.

When the spider, led by the Awwakkulé had left, and the others had returned to their rooms – and locked their doors – Jenny went to |Xi!xu‡qe. She was still trembling when he put his arms round her shoulders.

"How did it get in there?" she whispered into his neck. He tightened his grip on her shoulders and his brow furrowed. A good question. If the thing was not native in North America, what was it doing there? In a closely guarded and secret base. And why in their quarters? Clearly, the Awwakulé had not known it was – could be –there.

ǀXiǃxuǂqe saw her back into her room and shut the door. Then he settled down in the corridor outside for the night.

No one slept much. Everyone who had seen the tarantula looked a bit droopy in the morning but they recounted the events of the night animatedly to those who had slept through it.

"You could have woken me and warned me!" Wattanee's high voice could be heard berating a Yunwi Tsunsdi. None of them were particularly inclined to eat breakfast.

"And then you would have slept better?" sneered the Elf.

Later, in the secure office of the communications room of the facility, General Danny – as his staff called him – and ǀXiǃxuǂqe discussed the task of re-establishing communications with GCPP in Europe with the chief technical systems analyst. Most of the discussion turned on how much of the USB would be visible to the computer technicians and how much they could access. "It is absolutely imperative that I remain in the room and with the technicians. Come to think of it, it need be only this technician – sorry, Donny, right? – for the entire operation. Can you do it on your own?"

"It seems like it is a static code analysis tool and then merely the installation of a software patch," replied Donny.

"There must be no copying of information from the USB or attempts to access the second file. GCPP were absolutely insistent about that," ǀXiǃxuǂqe warned.

"Of course not, Sir," replied the technician.

"He wouldn't dare! I give you my word!" cried the General, who had been lost after 'static code analysis'.

"Let us be under no misapprehension, Danny," said |Xi!xu‡qe in a low voice, producing from his skin bag the sheet Eoin MacBhreithiún had given him with the USB and handing it to the General, "these orders are clear."

The General smiled, opened it and read. His face went pale. He gulped. "Treason?" His voice rose an octave: "Life in prison? Death penalty? Certainly, Sir," he said and turned to the technician, "Donny, you must talk Mr...er...Kiku through everything you are doing. He must understand and follow every keystroke. Understand?"

|Xi!xu‡qe turned to the technician, Donny. "Understand very clearly...," he paused, "What is your vision quest name?"

The technician looked at him, surprised that the Sān knew this of Nimerigar culture: "Sore Belly. After the great chief: I am Nimerigar," he said proudly. "And also because I used to get a lot of indigestion. Being an anxious child, you understand? But the people here call me Donny."

"Okay. Donny Sore Belly. Understand very clearly that what we are about to do will have enormous consequences for Little People the world over – and even for the world itself, eventually. It is vital that you get this right, which I'm sure you will, and that *you never tell anyone about what you have seen here this morning. Anyone. At all. Ever.* Do you understand?"

"I understand. Sir." The Nimerigar looked serious.

"If you do, the consequences will be terrible. Especially for you. You can expect imprisonment. Deep interrogation. Possibly a death sentence."

Now the programmer looked positively frightened.

|Xi!xu‡qe felt guilty about the heavy-handed threat but was finally confident enough to turn the USB key over to him. The master console stood in front of a window wall,

looking down into the dimly lit well of the hub that served the Far Eastern Region. General Danny flicked a rocker switch on the console: "Attention. All personnel are to vacate the IT suite immediately." He released the switch, looking pleased with himself.

Donny leaned over him, "I beg your pardon, Sir," he said deferentially, flicking the switch back: "Before leaving, save your work and log off your terminal. Ensure any TSRs and their connections are terminated. Then shut the terminal down and leave. A confirmatory test will be run. You do NOT want to be the one who has left an open line. This procedure is classified and you are prohibited from talking about it to anyone – even your opposite numbers on the night shift. Penalties for breaking this protocol are severe."

Heavy-handed, thought |Xi!xu‡qe smiling at the universal human desire to exercise authority. And, if he knew that human nature at all, an approach most likely to provoke curiosity; he said nothhing. Below them, the technicians' heads went down as they cycled through the disconnection and shut-down procedures. In five minutes, the last white coat had left the room.

"Right. Sirs," said Donny turning to the two officers, "I think it would be wise to run the sniffer. Do you agree?"

"The what?" the General was relieved to hear |Xi!xu‡qe ask.

"Sniffer. It's a program I wrote when we had a software intrusion shortly after the…"

"Sore Belly! What does it do?" snapped the General.

"Sorry, Sir. It goes into all the console connection logs and determines through passive tracking bots that I installed…"

"Donny, I think it might be better to use words that we will understand," |Xi!xu‡qe urged gently.

"Yes, Sir. Erm, I'm going to search all the connections that have been made on our terminals since you arrived. Then I'll be able to close any outgoing links. Except the one we're going to use, of course."

"You'd better warn everyone in the HQ that they're going offline, hadn't you?"

Donny looked at the Sān agent with renewed respect. "Good idea, Sir!" he pressed a button and rocked the communication switch to make the announcement. "We'll give them two minutes. In the meantime, Sir, may I ask what…"

"No," snapped the General. Donny Sore Belly looked crestfallen.

"You'll have heard of the GCPP climate summit that never happened?" said |Xi!xuǂqe, relenting. "And you of all people were probably aware of the break in communications that prevented it? We believe," We? thought |Xi!xuǂqe, feeling a fraud, "that the interruption was an act of sabotage of systems in the Eastern department – including but not only in North and South America. Your system here handles much of that traffic. Except for South American HQ, the Pombero – and the Trauco base. For some or other reason, their system is not on the same network but they were affected anyway…"

"Oh, yes, Sir," interrupted the programmer, "that's because the commander there is all but a luddite and his system seems to only let email traffic in, it's so outdated. He's only Head their because…" he stopped, "Well, they never reply anyway. With respect, Sirs, they're a bit backward down there. Sir."

"Then how…?" began |Xi!xuǂqe.

"But their technical lead, Ka'akupe is a good programmer. I mean, he's really clever. But his systems are archaic. It's almost impossible to make a connection to Trauco HQ. He can't be bothered."

"I see," said |Xi!xuǂqe. "I suppose I'll have to deal with that personally when I get there. In the meantime, we'll do what we can do from here, yes?"

The technician rubbed his hands with glee, to show his earnest enthusiasm but also pleased not to have been pulled up for insulting Millalobo, the Head of the Trauco[ii8] mission in Chile. "Right. Let's restore the protocol for the link between the North American Bureau and GCPP in Europe."

The first order of business was to load the repair program from the USB. In the doubly secured communications centre of the underground HQ, |Xi!xuǂqe sat beside the lone technician and handed him the silver bar.

Donny slid it into a port on the console.

Immediately, a small window opened at the bottom of the computer screen: 'Password:'

|Xi!xuǂqe took the keyboard and typed the password in: '**************'. When he hit return, there was no hint of the operating system's elaborate file storage system that would normally pop up. The screen showed two files.

1. LPSMTP/LPIP
9. MDEW

"Choose '1. LPSMTP/LPIP'". DON'T, don't go anywhere near number 9."

"1," said Donny, pressing the key clearly and carefully with one finger.

"Now, 'enter'," said |Xi!xuǂqe.

---

ii The Trauco: Chilean Pygmies.

"It's running, Sir."

"Good. I don't know how long it will take. Push the keyboard away from you. Right. Don't go anywhere near it." During the run, a series of selections had to be made. The Sān watched carefully as the technician entered them, not allowing him to press 'enter' without reading everything carefully. For some, he asked for explanations. It was as well to know what to expect when this was done again – and it seemed likely that he would have to take charge of the process in South America if what Donny had told him was true.

General Danny had feigned interest at first but given up when he could not follow what was going on.

However, while the program was finishing ǀXiǃxuǂqe turned to the technician and asked a question that had the General all ears.

"One more thing: did you notice anyone unusual in the HQ complex in the days leading up to the communications failure? Any Giants, or Pygmies who you didn't recognise or wouldn't have expected here?"

"No, not all, Sir. Everything seemed perfectly normal. And then we just started getting fewer communications. But after a few days, it was all back to normal. I ran my sniffer anyway, Sir. It came up with confirmation that our network connections had been reduced. And then they started up after one particular email series." He hesitated as if remembering, "There was some really strange language in the first email that arrived. I couldn't read it. Like this," he drew some symbols on a scratch pad. To the Sān agent, they looked Cyrillic. "And in the metadata the HTML specified a mishmash of conflicting character sets in the body but the header had specified charset UTF-8. That's Russian Cyrillic writing, Sir. It wasn't until much later that we were told that the communications regarding the Nature forum were all wrong. Perhaps the General knows more, Sir."

"The strange email. Do you still have it?"

"Oh, yes! I log them all. Protocol, Sir." He reached for another keyboard and typed in a command string on a different screen. A set of columns came up, listing date, time, sender, addressee and subject. He scrolled down. Then up. Then down again. "That's funny, Sir. I can't find it. It was here. The General said you'd want to see it so I checked on it just before you came yesterday. It was definitely here." Donny was sweating under |Xi!xu‡qe's doubtful gaze.

"Keep looking. We'll be around until after lunch so call me if you find it. Otherwise, forward it to the Pombero at South American HQ. Better add a warning not to open it until I get there: it looks a lot like someone installed a worm on your system."

"Oh, no, Sir. I ran all the security protocols. I even attached them to my sniffer so it followed the traffic on the connections before, during and after the interruption."

So, it appeared that there had been no breach on this side. And it came from a machine set to use Cyrillic characters. Whatever had done it had come in, done its job and erased itself – or been erased. But by whom? Wuttunee had been with him since Billings, before, even. And if the Nimerigar here was right there had been no incursion. Thinking back to the names on the board at the GCPP, he thought, the email with its illegible language had looked distinctly eastern European and was probably Cyrillic, given what he had seen and Donny's report.

The silver USB stick safely concealed in his buckskin bag, |Xi!xu‡qe returned to the others. It was lunch time and he, like them, had regained his appetite. He couldn't help noticing as the Yunwi joined the hubbub of lunch that Wuttunee came into the canteen alone and from a different direction. Puzzled, he turned to Jenny.

"I heard Wuttunee on the phone this morning, Kiku," she whispered to him. "I think he said, 'It must be done by now. He isn't out yet.' At least that's what I think he said."

"His mobile...cell...phone? I thought there was no signal."

"Well he was talking..."

"Who to? We need to get that phone. It could be a satellite phone, I suppose, but that would have worked on the bus, too."

After lunch, Jenny made a show of announcing that they had all been invited to enjoy a swim in the Centre's sports complex. "The general said 'ALL'! I think it would be a major insult if we didn't accept what is clearly a mark of honour. That includes you, Sequoyah! I see you sneaking out!" And she would brook no refusal from anyone.

The changing rooms were all male. "Typical!" snorted Jenny, who had counted on that being the case. "I'll wait for all of you to get changed first."

Once alone in the steamy changing room, she sought out Wuttunee's clothes and slipped his phone into the pocket of her own. Outside ǀXiǃxuǂqe – who had pleaded an urgent official Wavel meeting – took it from her. After their swim, she would change first so as not to have to wait for them. "It's only fair, after all," she protested.

And it would give her a chance to get the phone back from ǀXiǃxuǂqe and return it.

In the tech suite, ǀXiǃxuǂqe and Donny broke into the Mannegishi's phone.

After an hour, the guests had had enough of swimming. Jenny went first. "Can't have you ogling my underwear!" she laughed. There were mixed whistles and protests of "Eurgh! Gross!" but it was all good humoured. The Yunwi returned to ducking each other and 'bullfighting' on one other's shoulders.

Jenny changed quickly and slipped out to collect Wuttunee's phone from |Xi!xu‡qe. Then she replaced it where she had found it and called the others to change.

The contents of the Mannegishi's phone were puzzling. There were several calls to the PPSS HQ in Europe from Wuttunee's phone. That was noteworthy but could be explained. Positively suspicious, though were a number of calls directly to someone called MiniMan. Was Kleynmans 'MiniMan'? |Xi!xu‡qe thought it was likely, from the Afrikaans. Some of the calls had been made in a time frame that would have allowed Kleynmans to catch them, easily. But he hadn't. Did that suggest MiniMan was a Pygmy agent?

More puzzling was that the calls to PPSS Europe seemed paired with them but were always made a little before. Was Wuttunee betraying them to two different people? Was he informing someone in Eastern Europe about their movements and someone there informing Kleynmans? That might explain why the Giant was always a little too late. But who *was* MiniMan, then?

One fact was unavoidable: all this fooling about swimming and breaking into Sequoyah Wuttunee's phone had made them hours late for their rendezvous in the Reserva Natural del Bosque Mbaracayú[iii] – the site of the main South American HQ, their next stop according to the not-unexpected, sealed, brown envelope General Danny had

---

[iii] The Mbaracayú Forest Nature Reserve in Paraguay, on the border with Brazil.

hurriedly thrust into |Xi!xu‡qe's hands after the "swimming recreation".

Where he had got them, he would not divulge.

The journey was long and would have to be made in hops – it was too dangerous to travel from the US to the Paraguay/Brazil border on Giant transport. That being the case, it would be difficult to keep their destination hidden from Wuttunee for long.

When the light plane lifted off from the airstrip - concealed in the woods three miles east of the Pryor Mountain hideaway of the North American PPSS HQ – the four heaved a sigh of relief. Pi and Jenny fell asleep almost immediately. Sequoyah Wuttunee complained to |Xi!xu‡qe for a while – "Why couldn't we fly into here? What was the point of the stupid school bus?" The Sān explained that they had to use small aircraft to small aerodromes and that too much flying in and out of them was bound to raise suspicions and, besides, the overnight stop in Billings had been designed to create a smokescreen for anyone following them. The latter was untrue, of course, but might give the Mannegishi something to worry about.

Chapter 15 In the Back of Beyond

The journey to the Reserva Natural del Bosque Mbaracayú took ages. Even though they were flown straight to an airstrip – Pygmy, of course – outside El Calabozo in Mexico, the little plane took nearly five hours to cover the 1,000 miles. Once there, they were put on a shiny Gulf Stream G650 and, in luxury, completed the 4,500 miles to the HQ in under 8 hours.

On arrival, the exhausted travellers were greeted by a small, hairy man with an enormous grin. "Greetings, Kiku of the Sān, I am Karai of the Pombéro, Head of South American PPSS HQ. Welcome to South America." He said in perfect English. He leered at Jenny, "We have prepared a huge feast for you tonight. You must get some rest first, though!"

As they were led down the by now familiar forest green of a PPSS HQ, Jenny leaned over to ǀXi!xuǂqe and whispered, "My! He's not very good looking, is he?"

"Don't be fooled, Jenny Miler. The Pombéro are famed for their seductive powers. It is said they can put an unwilling woman into a trance of … well, a trance." He stopped in confusion. Jenny giggled. "Just don't let him – or any of them – catch you alone for too long!"

"You don't really believe that?" she replied. "I'm not a child, you know!"

"No. But you are a woman and that, I am told, makes you fair game. Now, you go into your room and lock the door!"

"Where are you going?" she cried, suddenly less confident.

"I have my work to do. I'll fetch you at 7. For the banquet. Oh, that's another thing: the Pombéro are absolute sots, to a man. They will drink until they can't talk then just get sober again at a particular blood alcohol level. It can be very disconcerting and, unless you can do it, too, dangerously disarming. The leading cause of death among them is cirrhosis."

In the antechamber of the Pombéro communications suite, the station head greeted him again. "This is my communications chief, Pyhare[i]. A codename, obviously. He is a master of the dark arts of computing and all that stuff. He'll help you do…whatever it is you have to do." The man's tone was enquiring.

Interesting, thought |Xi!xu‡qe, that he had not been told the cover story about the nature of the mission. But what harm could it do?

"It's nothing, really, Karai[ii], just re-establishing the communications protocols to Europe and North America. No need for you to be there. Boring and longwinded. Lots of waiting. Pyhare will handle it without difficulty." The Pombéro chief looked disappointed, then relieved.

"Okay. You two do your thing and then I'll meet you in the bar for a drink! How does that sound?"

"Perfect." The Sān watched the hairy chief lurch off into the passage, shouting after him, "Then I can put through that Wavel to the Trauco and maybe get hold of GCPP to

---

[i] The name means 'of the dark'.

[ii] His name means 'lord'

114

report." |Xi!xuǂqe was fervently hoping that Karai would remain sober. Or reach his limit and sober up. He wouldn't have put a bet on which one the Chief was going for. Still, he feared for Jenny who seemed entirely too complacent about the Pombéro.

Inside the computer and communications hub, |Xi!xuǂqe took the tech through the process exactly as he had done the Nimerigar tech. He watched Pyhare as he spoke. There was nothing dark about the man's open, almost gormless face. But |Xi!xuǂqe had met a few computer technicians and knew it was risky to make judgments too quickly. Well-groomed, efficient, social ease did not invariably add up to professional competence; likewise, the fact that a tech was a corporate, or social, climber, didn't mean he was incompetent. And vice versa. Pyhare's frank gaze might hide anything, or nothing.

"The whole thing," groaned |Xi!xuǂqe, "is like watching paint dry. Or a lizard on a log." Pyhare glanced up, quick to smile at |Xi!xuǂqe's patronising witticism. It is like talking to a younger brother, thought |Xi!xuǂqe, fondly. Even the sleek comma of silky black hair and the delicate ears suggested innocence and a sincere desire to be useful. No more.

Except for the pencil. Pyhare held a pencil, new, sharpened and with a rubber on its tip, that he constantly wobbled between his thumb and forefinger. His wrist rested on the computer desk, where there was no paper to write on, and occasionally the rubber tip bounced on the table-top in a rapid tattoo. After the first few times, |Xi!xuǂqe realised that this happened when he was telling Pyhare about technical features. Puzzled, he eventually told himself that Pyhare was simply impatient about technicalities being explained by a non-technical 'boss' but was too polite to stop him.

In spite of his questions about the Pombéro, though, |Xi!xu‡qe was pleased to note that the tech made no attempt – appeared uninterested in – the file numbered 9 on the drive. In order to make good his fib about the tedious complexity of the process, the Sān agent spent half an hour making small talk with the Pombéro tech. During their chat – t-t-tap, tap, tap – the Sān established that there had been no apparent intrusion in 'my tech suite' and nothing obvious anywhere else on the base. Other than the substituted email. He did learn, though, that the process for re-establishing the connection could be 'reverse engineered' from a central computer array such as the European one. A little questioning revealed that changing the Far Eastern protocols didn't need anyone to be on site. So why was he there? Or, more accurately, he thought, the Pombéro tech must also have realised it and wondered why |Xi!xu‡qe was actually there. Fortunately, the boy gave no sign that the thought had occurred to him...unless the pencil...?

It was the former idea, though, that really troubled the Sān agent: why had he been made to complete this troublesome and dangerous journey? Not just to deliver the Earth Worm. It had been given to him in Ireland, in Europe. If it had to be installed on a central computer in a B.O.S.S. facility, why was he carrying it around the world. Especially given that the communications protocol could be engineered from a facility of the Grand Council of Pygmy Peoples, probably in Ireland? It occurred to him that he was not carrying the Earth Worm at all; that the whole mission was a ruse. For a moment, he was on the verge of telling Pyhare to open the forbidden file. 9. He struggled with himself for a while but, lost in a maze of deceptions and covert contradictions, gave up. There was only one thing to do:

contact the Grand Council. Eoin MacBhreithiún and Mrs Donoghue would have answers.

Just then, Karai came barrelling into the room, "Great kid that Jenny!" he enthused, "You're missing a great party! Come and join us – you must be finished by now!"

ǀXi!xuǂqe found it hard not to show his irritation. 'kid' indeed! At least Jenny wouldn't be fooled by the someone who called her a kid! Someone who used 'great' like that!

It was as well that the Pombéro station head had arrived, though, thought ǀXi!xuǂqe. "I need to make a priority call to the Grand Council. It will have to be done by me, alone, in this room since it involves a matter of high security."

"You? Alone in my tech suite? Unchaperoned? Not bloody likely!" The chief was smiling but there was no doubt as to his sincerity. "This is a central station. This computer network has direct access to the whole Pygmy network. There is no way on earth that you are going to have unfettered access to it. Even Pyhare here isn't allowed in here alone. Nor am I for that matter!"

"But it's just a Wavel call!" objected ǀXi!xuǂqe. "I can't use my mobile because there's no signal!"

"No. No chance. Come and join the party!"

"I have to clarify something about my mission, though…"

"So phone them."

"Much too insecure. I wouldn't need to speak to Eoin MacBhreithiún in person if it were not highly sensitive!"

"As highly sensitive as the integrity of the Pygmy network? We've already had one security breach and you know what chaos that caused…Pygmy delegates appearing at different places and at the wrong times…or not at all. No.

The HQ directive was explicit: no one but appropriately cleared staff in here *in pairs*. You should count yourself lucky I trusted you in here with this scoundrel! Eh, Pyhare?" The big Pygmy slapped his subordinate on the shoulder, laughing. It was clear that |Xi!xuɬqe would not be allowed to make the Wavel call. The Pombéro must have caught the sense of defeat in the Bushman's eyes: "Here," he said, reaching into a pocket and withdrawing a brown envelope, "Perhaps you don't need to talk to Mac. Take this. It is for you to open. Your orders. Now come and join the party."

There was nothing for it but to join the raucous celebrations.

The contents of the brown envelope ordered him to the Trauco HQ to "complete his information mission" and leave "with all possible expedition on the transport provided" – odd wording, he thought. The orders didn't explain much: why the hurry? And where to? Not for the first time, he was struck by the flagrant disregard of operation rules. He'd still love to talk to Mac, he thought.

The next morning, |Xi!xuɬqe got Piyêsîs, Sequoyah and Jenny up early. Try as they might, they could rouse none of the Yunwi Tsunsdi, who had passed out in a heap in their dormitory. They made the 100 mile 'hop' to the Trauco base in Chile alone. It was tiresome but uneventful. Their first view of the setting of the base from the air showed a ridge with a peaceful valley stretching southwest. The sun was high and the green strip of the valley appeared as an oasis in the vast brown of the arid mountains that sheltered it. And it was in Argentina, not Chile. "It ought to be in Chile," laughed their pilot, "but hardly anyone knows it exists, let alone where!"

It was a beautiful scene – until he took the ancient Beechcraft Bonanza into a screaming descent that had them skimming the crest of a ridge and plummeting to metres over a stream before the runway even came into view. Wuttunee, eyes shut tight, clung to the armrest.

They were greeted at the entrance to the forest by a scruffy Pygmy carrying a stone-headed axe[iii] and staff. "Greetings, Bushman, you are welcome to our humble abode," he intoned in heavily accented English, unusual for a Pygmy. "I am Millalobo, bureau chief here." The Trauco chief looked at the 'Bushman' from his full 1meter 27 height. Somehow, though he was at least 20 centimetres shorter, he gave the impression that he was looking down on |Xi!xu‡qe. Millalobo did not spare Jenny even a passing glance.

Suddenly, there was another figure beside them. "And I am Fiura[iv], 2IC to this troglodyte harebrain," she announced pleasantly. She leaned towards Jenny and stage-whispered, "Don't be efended if he does not look achoo. He believes that he is irrisitible to wooman. So he's afraid dat you become besotted wit him. Of course, he would seduce you in a shot if he could – though he can't! I am not worried! Ha Ha! – but he's terrifié of what the GCPP would do. You two are celebrates, you know?"

"Celebrities?" said Jenny turning to Fiura, "I don't think Kiku will like that!"

"Kiku? Is dat how you say? We are all complete boffled!" She pronounced her mangling of the 'baffled', 'boff-led'. "Oh, you must no worry – it is only among officers in this be-niggeted place."

[iii] In the myths, the Trauco man supposedly carries a small stone-headed hatchet that he uses to strike trees in the forest to symbolize his reputed sexual potency.

[iv]. According to myth, the Trauco's wife is "the wicked and ugly Fiura." https://en.wikipedia.org/wiki/Trauco

They were given a rather frugal lunch, presented to them as the pinnacle of Trauco cuisine but which Piyêsîs warned them was not what it looked like. Wuttunee advised them not to ask what it was. Afterwards, there was an uncomfortable silence – it seemed the Trauco high command were not big on conversation – the Sān agent told the sullen bureau chief what he needed.

"Of course. I barely know how dis ting works. Ofcoursid ('accursed' Jenny supposed) Giant mahia! ('magic, Jenny assumed) Why not use the sea creatures (cree-ay-too-a-raz) we always have? Instead dey..." Before he could launch into what was obviously a pet gripe, he noticed his wife – as his '2IC' had turned out to be – rolling her big dark eyes. "The feelty ting is over in dis compter bolding across parody ground." He flapped a hand at a morose Trauco at the end of the table, "CoiCoi – is name Ka'akupe, 'behind the forest' – take you to. He knows how works it, but I think you do, too."

"Somehow," Jenny whispered, giggling, "I don't think that was meant as an expression of admiration!".

|Xi!xuⱡqe turned to her, "This should be quick. An hour tops. I've let the pilot know that we'd be flying out this evening but I haven't had any orders and I'm not sure where we're going or what happens next. Pi hasn't heard anything but I'll know more when I've Wavelled CCPP – it'll have to be through the computer system." He leaned over to her and whispered: "The sooner we get back to civilisation the better!"

In the 'compter bolding', |Xi!xuⱡqe told Ka'akupe that he needed privacy for a secret conference. The Trauco, who had perked up when asked to guide the 'steem-ed gust' (esteemed, |Xi!xuⱡqe guessed, fervently) across the clearing to the only brick building in the compound, looked crestfallen when he realised he was not invited. "It is PPCC business with the GCPP," the Sān agent explained, using as many initialisms as he could – always good for frightening the ignorant! The Trauco's eyes grew big. "I have to speak to the Prime Minister and Mrs O'Donoghue in secret." As he had hoped, Ka'akupe's mouth dropped open, his eyes grew even bigger and he hastened to the door. The poor man was almost apoplectic with respect.

"I bees outside. Long way outside. If you need me, Sir. Oh. Is dialup modem."

"Dialup? What? You can't be serious! Why, CoiCoi?"

"Secure," was all Ka'akupe said before he disappeared, practically slamming the door in his haste.

The moment he saw the machine, ǀXiǃxuǂqe realised it was archaic. However, it started well enough. Pisamboro! Windows 10! But then it took him twenty minutes to work out how to connect a dialup modem to make connection to the outside world. He cursed his foolishness in sending Ka'akupe away. Probably – well, perhaps, at least – the Pisamboro would have known how to navigate the archaic operating system. When he finally got onto the internet, the computer informed him that there were 32 updates to install. Try as he might, ǀXiǃxuǂqe could not convince the computer not to install the updates. That was another thing Ka'akupe might have been able to do.

Ka'kupe clever? Really? Donny had truly had the wool pulled over his eyes! Cursing the Trauco, and Ka'akupe in particular, for not maintaining systems, he sat back to wait.

Four hours later, the last update installed. ǀXiǃxuǂqe sat forward, breathing a sigh of relief. Time to find out what his mission was all about, why he was traipsing around

South American Pygmy bases when his mission had to be completed in a B.O.S.S. central computer array – had already been, for all he knew. He could see why *this* machine might need someone competent on site but not why Eoin MacBhreithiún had ordered him to install the message reconfiguration application on the North and South American HQ computers when it could be reverse engineered from Europe.

Computer restarting.

Do not power off or unplug your machine.

He stared at the green legend on the screen. A lesser man might have wept. A man with longer hair might have tried to pull it out. He took a tighter grip on the knobkierrie that never left his side, sat back and waited.

"Kiku!" Jenny's voice came from outside the door. "Where are you? Why are you taking so long?"

He opened the door. "You would not believe this computer! I don't think it's been started since…God knows when!"

"But we were supposed to leave! It's 6 o'clock. We must go. They've sent that jet for us. The pilot says it's all ready. We can go now."

"Jet? Good. I won't be long. I'm afraid I haven't managed to get through to MacBhreithiún yet. I need to know what our next move is. And why he's sent me on this wild goose chase!"

"Oh, can't you ask him when we get back?"

"Get back where, though? I'm not sure he hasn't got some other plan up his sleeve. I don't know what my orders are. He must have meant me to contact him. That's all I can think of. Only he didn't know what a backward communication system they had down here. It's really quite strange that nothing was waiting for me here…no, actually," he looked back inside at the quietly humming antique, "it's not at all surpris…."

"KIKU! You're not listening. They sent a jet! Let's go now. Please? Please!"

"Jen, why are you in such a hurry? I know this is not a very comfortable place but I have my mission to fulfil, orders to follow…" Suddenly he noticed that her eyes were brimming with…tears? No. Rage! "I promise we'll go as soon as I've talked to Eoin. Promise. Besides, I don't know where to tell the pilot to take us." Firmly, he closed the door, blocking off her pleas. He regretted excluding her. After all, he thought, she is only a girl and the turn her life has taken in the past few days is bound to have unsettled her. She wants to get back to civilization, of course…. He turned to the machine. "Ah!" something was happening. He sat down in front of the screen. *Command prompt*! He remembered now. It took a moment to remember how to get there but it was definitely the fastest way of getting into the communications system. He opened a DOS screen and connected to the portal in Ireland. In a few minutes, the jocund head of MacBhreithiún bobbed on the screen. ǀXiǃxuǂqe's relief was huge, even though the Pygmy PM's head was wreathed in green locks instead of the red ones. Of course, green screen: a cathode ray tube monitor, of course! Good grief!

"Ah! Eoin! It is so good to see you! I never thought this damned Trauco machine would start."

"Kiku, what the hell are you doing in Chile? You were supposed to be on your way to …."

"But I haven't had any orders. The Pombéro in Paraguay wouldn't let me use their system to contact you…

"General D gave…was meant to give… I made a clear order… the pilot… Never mind. You have to get on a flight to London!"

"London?"

"Yes. London. London. How many times do I have to say it? Do you have the MEW with you?"

"Yes. In fact that's what I wanted to ask you about. It's why I had to be alone when I spoke to you. Which is why Karai – that's the section head of…"

"Yes, I know who the bloody section heads are, ya feckin' eejit…. Didn't Fiura just send someone to get yer?" shouted MacBhreithiún, uncharacteristically. "Agent |Xi!xu‡qe," MacBhreithiún's voice took on an entirely different tone, so different that the Sān agent didn't even register that the Clurichaun had pronounced his name perfectly, "here are your *express* orders: you are to enplane immediately and make all haste to Brasilia airport. There you will find two open tickets in yours and Jenny Miler's names…"

"Jenny Miler's name? Why? How do you know she even wants to go to Europe? Wait, how do you even know she's with me?"

"Do not question me. The ticket will identify her as your mother, as will both your passports. You will be given these at Brasilia BSB. Leave. Now." The screen flickered to a dull green, the DOS cursor flicking in the top left corner.

|Xi!xu‡qe sat looking at it, stunned.

That's when he heard the unmistakable whine of retrostabilised helicopter engines in the distance and felt the agitation of the forest animals ripple through the forest, up the valley. There was a tang of radio waves, bitter and metallic on his tongue.

Chapter 16 Battle of the Jogahoh

In the lead helicopter, Kleynmans grinned in satisfaction. There was no way they could have got away from this wilderness without being picked up on his radar or IR scans. If they had come here, as Sparrow had assured him they had, they were still here. He had them. All he had to do was locate them. And his noose was tightening. He chortled.

In the little valley ahead of him that would not be a difficult task, he estimated.

"Put two choppers down on the north flank of the valley, two on the south. The other two come down with me into the valley floor. Then we sweep northwest up the river till we get them."

"Kiku! Kiku!" Jenny's fear pierced the door like a drill.

The noise of the chopper blades was much louder now, a jackhammering thudding up the little valley, underpinned by the turbo whine of retrostabilisers.

Then there was another noise.

ǀXi!xuǂqe recognised it with a shock: the sound of boots in unison, the cocking of automatic weapons. At least there was no gunfire as yet. The Sān clutched at his knobkierrie and opened the door. Jenny was outside, urgency in her eyes but, he was glad to see, not panic.

"There are helicopters, six, landing down the valley. The Trauco are going there now. There are hundreds of them, Kiku! Where did they come from?"

"It's a garrison, Jenny. Look!" He pointed at a phalanx of Pygmy figures in camouflaged fatigues and drill order, weapons cradled and heading at the double to the southwest of the valley. In addition to a rifle, each had a pahueldún – the axe-shaped equivalent of his kierrie that he had seen Millalobo carrying – across their back. The rays of the setting sun sloped down to their right, making shadows that seemed to increase their size and numbers. They disappeared into the shadow of the mountain. "And look! There," he pointed to the left, another phalanx was appearing into the light, heading up to the high ground.

Suddenly the neat rows were surrounded by splashes of dust and they shattered and disappeared. A few figures lay still on the hillside.

"They need me. MacBhreithiún can't have known about this! Where are Piyêsîs and Sequoyah? Find them. Tell them I've gone down the valley, along the riverbank."

"Kiku, no, it's dangerous and we need to get away. You cannot be risked. Nor can the MagDhuibhfinn Earth Worm! You have to come!"

"Jenny, you go and make sure the jet is on the runway. We can't just leave Pygmies in danger like this. Get Piyêsîs to bring a vehicle to fetch me when you're sure we can fly immediately. Until then we have to hold them back. Hurry!"

In the haste and urgency, in the passion of battle, he didn't fully take in what she had just said.

She looked at him. For a moment it seemed like she was taking her last look. Then she turned and ran across the parade ground to the main entrance.

Shouldering his bag and drawing his kierrie, |Xi!xuǂqe moved towards the river – little more than a stream – and started making his way through the thin forest on its banks. The small trees and low brush afforded some cover and something about them made him feel more confident – as though his First People ancestry recognised the safety of forest-land. He moved towards the sound of gunfire, now almost incessant. As it got louder and his senses integrated with each other, the sound began to break in his mouth like lemons bursting. A bitter blue colour streamed from his right and he moved towards the still figure of a Trauco soldier. The Pygmy was dead, his weapon unfired. |Xi!xuǂqe stooped to retrieve AMP-69. More use than a kierrie against an army. As he did so a stream of tracer arced from behind a low ridge, slashing violet furrows like pain across his back as it passed, almost leisurely, into the brush behind him. He felt the site of the pain. Nothing. Sometimes, being a synesthete was a liability.

On his belly, making himself as small as he could, he crawled along a shallow depression towards the right of where the tracer had come from. Every few seconds, a fresh rush of fire would come. At first it was near him, then its direction was more erratic. Clearly the shooter had no idea where he was. |Xi!xuǂqe shuffled closer to the gunfire. Suddenly, he saw the Giant, squinting through the sights of an HK MG4. He was moving the barrel to and fro across an arc in front of him, every few seconds letting loose a stream of death. He had no idea where his target had gone.

|Xi!xuǂqe raised the machine pistol, shouldering the shortened butt, and fired once. The Giant stopped moving. The barrel of his weapon tilted, uselessly aiming at the hillside. A deep purple washed from his right and a bitter taste washed into his mouth as the bush came suddenly alive

with camo forms. He shuffled round till he was beside the dead Giant and facing the same way. The Giant's platoon had overtaken the more intense sounds of battle.

He was witnessing a flanking movement by this LMG platoon.

By combining his sight with his smell and hearing, |Xi!xu‡qe adjusted his vision to emphasise the ultraviolet. Five men stood out, clear as day: their camouflage as bright as pollen flowers to honeybees. He rolled the dead Giant over, "|Ûba te[i], brother."

He felt the canvas bag of ammunition that hung below the weapon. Plenty.

With the underside curve of the weapon's butt over his shoulder – it was far too long for him – he took aim at the furthest Giant. The weapon leaped in his hands but he held it firm, redirecting his fire at the panicked Giants who had little suspected that the right wing of their pincer movement would turn on them. They fell quickly, only the nearest making it to cover before the raking fire shredded the bush where he had been.

But |Xi!xu‡qe was already up and moving, his kierrie in his right hand. He planted it in the ground in front of him as a pivot. In two cartwheels, he reached the Giant, now hysterically firing at the ground where |Xi!xu‡qe had been. He had not expected Pygmy death to arrive at him from the air. But it did.

Moving quickly through the undergrowth he began to come across more signs of battle. There were some Trauco killed by bullet wounds but also Giants, some with the shocking skull injuries he would have expected from a kierrie. But narrower, deeper: pahueldún.

---

[i] Sorry.

Something pale grey whipped through the leaves and thudded into a tree trunk nearby in a splash of orange and sark grey. Cursing himself for standing still, |Xi!xuǂqe flung himself to the ground. Across the valley the hillside was marked with occasional glowing golden blossoms that sparkled and then vanished. Immediately, he could sense the pale grey streaks of the rounds crossing the 200 metres towards his position. Then he heard the maroon thud of brass burying itself in the earth. Most of it was aimed down the valley. At least he knew now where the thick of the battle was. He moved, keeping low to the ground, a brown streak like dead leaves across the forest floor.

As he approached through the more densely wooded western bank, |Xi!xuǂqe realised that he was behind the Giants. Their flanking motion had been intended to cross the stream higher and attack the Trauco position. Looking down, he saw Piyêsîs and Sequoyah trapped in a narrow strip of bush on the eastern bank of the stream. It was impossible for him to reach his friends through the Giant forces! With a shock, he realised that there were Giants around him. Focused on events before them, they had not seen him. He froze. To be spotted now was certain death. If the snipers across the valley had seen him, they must be hesitating to aim their fire here for fear of killing their own forces.

The Sān made himself as small as possible and started slithering backwards.

There was a cry from the opposite bank: "Pi! Pi!" It was Wuttunee. |Xi!xuǂqe risked looking along the sight-line of the Giants. What he saw froze his blood.

Beneath an intense crackle of suppressing gunfire from the Trauco, Sequoyah was struggling to manhandle the form of Piyêsîs across a clearing. The tiny figure of Sequoyah struggled with the inert weight of his Giant friend.

For a moment, the battlefield seemed to hold its breath and the return fire stopped. Perhaps the attacking Giant force thought the Mannegishi was trying drag one of their own to safety.

There was no movement in the body of Piyêsîs.

Then all hell broke loose. From behind, |Xi!xuǂqe sensed a red lattice of rounds streaking into the Giants amongst whom he was hidden. Had the Giants across the valley gone mad? Been ordered to sacrifice their comrades?

Now the Giants around them were screaming, fleeing in panic. One or two fell. They were left writhing where they were as their comrades fled. The web of crimson and grey followed them south down the banks of the river, away from |Xi!xuǂqe. Cautiously, he turned around and peered at the sandy valley floor. Hundreds of tiny figures were charging in a formation rapidly wheeling southwards, sweeping into a front that spanned the width of the valley.

"Are you alright, Sir?" asked a voice at his shoulder. |Xi!xuǂqe spun round to find a Jogahoh in an officer's uniform.

"Kaggen! I nearly died of fright! What in the name of Pisamboro are the Jogahoh doing here?"

"Sorry, Sir," said the officer, "we are late but we were on our way when we heard that you were still here and that the attack had begun. We made all haste. I am glad that you are alive, Sir."

"Wait! What do you mean you were on your way here? How? Why? And how did you know I was even here? And what do you mean '*still* here'?"

"MacBhreithiún," the officer said, as if that were all the explanation needed. "I have express orders to evacuate you, Sir. By force if necessary, Sir. The jet is on the runway. A helicopter is on the way to fetch you. Anyway, I don't think the Giants represent any danger, now. Or, not for long."

|Xi!xu‡qe looked around. There was no sign of the other army. A wave of Jogahoh and Trauco swept south down the valley, firing. They moved past the Giant helicopters. He could only stare.

The rock-hard pulsing of a helicopter's blades like stones being thrown slowly broke through the post battle fog of his senses and then he was on board, rising above the battlefield. He could see the Trauco and Jogahoh holding-positions as the machine carried him aloft.

As the helicopter circled, the figure of Sequoyah Wuttunee appeared from behind a tree, standing astride the motionless figure of Piyêsîs. The tiny figure looked up and raised his hand in farewell, or despair.

Brave Mannegishi, valiant Cree, thought |Xi!xu‡qe as the machine wheeled north to the runway.

At the runway, he was hustled onto the G650. Still in a kind of shock, he was so relieved to see Jenny in the doorway of the aeroplane that he did not even notice when a Trauco soldier relieved him of the AMP-69.

As the aircraft arrowed through the sky, they watched the sun finally disappear, and then the machine turned east.

"Where are we going?" the Sān asked an attendant in NCOs uniform.

"Brasilia, Sir." An officer appeared behind him.

"We have orders to get you on a flight to London, Sir. Do you still have the item?" |Xi!xu‡qe almost reached for the small bag at his side but resisted. He sensed its presence instead.

"I'm sure of it," he answered, expressionlessly. The officer looked relieved.

"We have a two-and-a-half-hour flight. You must be tired, Sir." He turned and left.

Alone in the lounge area, food and drink on the table between them, Jenny Miler and |Xi!xuǂqe compared notes. Though the Sān had innumerable questions, he knew Jenny could have no answers. She was furious with him but also overjoyed to see him.

"Why didn't you come? I tried to tell you! Pi followed you. And Sequoyah! You should have come!"

"I'm so sorry that I dragged you into this, Jenny Miler. It was not meant to be so dangerous."

"That's not the point! You put us all in danger and Pi and Sequoyah...I hope they are alright!"

|Xi!xuǂqe could not tell her what he had seen. Ashamed, he changed the subject: "I do not understand how Kleynmans got to the Trauco base. I cannot believe he was guided from GASP or B.O.S.S. Even we did not know where we would be yesterday." But the envelopes, he thought. "And another thing, how did the Jogahoh know?"

"I don't know, Kiku," said Jenny. She looked at the table in front of her, touched the polished wood. "As long as you're safe."

Although |Xi!xuǂqe knew it was not an accusation, he felt it like one.

Jenny looked around the empty cabin. "At least we won't have to worry about Wuttunee and Kleynmans. They can't possibly know where we are. Or follow."

"No. We will not have to worry about Sequoyah. But I do not believe he was responsible anyway," replied the Sān.

She looked at him for a long time. "I don't know what is going on but it's the most exciting thing that has ever happened to me – anyone! – and I'm so glad to be here with you. I was terrified back there. Especially when you went haring off like that!"

"You are right. My superiors will not be pleased with me. In doing that, I put the whole mission in danger, even if I don't exactly know what the mission is."

"Was the 'item' that guy asked about…?"

"The USB key. It is nothing for you to worry about, Jenny Miler. But," - a memory of something earlier flashed in his mind…something she had said at the Trauco computer building: what? But it eluded him so he dismissed it. He stopped to choose his words, "I have some difficult news: Piyêsîs was wounded in the battle. He was not moving. Wuttunee was with him." Then he told her the story of what he had seen, of Wuttunee trying to drag Piyêsîs to safety in the face of the Giant attack, of how the battle had paused as if in respect for his bravery. "I…I think Pi may have died, Jenny."

"Oh, no! that can't be! Not Pi! He was so…" Jenny broke down. |Xi!xu‡qe reached across the table and held her hand. "What about Sequoyah?"

"I doubted the Mannegishi," said |Xi!xu‡qe looking out of the porthole at the clouds sliding by, "He was so bad tempered. And I thought it odd that we were so closely followed by Kleynmans. But then…then I could not understand why Kleynmans never caught up with us. Until today, of course. And Sequoyah did not know where we were going after the Pryor Mountains, nor the Pombero. I doubt he even knew where the Trauco base was – on a map, I mean. We certainly didn't. Then he risked his life to rescue Piyêsîs. I cannot believe he was a traitor. It is all very odd."

Jenny sat quietly, dabbing her eyes with a tissue. |Xi!xu‡qe looked out of the window at the darkening sky. Eventually the two fell asleep in their seats.

When they awoke they were on the approach and there was a carpet of the lights that was Brasilia and its extravagant architecture, brightly lit and set in curving parks.

And next they were through check-in, with the help of a smiling British Airways steward fussing alternatively in in Portuguese and English, who settled them into business class seats and brought him a colouring book.

Finally, the flight was airborne. ǀXi!xuǂqe looked at Jenny. "Jenny? I have a question. What are you really doing here? You say it is exciting but…"

"It is. It's an adventure," she replied, "and much better than my boring life in Canada. Until…" she seemed to remember, then continued, 'I mean, what was I going to do? Graduate, get a job, become a wage-slave? This is something that I can believe in. I can believe in you, right? And, besides, I like you – and you look like you could do with the help!"

"Oh, I do, do I? I look helpless to you?"

"Well, let's face it, you wouldn't have got onto this flight without a Giant mum or dad…"

"I'll have you know that I am quite capable of travelling without a Giant. People are very cautious about questioning your height – they are afraid of offending a person who they see as born with a disability. They think I have achondroplasia."

"What?"

"A Giant born with what they call 'dwarfism': short limbs, mainly."

"Ah, well," she said, looking out of the porthole so he couldn't see her smile, "you saw how smoothly the airport all went, didn't you? If people are worried about…er…. dwarves – yes, yes, I know: Giant woolly thinking – they are twice as worried about mothers with spectacularly ugly children!"

Chapter 17 A Matter of Trust in Skulduggery Alley

At that moment, the Grand Council of Pygmy Peoples was in session. And they were talking about ǀXi!xuǂqe.

Holding the floor was Inina of the Taotao Mo'na representing Micronesia.

"After all," she shrilled, "what did we know of this Kiku before he came here? There was meant to be a meeting. It did not happen. Why? We do not know but are told," she looked at MacBhreithiún accusingly, "that someone has penetrated our communications network. Who? We do not know who. Then suddenly, there appears this half-Giant, half-Pygmy Kiku, a half-height –" The delegates shuffled uncomfortably on their chairs.

"Inina, that is not language that we can use in this chamber. Unlike Giants, we do not hold the physical attributes of people against them!"

"Yes, MacBhreithiún, and we all know where your sympathies lie. And your emissary, this…this Bushman! travels the world in the name of the Pygmy people. He causes mayhem in Canada, in America. There are deaths! Deaths in our name! And in Mbaracayu forest a massacre. At a PPSS HQ! It is hard to imagine how he could have brought more attention on us from the Giants!"

Delegates were now beginning to look decidedly angry.

"I say," began ÓCléirigh, "ahem, I say, that is nothing more than conjecture…. The Giants already knew of the whereabouts, through someone's treachery, no doubt, of the mission and…"

"Oh, shut up, you mumbling fool!" shouted Hugh, "What do you know about anything? And besides, Inina is right, how did they know where that," he struggled to pack his voice with all the venom he could muster, "Highly Secret Pygmy Location was? And who knew he was going there? Only one person – Kiku!"

"Not true, Hugh of the Brunaidh," retorted MacBhreithiún, though he knew he could never reveal enough to challenge this attack, "We also knew. Officers of this council. Why do you not believe one of us…" His voice was lost in a chorus of rage.

"Absurd!" shouted Afallon, "and besides, the moment he came here he began to sow discord with that outlandish name of his – clickety-clackety, hick-hock, hot-and-tot! don't you remember? He suggested that we were all against Pygmies because he couldn't pronounce our names!"

"I agree, it was a deliberate ploy. Avalon is right!" shouted Locryn. It was not lost on Afallon on that Locryn did not pronounce the uvular trill that made the second consonant in his name but this was not a time for petty disagreements. She was going on: "There is some skulduggery going on here. The Grand Council has not been kept properly informed, maybe even misled. A Pygmy agent on a supposedly secret mission is accompanied by two Giants, the Cree Piyêsîs and that…woman, Jenny Miler. How secure is that?"

"And what's more," Arsenei, the Belarusian was on his feet, "every step of the mission is followed by a B.O.S.S. agent, this Kleynmans! He was on the ferry before Kiku even reached us, before we knew about him, even!"

"Absolutely true! That is absolutely true. Why didn't I think of it?" Hugh exclaimed, smacking his forehead, "That's brilliant Arsenei! How do we know the B.O.S.S. agent was not told where this council sits? Are we all in danger like the Trauco? I propose that we send someone to intercept the half-height and find out what he is doing."

"I second that!" shouted Peyton, the English Brownie. Continuing, her voice, dripped in sarcastic acid, that favourite tool of the English Pygmies, "Arsenei's analysis is exactly the kind that should have been made by our Esteemed Prime Minister and his Minister of Environmental Affairs, not to mention the bumbling clerk ÓCléirigh!"

Mrs Donoghue looked from MacBhreithiún to ÓCléirigh. "It seems that the council is set on bringing its agents to heel," she said, "and we must abide by the majority finding –"

"Since when is the ill-informed rancour of a few delegates and agents a majority –" started MacBhreithiún, but Mrs Donoghue was not to be stopped.

"– but let me be clear that the operation currently underway is of critical importance. The fact that its details have not been generally divulged should be testament to that. However, while I agree that Kiku has been most…er…unfortunate, I cannot believe that it is the fault of Eoin MacBhreithiún or any officer of the Grand Council. And I wish it to be placed on record that both he and his clerk have my full confidence in this, as in all matters of the

Council." This speech seemed to suck some of the venom from the proceedings and matters calmed down.

She leaned over to MacBhreithiún and whispered dramatically from behind her hand, "And you will have noticed that it is the mainlanders who are crowing most loudly, will you not?"

"We must not," MacBhreithiún spoke aloud to the whole chamber, "allow ourselves to be divided. If we do, we are lost. That was true among the Pygmies of the Americas, against both the Conquistadors and the New England settlers. It was true among the Southern Asian and Melanesian Pygmies. It has always been true. Unity is all that is left to us: the Giants have seen to that."

As usual, the Pygmy Prime Minister's clear view of the broader picture and the soothing tones of his voice brought a kind of calm to the chamber.

Hugh got to his feet. "I hear and agree, Eoin MacBhreithiún. I too call for unity. But we must be careful. We are as ever just a stone's throw from disaster. If there are members of the Giant security community who are able to reveal the true nature and extent of the Pygmy peoples, the fate of the Trauco may easily be ours. And the Grand Council. And this hallowed hall," he waved up at the chamber's ceiling, knitted with the ancient roots of the trees above, "If this were to fall, we might never survive the calamity –"

"That is not so. It will not happen –" began ÓCléirigh but he got no further.

"– I say, if it falls, Pygmydom, worldwide, will suffer," Hugh continued portentously. "At the very least, we have to negate the threat of Jenny Miler and establish a clearer line of communication with Kiku so that he cannot do as he wishes." There were murmurs of assent around the chamber. "To this end, I propose the Zlydzen Arsenei to act as our agent in Europe: not only is he a trained PPSS agent, but he knows that ground and has some acquaintance with our most implacable enemies, GASP, that may ease his passage."

The vote that followed was not as close as it should have been, thought ÓCléirigh but it was binding. Arsenei was taken off to be briefed.

Outside, some of the delegates went off to the pub, some returned to their dwellings. Afallon, Hugh and Locryn sat together in the shadow of a great aspen.

"Well, I think we can say goodbye to Kiku and Jenny," said Locryn, peaked little ears almost trembling through her long blond hair.

"And the bloody MagDhuibhfinn Earth Worm!" snorted Hugh.

"Mmm," Afallon chimed in, "I hope that we are not making a mistake, "There is only one and, we have to admit, it's a brilliant idea: the Giants are screwing up the planet hand-over-fist and we have precious little say in the matter, especially since we weren't even able to establish a Climate Committee, let alone feed into their Cop31."

"I wouldn't be too worried, Afallon the Worrier," teased Hugh. It was a widely held view that the Bwca had acquired the characteristic, superhuman propensity for worrying of their occupiers – the Welsh Giants. "Can you imagine what would happen if the Giants found out that we had infected all their computers with a worm? The retaliation would be total –"

"Yes, but Arsenei…he's a Zlydzen. You know what they're like: a vicious lot. Violent. And they enjoy it. What if…"

"There you go again, Afallon," Locryn, her voice melodic and soothing, "seeing in the inevitable only roots of failure when what lies before us all is a golden road of peace and calm. Fret you not."

When their flight landed in London, |Xi!xu‡qe and Jenny were whisked away in a Pygmy Secret Service vehicle, just as |Xi!xu‡qe had expected. The darkened windows obscured the built-up seats and the driver's enhanced steering wheel controls. The streets of London soon took over from the M3. Traffic was all around them.

"This feels nice and anonymous," said Jenny. "After all those mountains and trees and that disgusting spider, I'm glad to be safely back in a city!"

The car drove past blocks of old buildings, mostly darkened now. The limousine slowed to a crawl and the driver's partition slid silently open.

"This is where you'll be staying, Sir," said the chauffeur, "The St Ermin – long the preserve of PPSS, though the Giants use it, too."

"Really? Isn't it a little risky to put us in a Giant hotel?"

"Oh, not just any Giants, Sir, all the agencies use it: B.O.S.S., P.E.D., NSA, CIA, GASP –"

"What! That sounds remarkably foolhardy."

"It's completely crazy!" Jenny cried, her eyes wide, "Kiku we can't possibly stay here!"

"Oh, you don't need to worry," the chauffeur said soothingly, though |Xi!xu‡qe could hear the smile in his voice, "It's been going on for decades, maybe a hundred years. They all think that whatever happens here is some kind of skulduggery by one of their own agencies – Giant, I mean. It never crosses their mind that there are Pygmies.

Few of them 'believe' in Pygmies anyway and, besides, and this is cleverest of all, there have been innumerable renewals and changes of the décor. During them, Pygmy architects and builders have…er…sequestered whole spaces between rooms that are comfy for us but… well, you get the idea."

Outside, the brightly lit, almost golden grandeur of the old hotel's entrance was sliding into view. Ornate statues, one of an unidentifiable beast and one of what looked like a cougar to Jenny, stood on carved pedestals, guarding an ornate wrought iron gate. Beyond it, down a brightly lit drive was a red brick, white-windowed façade flanked by cupola surmounted wings. Above the wide portico was the name: ST ERMIN'S HOTEL.

"You're not going to drive us in there, are you?" Jenny said, "We'll stand out like a sore thumb!"

"Oh, they're very discreet here," said the chauffeur, "there's even a bee hotel…"

"What! You're joking!" |Xi!xuǂqe exclaimed.

"Don't you worry, Sir, the bees are outside. In fact, the courtyard where they are kept is inaccessible to anyone – and guarded by the bees – because it overlooks some of the rooms that the PPSS keeps. Stops people looking in, don't you know!"

"Thank Pisamboro for that. But you aren't dropping us at the front door, are you?"

"No, Sir, indeed not. The entrance we will use is round the corner in St Ermin's Hill." The limousine slid smoothly into a grubby little street and stopped in front of a row of blue bins. They trundled gently aside to reveal a low, non-descript black iron door, which opened. The ground tilted down from the single yellow parking-restriction line into a downward ramp and the vehicle, which had looked too high to get into the entrance, glided down it into the bowels of the hotel.

Within ten minutes, the two of them were in their room: "Sorry, Sir, we were not aware that the young lady would be accompanying you but we have upgraded you to a twin room!" simpered the maître d'. He handed |Xi!xu‡qe a small brown packet and skated backward, closing the doors behind him.

"I'm bloody sure he was laughing," said |Xi!xu‡qe, putting the envelope on the table and picking up a smell book, "Sorry about this."

"Who says I mind? It's lovely. Cosy. And the décor! My God, look at those drapes. Is that gold thread?"

"Gold brocade, I believe," he said, paging through the booklet, "But it says here you can't open them. It's just a wall. Secrecy, supposedly. I suppose you can see the point. What I don't understand is why they even have a book – like a guidebook, or something!"

"Maybe people come here just for the thrill of staying in the hotel where spies stay."

"Pygmies – tourists? Surely not. Well…maybe. There's a whole history, here."

"I suppose I'll have to read that. I don't suppose we can't just go out." She looked sidelong at |Xi!xu‡qe, hoping he would contradict her. Nothing. "I'll go stir crazy. How long will we be here?"

|Xi!xu‡qe didn't know but supposed they would be contacted soon. He still had the MagDhuibhfinn Earth Worm, after all. He still had his mission. But he recognised Jenny's excitement and was pleased.

"I'll get us some room service. Champagne, Miss?" he smiled.

"You devil you!" Jenny giggled, assuming a seductive pose on one of the ornate beds. "What's in the packet?"

"Mmm. A mobile phone. That's all. It's got no stored numbers. I suppose *they'll* call *us*."

The next morning, after delicately juggling access to the ensuite bathroom, they were sharing a continental breakfast that had been brought by a neatly clad waiter – a bellhop, Jenny called him – when the mobile phone bleeped.

|Xi!xu‡qe looked at the message on the screen: "Calling in 5 minutes."

"Why do they think you need warning?" mused Jenny, a wicked look in her eye.

"Maybe they thought I would be in the shower, or something?" |Xi!xu‡qe parried, a little uncomfortable.

When the phone rang, the tiny screen popped open into a much larger holographic image of ÓCléirigh. "Er, who's that?" were the secretary's first words. Although Jenny was opposite |Xi!xu‡qe, ÓCléirigh could clearly see that there was someone.

"Jenny Miler. She's safe. She's been with me since…"

"Oh, yes. I know about…well, that is to say, I've been briefed…"

Clearly, ÓCléirigh was uncomfortable, and it wasn't merely because of the presence of Jenny. "Listen, things have taken rather a sinister turn here," he continued. He turned to look over his shoulder. His eyes seemed constantly to move around the room he was in.

"What's going on, Mr ÓCléirigh?"

"ÓCléirigh, just ÓCléirigh. I'm only a clerk, after all." There was irony, even bitterness in his voice, "so, just ÓCléirigh. But that's enough of that. There is a significant group – almost a faction, I would call them, Arsenei, Peyton, Hugh and them – in the Grand Council who are convinced that you are no longer to be trusted."

"Oh, really? Why do they say that?"

"Kleynmans." Clearly, ÓCléirigh was hoping that the explanation could end there.

"How is Kleynmans a reason for me to be distrusted? I would have thought that being hunted by your enemies is a mark of trustworthiness to your allies."

"Yes. Of course. Usually. But in this case the reasoning goes that he always seems to know where you are going."

"That makes no sense. He never caught up with me. If I am acting in Kleynmans' – B.O.S.S.'s – interest, he would have caught up with me."

"He did."

"What! Do you mean at the Trauco HQ?" |Xi!xu‡qe's voice had gone up an octave, "Do they think I lured myself into a trap that resulted in the deaths of both Pygmies and Giants – some of whom I killed myself! – and then escaped? Why? What could he, or B.O.S.S., get out of it? An international diplomatic incident?"

"Ah. Yes. Well. Erm, not necessarily you. They argue." ÓCléirigh's eyes made an odd circling motion.

"You don't mean…. They can't possibly…. Why?" Suddenly, they were both acutely aware of Jenny's presence but couldn't dance around the issue anymore.

"Well, she is a Giant…. THEY say. And how did you meet? And why did she go along with you so willingly? And she's even with you now, in one of our safe houses…"

"It's not a house…" was the pathetic best |Xi!xu‡qe could come up with. The fact was that he could not think of any rebuttal to their suspicions. He had asked her the same questions.

Jenny went into the bathroom, softly shutting the door behind her.

"Anyway, an Taoiseach MacBhreithiún…"

"an what?"

"The First Minister. Anyway, he's had to agree that the USB key with the MEW should be transferred to another operative for delivery and installation. As soon as possible."

"Really? Does he not trust me, now, either?" |Xi!xuǂqe couldn't help himself assume some of the lilt and language of the Leprechaun. It was a measure of his stress. "And who is it that will take the MEW forward? In defiance, I might add, of the express instructions given me - in person! – by MacBhreithiún!"

"At the moment, I am obviously not at liberty to divulge that…" ÓCléirigh's chin tilted up and his abrupt switch to formal language meant one of two things, thought |Xi!xuǂqe: either someone else had come into the room or the clerk was offended by the Sān's suggestion that this call might itself be suspect. "You will be contacted and told how to proceed when arrangements have been put in place for the transfer." Suddenly, the little clerk was almost in tears. "Kiku? Kiku it's better like this, believe me."

|Xi!xuǂqe grunted dismissively. He didn't feel like indulging ÓCléirigh's self-pity. He had his own grievance to nurse. When he shut down the phone, Jenny came out of the bathroom; she was looking at him with big, teary eyes. "Kiku I'm so sorry! I've been so selfish. All I thought of was having an adventure – and, and getting to know you – and I never thought about your work. Oh! How could I think they would just ignore me!"

"Do not worry, Jenny Miler, none of this is your fault. And, you know, they are right…"

"What? You also think I…"

"No. No. Not a bit. However, after the Bosque Mbaracayú thing, at Trauco HQ, even after Billings, I should have thought, realised, how dangerous my mission was becoming, what danger I was taking you into. And to tell the truth, I am not even sure what my mission is. It certainly does not make sense to me. That is why I was so desperate to get hold of Eoin when we were at Trauco HQ…"

"But it was just…if we had left when you said we were going to…."

"Yes. But how was anyone to know Kleynmans was so close? That we were there even?"

Jenny slid over to the Sān and rested her cheek on his shoulder, an awkward act that involved bending down. "Oh, Kiku, I'm so sorry. Tell you what, I'll leave. Right now. I can just get a plane back to Toronto. Then I'll be out of it completely and you can finish your mission. What is your mission anyway, do you think?"

It was all |Xi!xu‡qe could do not to laugh out loud. Smiling, he said, "As I said, I'm not sure what it is myself. I don't know why I was ordered to America in the first place. It made sense at first – we had to reconnect the Far East. That's the Americas and the Pacific from the Pygmy point of view – but then Eoin gave me something else…" He stopped.

"What, Kiku? This 'mew' thing, or whatever? Sounds like a kitten."

"It's an acronym, Jenny, and I can't tell you anything more. It's a secret, you might be surprised to know…and not in the least feline!" Now where had she heard "mew"? he wondered. Anywhere, he supposed; they'd been travelling together long enough and there had been enough communication. He must have dropped the acronym – certainly, she had thought it was a word rather than an initialism. Quick of her to pick up on it, though. Impressive. Something else, a memory, played at the corner of his mind like a moth just escaping a spider's web...

"You're laughing at me!" Playfully, she slapped his arm. "Brute!"

"No. No. Sorry, Jenny Miler. I did not mean to mock you," he chuckled. Everything seemed alright again. Then, suddenly, he was serious, "But it is dangerous for you to know about it."

"But what is it? Is it..."

"Jenny, it is best that you do not know.... there is real danger.... You know...Piyêsîs..." |Xi!xuǂqe trailed off, he did not know what to say to her but there were many reasons not to share too much with her.

"You don't trust me!" she yelped, lifting her head from his shoulder and taking a step back. "You believe him – ÓCléirigh! You think I have been selling, trading, giving away, oh! whatever! your secret!"

"No, Jenny. That is not true. By Kaggen," he did not often invoke the creator god of his ancestors and he felt the weight of it now. "I promise that is not true. But there *is* danger, *great* danger!"

"Danger! You didn't think of that when we were in Billings. That man was clearly following us there. We went into that alley in Toronto! And you already didn't trust Sequoyah! Or did you? But you don't trust me, instead! You've just used me as a way of getting onto planes and trains and things and getting around without being questioned or noticed – a little boy and his mother! It's all a lie! Your world, the 'adventure' you got me involved in…and all because I helped you when I thought you were lost!"

As she spoke, she had been flinging around the room, gathering together her few things. "Well, I'm done, eh! Ouda here!" were the last words she spoke, standing at the open door and slinging her little bag across her shoulder.

"Jenny Miler! Stop! None of this is true…"

"Well. Well, I'm going to enjoy myself anyway. Keep some lunch for me or I'll starve. As if you care! I've got to London and I'm going to see stuff – the London Bridge, Big Ben, the Thames, the, oh, Eiffel Tower…."

|Xi!xu‡qe smiled involuntary, "Well that's going to be more difficult than you imagine…" he quipped in his most suave, James Bond voice.

"Oh, shut up!" she shouted, slamming the door behind her.

For much of the rest of the morning, |Xi!xu‡qe went over the exchange with Jenny. He was hurt that she had been upset, worried that she was out on her own. Did she even have enough money? They – she – had only drawn a small amount at the airport, had not expected to need much. But at the same time, he poked and prodded at her motives: why had she dropped everything, her whole life, at the drop of a kaross? And the MEW, what did she know of it? Why was it so interesting to her? He smiled, remembering her joke about a kitten. But then he contrasted the childish joke and her fury when he had refused to tell her about it. Surely that was more than just wounded pride? What more? It would make sense if she had a deadline, if there was some urgency to finding out. Or, what if it had simply been that she had expected more of his feelings towards her? If she was falling in love, believed he loved her, the refusal might have seemed a lack of trust, a betrayal…. |Xi!xu‡qe was perplexed. It was true that her curiosity, willingness, anger, naivety – the argument – had made him feel closer to her than ever. That he could no more mistrust her than send her away.

It never even crossed his mind that she might have intended him to have those feelings. That she was afraid he was beginning to know her too well.

By early afternoon, she had not returned. He had convinced himself that she had meant to come back, that she had been injured or worse: "save me some lunch" or words to that effect, she had said. She had meant to come back. And some time before.

|Xi!xuǂqe called the desk. They had not seen her come back into the hotel. They searched the public areas frequented by the Giant tourists. She was not there. Eventually, he got hold of the porter who had showed them into the room. A little questioning revealed that she had told him she was going to let the 'brute stew'. A lovers' tiff, the porter had concluded, but not ill meant. She had even told him that she would be back for lunch. In their room. Because she did not have money to buy lunch for herself. Alarm bells started to ring in |Xi!xuǂqe's mind. "Can you make sure I have enough money, please, there's an expense account...I'll be down at the desk in 5 minutes."

Out in the streets, few looked at him. In this huge, cosmopolitan city where people walked in jeans, djellabas, mandarin skirts, denim jackets, souk jackets, puffer jackets, salwar kameez, bourkas, pinstripe trousers and track suits no one looked at a little, dark boy in jeans, with a leather bag and an excited smile, even if he seemed to have an odd-looking crutch. The English in the places he checked were much too polite to pry. And he went to all the places she had mentioned – except for the Eiffel Tower – and asked a policeman (who offered to find his mum) and street vendors, shop assistants in the kinds of shops he imagined she might have visited, waiters in pavement restaurants, old men sitting on benches on the banks of the Thames. Mostly, he sought the figures huddled down alleyways or in seldom-used doorways, the down-and-out, the neglected and unnoticed. There were many of them, even in this 21st century, thriving, modern economy. |Xi!xu‡qe knew that these people, who had little to do but spot opportunities to seek help, would have noticed a lone woman of unusual size, would have recognised a tourist.

Finally, returning to the hotel from the other direction, he encountered a grubby faced girl, sitting cross-legged on a grimy sleeping bag, watching him. "Hello," he said, approaching her.

"You wif 'er ven?"

"Who, exactly?"

"Little woman. Dark, like you almos'. Looked grown up but…li'u" ('little' he guessed), "like a child. Walked like a grown up, buil' like a child. Like you. You're dwarves, i'ntcha?"

"Yes, well. You saw her?" He described her clothing.

"Yeah, sure." The girl stopped talking, looked down and started rolling a cigarette.

|Xi!xu‡qe took a £10 note out of his bag. She looked up.

"Where did she go?"

"Funny va'," said the girl, holding out her hand. |Xi!xu‡qe hesitated. "She asked me which way ve 'ahses of Parliament was. And Lum' Bridge, and ve Thames. I mean!" The girl grinned, rolled her eyes.

"The Eiffel Tower?" It was all |Xi!xu‡qe could do not to sob with relief.

"Wha'? Don't be daft. 'sin Paris, innit.. Why'd she ask va'?"

"Never mind. which way did she go?"

"Way I showed 'er, course," The girl gestured and reached for the money. |Xi!xuɫqe surrendered it. As he started off in the direction she had indicated, she said, "Din't cha wanna know bah' ve uvver one?"

It was his turn to say, "What?"

"Yeah. 'im too. Li'u, loi' you. No smallah. He come past jus' after. Din give me nuffink, little bleedah, wif his stupid ha'. Jus' went after her…"

|Xi!xuɫqe thrust a £20 note into her hand, "Anything else? What did he look like?" He was in a hurry now.

"Cor! Fanks, mate! Yeah, 'e was wearing va' ha'. Green, ridic'lous, like a li'u porkpie perched on 'is 'ead. No. like those ones vem blokes in levva shorts wear. German, or Austrian. Wif a couple o' li'u white fevvas n ve band. Shor' he was. Shor'tr'n you, no offence."

"Any other details?" Though he had an idea he had seen such a hat at the 'summit' in Ireland.

"No. Wish there was, ma'e!"

|Xi!xuɫqe spent the next hour searching in a fan spreading out from where the girl had been. He rushed down all the little streets between Birdcage Walk and Victoria Street, leading away from the hotel. Then through Parliament Square and down Abingdon Street. Turning left down College Street, he got lost in the maze of little streets. It didn't bother him; she was as likely to be there as anywhere else.

Eventually, as he turned onto Old Pye Street and was led back into Victoria Street where he saw signs to St. Ermin's, he realised that he had no plan and no ideas.

He gave up the search and returned to the hotel. Maybe she had just lost track of time and finally gone back there.

But she hadn't come back - at least, none of the staff had seen her. He desperately wanted to ask the Giant staff but the Gnome maître d' on the front desk nearly had apoplexy. Although the man maintained his suave composure outwardly, |Xi!xu‡qe saw his true reaction as a dark mauve and lime green emanation when he suggested it. "Most unwise, Sir. Most! I'll contact someone who can ask those sorts of questions again, Sir, and tell you what I find out. Maybe it would be better to go back to Sir's room now?" Without even waiting for an answer, he snapped his fingers at an Elf, "Ian! Take Sir up to 216b, please!"

|Xi!xu‡qe was left in no doubt as to the status of that order.

Back in the room, any last vestige of hope that Jenny might have slipped in without anyone noticing disappeared. The room was empty. He waited. The room phone rang. It was the concierge. No one, either on the Pygmy or the Giant side of the hotel, had seen her.

Chapter 18 Second Contact

He was going over the argument for the umpteenth time, trying to remember where she might have wanted to go, when the phone rang in his bag. It was a voice call. No video.

"Identify yourself, please." The voice was flat, accented.

"ǀXi!xuǂqe," he said, giving the clicks their fullest expression.

"Ha! Ha!" was the unexpected response, "No need to ask more qvestions. Only you could say that! Ha! Is brilliant! Better than password. Here is Artyom, Domovoj, of PPSS, too."

ǀXi!xuǂqe vaguely remembered Artyom from the meeting in Ireland. "I recognise your accent. I think I remember you from…"

"Never mind, this line is secure but no need to share more information than we need, right? I have message from Eoin Brown – Mac an…. Oh, these names! Why can't all be simple like Domovoj? He say about Magoofin Ert Vorm. It must be handed on. GCPP members no longer trusting you and he must make sure is safe. I am to deliver to agent who will be able to install it on B.O.S.S. central computer."

"Really? That seems unlikely. How will a Pygmy get to the computer?"

"Is not Pygmy agent. He says is sympathetic Giant. Some are. He says you met some: Piyêsîs, спасти его душу, is one."

"What does that mean?"

"'spasti yego dushu'? Is nothing. Is mean 'save his soul'. Just Russian superstition. Never mind. There is more Giants to help, especially about stopping climate changing. Cop31 has not been success. You hear? Like all since Cop26: Giants promise much to avoid giving anything."

"I read something," he answered drily. "What does MacBhreithiún want me to do? Why not phone me himself?" There were many questions. So many, he thought.

"Is not secure from EU – like Ireland, since stupid Brexit there is no trust even now UK back in EU. You must get USB key to me. I must deliver to agent for installation."

"I could do that. Where are you?"

"Not far from you. Can meet in café or, better, bar! Heh, heh!"

"But how do I know I can trust you? You could be…"

"You choose where we meet. Also, I have credentials from MacBhreithiún…Oi, that name!"

"Ok. I saw a café earlier on…. But first there is a problem. My companion has gone missing…"

"Jenny Miler?"

"How do you…"

"Is not secret. Anyway you did not hide her very well!"

"Well, she went out and hasn't come back and I can't find her. Only one person saw her…"

"You trust this person?"

"…a girl sleeping rough on the street…"

"Ah, yes. Best eyes, those type!"

"She told me she was being followed by someone – I think a PPSS agent, the Russian, I saw him in Ireland. Little green hat with a feather…"

"Hah! That Arsenei. Is not Russian. Is Belarusian. Is insult to Russian! Now why he was following Jenny? Definitely following? Not with her?"

"It doesn't seem like it. Can you find out where she is?"

"I will look. When you can give to me USB key? Where?"

Suddenly |Xi!xuⱡqe saw in the Domovoj's - GCPP's - concern an opportunity: "I'll hand it over when you have some information about Jenny." "What? No. is impossible! MacBhreithiún …"

"You tell him that's the deal. Otherwise…"

"Ok. Listen. I call you in one hour. Do not go out. Wait."

"Believe me, I will wait!"

Exactly an hour later, the mobile phone rang again – |Xi!xuⱡqe admired the precision, recognising in it another sign confirming Artyom's credentials – and the Russian Gnome launched straight in. |Xi!xuⱡqe took that as yet another sign of authenticity: how would Artyom know who he was talking to unless this was the only, and secure, phone and he knew only the Sān would be answering?

"Listen. I have been successful. MacBhreithiún will search. He has some Giants searching, too. MacBhreithiún says 'not at the main gate this time'. I do not know what this means…"

"I do," At the main gate at midnight – the meeting when MacBhreithiún had explained the significance of the MagDhuibhfinn Earth Worm and given him the USB key…and sent him on the wild goose chase to the Americas.

Never mind. Only Eoin MacBhreithiún would have known that. "Okay. Good. When?"

"MacBhreithiún says not more than tomorrow morning. Will have information by then. Maybe sooner, but…"

"Okay. Tomorrow morning at 9 o'clock at Royal Artisan Bakery in Petty France. If you have earlier information, call me."

When he rang off, it was as much as he could bear to be away from the machine long enough to have a shower. He kept the phone near him as he slept, fitfully.

The next morning was misty and grey. He reached the bakery half an hour early and loitered over a cup of coffee in the Adam and Eve pub opposite. The landlord tried to object about his age but then relented, embarrassed at having assumed that a 'dwarf' was a child. There was nothing untoward in Petty France or down Palmer Street, as far as he could see. Some workers went into the buildings opposite – all Giants. Eventually, he saw a small figure wondering along the road from the opposite direction he had come. The man in the pub looked at |Xi!xu‡qe and then the approaching figure. Another dwarf, obviously. |Xi!xu‡qe smiled as if to say, that's my mate who I've been waiting for.

In the bakery, they found a table in a back corner and Artyom ordered a cake. |Xi!xu‡qe asked for a cup of tea but, when the waiter looked disappointed, changed it to cappuccino.

"MacBhreithiún says 'not at midnight this time'. Is password?"

"What has he found out about Jenny?" asked |Xi!xu‡qe, immediately.

"You have key?" The Sān looked in his leather shoulder bag and placed the USB key on the tabletop.

The waiter arrived with a tall cylinder that looked like it had had a Ferrero Rocher melted over it, and a cup of beige froth with what looked like a white feather artfully worked on it.

"What," the Sān repeated, covering the key with his hand, "have you got for me?"

"Seems there is agent with full knowledge. Jenny is captured by GASP. I do not know why but she – this agent, Blond – is finding out. She has contact in GASP and will give me written instruction when I give her USB key tomorrow."

"GASP! What do they have to do with it? How did they know? We have not been…. Is that all?"

"You have my word. I will get instructions, map, directions, details tomorrow, you understand? I phone you in morning. Now, I must hurry."

Unsatisfactory though the arrangement was to him, |Xi!xuǂqe realised that he had no choice.

As they left the bakery, he felt Artyom stiffen slightly at his side and pause. Following the Russian Gnome's eyes, he saw a diminutive figure disappearing round the corner into Palmer Street. "Is strange," said Artyom, "I think he had green hat. Like you said." They walked casually to the intersection but there was no one to be seen. Only the Giants coming from St. James's Park tube station. "I must be dreaming, huh?" scoffed Artyom, "Is too much daggers and cloak!"

|Xi!xuǂqe spent an irritable and impatient day in St. Ermin's. That night, he slept little. The coffee didn't help. Nor did dreams of the white feather that had been artfully reproduced on the foam of his cappuccino in the Royal Artisan.

When the mobile phone rang the next day, it was a woman's voice. "Kiku?"

Immediately suspicious, |Xi!xuǂqe hedged, "I wasn't expecting…. Where is our Russian friend?"

"I'm Blond, Jemma Blond. I have news of Artyom. A problem."

"Jemma Blond? Seriously?"

The voice sighed, "Jemima Blond! I get this all the time. Try to work around it!"

"He told me about a Blond. How do I know it's you?"

"A password? Really? How about: 'Is too much daggers and cloak'? Recognise it? A favourite saying of Artyom. Was."

|Xi!xuǂqe's mind went back. It was practically the last thing the Domovoj had said. "Okay. What about Artyom? Have you seen him?"

"Yes. Did you give him the USB key yesterday?"

"Of course. He said you would have instructions about Jenny Miler for him to pass on to me."

"I'm with Artyom now. Or his body, anyway. And the key's not here."

Cold panic spread through |Xi!xuǂqe's body. 'was', she'd said! "Where? How? When?" Thoughts tumbled through his head. He had put the whole of Pygmydom in danger. For a girl! Not just a girl, Jenny! But the MEW!

"I came to meet him this morning to make the exchange and he was here. Someone had slit his throat. What did he tell you about the rendezvous?"

"Nothing. And I didn't ask."

"No. I believe you. There are some things I have to tell you. Jenny Miler is being held at a hotel in Berne. By GASP. We believe, they took her as leverage, hoping to find out what GCPP were up to or to get the MEW. We don't know, really. I suppose this proves her innocence though there still seem to be powerful forces that do not trust her – or you. The Taoiseach seems to but.... Now they have the USB – if they have it – Jenny won't be much use to them. One other thing: at the murder scene, there was a white feather. I don't know what it means but when I mentioned it to ÓCléirigh, he got very agitated.... Seemed to think it was a disaster of some sort. Oh. And there is a till receipt for a café in Interlaken."

"Never mind that. What is the name of the hotel in Bern?"

"We have been given orders to go to Bern. To meet there. Have you got a pen?"

"I've got a memory." Instantly, he regretted snapping at her but he excused himself: he was worried, after all.

"Okay. Remember this: café Monnier Bern, Schauplatzgasse 26. This evening. Teatime."

"Teatime?"

"Four o'clock, obviously!"

In Bern, 'teatime' was damp and dark. The huge windows of the café Monnier Bern seemed a golden oasis in the gathering autumnal gloom. Nervous of how visible he would be in the café windows, ǀXiǃxuǂqe was spending some time window-shopping, first in the Gurtengasse then in the Schauplatzgasse.

Suddenly, he saw a short figure in a hat of the type he had seen in Ireland, on Arsenei. Like the one Artyom had thought he'd seen in London: a Tyrolean Mountain hat, Arsenei had called it.

He followed the hat. The wearer was very short, no more than 1m 40, but he seemed cheerful and unconcerned. Not like someone trying to avoid observation, or skulking.

Eventually, he disappeared round a corner into what a sign said was Bundesplatz. It was a square, looked over by a grand building with six columns and a huge, green fluted dome. And the square was filled with women and girls in dirndls and men – and boys – in Tyrolean Mountain hats. It was a festival of some sort.

Feeling a fool, |Xi!xu‡qe returned to the café and found an empty table. He ordered a coffee and pastry. As he sat watching the crowds walking towards the Bundesplatz and its festive crowd, a female Giant came over to his table. She rested her hand on the back of the unoccupied chair.

"Is this seat taken? May I share your table?"

Immediately, |Xi!xu‡qe was aware of the accent. It had nothing of the German lilt he had heard ubiquitously since arriving in Switzerland. It was English. British English. Educated British English. And he recognised the voice, too. Blond? Jemima Blond. He stared at the Giant. She was slim but there was something athletic about her shoulders. The wrist resting on the chairback seemed tensed, strong, easily able to shift the squat, upholstered chair – heavy, he knew from moving his own closer to the table. She was smiling, though, and there was a light in her green eyes that bespoke friendliness... and confidentiality. She sat down and ordered a pastry from a waiter who appeared suddenly at her shoulder; |Xi!xu‡qe wasn't really paying attention. He was studying the Giant. Her dark hair was cut in a short, boyish slightly messy style. Waiters, he guessed, were always appearing at her shoulder.

"Are you Kiku?" she asked.

"Yes, are you...er...um...that is...." |Xi!xu‡qe was lost, "You are...must be...." Looking at the brunette, his question seemed so silly that he imagined the whole café bursting into laughter.

"Blond. Yes. Jemma Blond. I'm glad to meet you. You've been causing quite a stir in the community."

"Community?" he played for time, getting his equilibrium back. Obviously she meant the intelligence community but where did she fit in? She was no Pygmy, that was certain, "And which particular part of the 'community' do you fit into?" he asked.

"Ah! That's more complex than you might think. I'm NSA, out of London, obviously..." she stopped. |Xi!xuǂqe had tensed, hand on the shaft of the knobkierrie at his side. "Oh, don't worry. I told you, it's more complex than you think. There are factions in B.O.S.S. Some of them are working to progress the Giant nations' climate security agenda..."

"Giant? I've never heard a Giant refer to Giants as Giants before."

"Again, complex! Not all of us are unaware of Pygmies. You know that: your friend Peechee. Also Piyêsîs. And my Pygmy contact Artyom..."

"Both dead."

"Sadly, yes. But we work side by side. We have the same aims. Mostly."

|Xi!xuǂqe found himself warming to the confident, breezy Giant. There was one test: "Jenny," he said. The word hung between them for a moment.

"Of course. Your first concern. You'll find her at this address," She slid a business card onto the table. On it was the address of a hotel in Bern and a handwritten number. "And now you have that, I was told, you will listen to what else is happening in the world. Yes?"

Ignoring her arch tone, |Xi!xuǂqe glanced at the card: Hotel Waldhorn, Waldhoeheweg 2, Bern 3013, Room 113, and slipped it into his skin bag.

Blond continued. "Firstly, you know the outcome of Cop31. Typical. The interests of fossil fuel companies have been almost impossible to dislodge from the agendas of most governments. The UNFCCC seems to be powerless. But the powers aren't. We're the powers. Carol Powell, Sharina Pressley, Bahrend Kopf are all aware of the need to shift the discussion away from national political consensus that has been so badly railroaded by lobbyists. Thunberg has made this abundantly clear.

"That's where the MagDhuibhfinn Earth Worm comes in. Yes, yes, I know all about it. MacBhreithiún briefed my boss. Unfortunately, that information was routinely shared with the CIA. That means their Europe Bureau chief, Jeff Heinzforth, knew as well. The Pygmy, Arsenei…"

"Arsenei! He was at the GCPP when I got to Ireland!"

"That's him. Apparently, he was sent to stop you by the GCPP when they thought you were…er…compromised. He was recalled but never acknowledged the order. There is some evidence that they were both in London at the same time: the white feather and the Interlaken receipt - the card number on it was traced to Heinzforth's CIA account. Careless of him, fortunately for us. You do know there's a major GASP facility near Interlaken?"

"I've never heard of anything like that; not my bailiwick. And ÓCléirigh mentioned that there were factions lobbying against me and Jenny in GCPP. He mentioned Arsenei, too. And Hugh? Peyton?"

"Really?" Blond looked thoughtful. "Have you ever heard of Freitag? F.R.S.T. Freitag? He's a GASP sub-director. He's met with these people, the ones you mention…"

163

"Hang on! Just how many people know about the Pygmies? And how much?"

"They are widely known among Giant government agencies like ours. We have some close links. Their existence has been blurred and denied by those agencies for centuries. All that stuff about Knights Templar and the Illuminati, hysterical claims about 'fake' moon landings, QAnon – much of it is manufactured or manipulated to conceal a truth: the existence of Pygmies. Given the way we've treated you and the First Peoples of Africa, the Americas, Australasia and the Far East, let alone Jews and Gypsies, it seemed necessary. And the least we could do. Just…not everyone is on board so we keep the links, and the knowledge in a very tight-knit circle."

ǀXi!xuǂqe was stunned. "Who else? I mean, who knows? Like who in B.O.S.S.? Kleynmans' boss, Bootha? That would explain why Kleynmans was always too late."

"Can't possibly say but I wouldn't imagine Kleynmans…. He seemed pretty deadly in his pursuit of you."

"No, of course. Ridiculous. But…"

"I don't think that this is what we should be talking about. As far as we have managed to work out so far, the MEW is in the hands of GASP. They – the same people probably, certainly Arsenei – took Jenny for leverage and information and, according to Freitag, in case they couldn't get the USB key…"

"The GASP sub-director – Freitag?" ǀXi!xuǂqe did not want to hear her say that Jenny might have told them about the transfer of the key to Artyom. How might they have got that information from her? Had she been in the room when the arrangement was made? No. Obviously not.

He had met Artyom to exchange the key for information about Jenny.

"Freitag works for us – a mole – he also confirmed that Arsenei and Heinzforth are working for GASP. Of course, the transfer plans were approved in London. Heinzforth was present. And that's how Arsenei tracked Artyom, killed him and took the USB. What he did with it, we have no idea. We'd heard Peyton and Hugh were involved, too. Now you've all but confirmed it. Anyway, Freitag tells us there's been a lot of activity at the GASP laboratory inside the Trugberg, east of the Jungfrau."

"Good. But, much as I'd like to get the key, and Arsenei, I'm not interested," said ǀXi!xuǂqe decisively, "I've got what I needed, or I will have when I get Jenny out of that hotel. After that, I resign. You seem to have all the help you need."

"It's really not as simple as that. The operation to mislead them – your taking the MEW secretly to the Americas didn't work as well as we would have liked: we think they knew you had it by the time Kleynmans attacked the Trauco HQ, at least. It seems he had CIA backing for that. The key lies with Jenny (sorry!) probably and we won't know until we talk to her. She might have nothing to do with it..."

"Obviously she doesn't. You said so yourself – they don't need her anymore. And besides she was with me...." And under his objection an idea formed: 'mislead'? he thought, 'mislead'?... He stopped, his mind making a leap to Jenny's plea before the battle: 'You cannot be risked. *Nor can the MagDhuibhfinn Earth Worm*'. That was the memory that had been eluding him! His blood froze. But the complexities and implications were swept away by what Blond said next.

"Exactly. All the time. From Toronto. At least. Whatever you might think, until we can be sure she was not speaking to anyone about it, we can't be sure the information came from PPSS agents in the GCPP who are working for GASP. And how did he, or they, know? There's something very deep going on here and I'm not even sure that what I know is accurate; like you, I'm only an agent. No, you have to get Jenny to settle that…. Until you do, we can't be sure who we can trust to go to the GASP facility to get the MEW back. That's your next mission."

"What! That is the most hare-brained idea I've ever heard of! The Jungfrau is one of the highest mountains in Europe. I'm not climbing that!"

"It's in the Trugberg. Not as high as the Jungfrau. And it's on the slopes of the valley. No more than 3,400 or so metres. A bit of snow, that's all. And we'll help you get Jenny back. This afternoon. Otherwise you're on your own. And we can't vouch for how many GASP and B.O.S.S. agents will be guarding Jenny."

|Xi!xu‡qe looked at her in horror.

Waldhoeheweg turned out to be no more than a few kilometres away. The Hotel Waldhorn was a building of a type |Xi!xu‡qe now found unremarkable for Bern. When they got there, he turned to Blond: "Right. Where are the others?"

"Others?" she said, her eyes big, "What others?"

"You said 'we'. 'we'll help get Jenny back'."

"Aah! I see where the confusion lies! You thought 'we' meant other agents. Actually, I meant the resources of the agency. Not actual people."

"Bloody Giants! All the same: untrustworthy! You said there might be a lot of guards…"

"Not really. I said we couldn't vouch for how many…"

"So? How many?" |Xi!xu‡qe was shouting in a whisper as they stood on the corner.

"Why don't I go in and ask for a room?" she said, calmly kneeling on one knee beside him and pointing down the road, "Why don't you go to the park? It's just down there. Spitalackerpark, it's called."

|Xi!xu‡qe stalked off, acutely aware of the old lady and her dotard husband on a bench at the park entrance, smiling at him.

It took an age. Twice, |Xi!xu‡qe walked to the corner of Spitalackerstrasse opposite the hotel entrance and peeped round the corner across Beundenfeldstrasse. The elderly couple looked increasingly concerned as he crossed the road and, apparently, 'hid away' from his 'mother'. He went back into the park. Out of the corner of his eye, he noticed the old lady watching him with alarm and pawing at the man's coat sleeve every time he moved. He started towards the complex junction of Spitalacker, Beundenfeld and Gotthelfstrasse. The old lady became more and more frantic. She was practically having apoplexy. The old man started looking around urgently. For a policeman, |Xi!xu‡qe supposed. He gave up and went back to the bench where Blond had left him. The old couple settled down and looked reassured. But every time he got up and made to walk towards the street, they started becoming agitated. Apparently they had turned themselves into his babysitters.

Eventually, Jemima Blond appeared at the door. She looked around her then crossed to the park.

"Well? Did you find her? Is she there? I swear if…"

"She's there. We just have to wait here."

"Are there many guards? How are we going to handle this?"

The way Blond looked at him suggested concern but seemed mistrustful and pitying at the same time, like a vet looking at the owner of a terminally ill pet. "That's the thing, Kiku: there aren't any."

"What? Is she alright? Is she still there? You mean she's gone? Was she there at all? What did the hotel say?"

"Yes. Yes. No. Yes. They gave me her room number when I asked at the desk."

It was |Xi!xu‡qe's turn to be puzzled and concerned. "No pseudonym? No obstructions?"

"Nothing. I went up, knocked on the door and she answered. As if nothing was wrong. Oh, she didn't know who I was and seemed frightened and a little confused but when I explained about you and…. Well, she just giggled and said she'd be down."

"I don't believe you! Where is she?" |Xi!xu‡qe's head was spinning. How could she not be guarded? Why had 'they' left her there? Why hadn't she contacted him? How could she have been expecting him? Worse, how had Blond known that she would be here – and unguarded? Or had she? She certainly seemed puzzled herself.

Just then, Jenny appeared at the door of the hotel, looked around, saw them, waved and started making her way across the street towards them.

As |Xi!xu‡qe started towards her, he noticed Blond nod towards the elderly couple. You cow! he thought.

But his mind was on Jenny. On having Jenny safely back.

Chapter 19 "It's a hare-brained idea!"

"I don't know!" insisted Jenny, almost in tears, "I don't understand why they left me there. All I can tell you is that the guy in the hat told me you would come and fetch me. I was going to see Big Ben and then an American said what a grand old building the Houses of Parliament was. He was very polite. He offered to show me some other sites. Knew all about Boadicea when we went to the statue. And the Embankment? That bit by the Thames? Cleopatra's Needle. Though I don't know I believed him. Then he said I had to see Pall Mall and we had to get a cab. There was a black one right there. That's all I remember. I woke up in a room somewhere."

The three of them were in a room of the Bellevue Palace, a few kilometres away. It seemed the British NSA kept the small suite they were in. Jenny was thrilled to back "at home". Her enthusiasm was short-lived, though.

"You mean they drugged you? for how long? Do you remember travelling? A plane? Train?"

Blond had been - aggressively, |Xi!xu‡qe thought - 'debriefing' Jenny for several hours and it was becoming increasingly clear that Jenny had no idea of what had happened. As if it hadn't been right from the start, as far as |Xi!xu‡qe was concerned. He was starting to think his judgment might be 'impaired'.

"There were phone calls – the leader, the American, spoke to several people. He was…polite…to some but not others. Different people…" Jenny seemed wilted but was holding up well |Xi!xuꟛqe thought. Very well. She was tough.

"What happened before they left you?" Blond remained cold, steely, "Think. Carefully."

"I had tried to get out. That's when they told me I wasn't in London anymore. That it wouldn't help if I escaped. Where would I go? They refused to tell me where we were. And they had guns. At first I made a bit of a performance and I heard them discuss whether they could get rid of me."

|Xi!xuꟛqe shuddered but he had been warned not to intervene.

"But later…I don't know how long…the American was on the phone again. Someone called. He was talking quite rudely. He seemed angry. Then suddenly he was happy. He said: 'They've got it.' Then they warned me not to leave the bedroom. It was guarded, they said. The American told the others, there were three of them, to check their guns. I was a bit frightened then. Then it was a long time till there was a knock on the door – when you came – and I came out when no one answered. It was all tidy. They must have left but I don't know when."

Finally, Blond was satisfied.

They left Jenny to have a bath and a sleep. She said she had had enough of being in hotel rooms but she stopped complaining when she looked out of the window across the river at the snow-capped mountains in the distance. And Jemima promised to get her some fresh clothes.

The two agents were discussing her in a salon, downstairs.

"She doesn't seem to have any idea who or what she was dealing with, though!" |Xi!xuǂqe insisted.

"Exactly. How can you not even be curious, at least?" Blond said 'you' but she meant 'she'.

|Xi!xuǂqe had no answer. Just another question: "And why did they let her go if she has nothing to offer?"

"'they'? Who are 'they', again. Anyway, it seems to have something to do with the USB. That's the key to the whole operation on our side so it makes sense that it is on their side, too. No matter who they are. If they got the key – from Arsenei, who killed Artyom for it in London – they might have decided they had no need for Jenny Miler. That suggests these were two separate operations. Perhaps even two different agencies working towards the same end."

"But why risk releasing her?" Like it or not, it was a question |Xi!xuǂqe kept coming back to.

"One of two reasons: first, she's too valuable an asset for them to get rid of. That suggests, Kiku, that she might not be all she seems, that she went willingly with them to help get the USB from you. That would suggest that she is working against the GCPP," she held up a hand as |Xi!xuǂqe made to object, "or that they know that you will walk away once you get her back and they need you out of the operation…or they're actually afraid of what you might have done had they harmed her!" Blond frowned and cupped her lower face in her hand, "Mmm! Those two seem to amount to the same thing."

"That's ridiculous! Once they've wiped the USB, there would be nothing I could do." |Xi!xuǂqe couldn't be sure whether she was laughing behind her hand.

"Maybe they don't want to wipe it," she paused, "After all, it's probably the only one there is. At least as far as they know."

"What makes you say that?"

"Well, if there were copies, why would we being going to such lengths to get it back to Europe and guard it so closely?"

"So," exclaimed |Xi!xuǂqe, "maybe they need it to work out how to neutralise it!"

"Neutralise what, Kiku? You don't neutralise information so what does it *do*? What is the MEW, actually?"

"Let's put it this way: if they could reprogram it, the results could be disastrous for the planet."

Blond looked at him, her green eyes narrowing, "Very well, don't tell me. But that leaves us with one clear conclusion: whoever has it is trying to stop the GCPP from actuating, or launching it, or whatever you do with it. At least that means it is a hostile B.O.S.S. related mission. That it is in a GASP facility here and that 'they' brought her here suggests that 'they' are part of B.O.S.S., more probably GASP, and that there are elements of Pygmy security, even GCPP, involved. Arsenei is acting with the American, Heinzforth: the CIA hate the Eastern Europeans but they hate the GCPP more…something about the first nations…"

"We have to get the key back, Jemima."

"Yes, we do. And that involves breaking into the Trugberg facility. We need to organise a team."

"No. Scratch that: *you* need to organise a team. I'm staying to guard Jenny."

"Not possible. You're the only person available who has ever seen what's on it. What it looks like. You have to come. But I see your point. If Jenny is leverage," Blond smiled at him, "then we can't let them get her again. If she's working for them…"

"No, she's not…"

"IF. IF she's working for them, the moment we leave her she'll tell them. She has to come with us."

ǀXi!xuǂqe goggled at her. "That is the most hare-brained, ridiculous, dangerous, insane proposal!" He stopped and thought. "But you do have a point."

And so it was that the Sān PPSS agent and the English B.O.S.S. agent were sitting in the suite's lounge, on a Wavel call to ÓCléirigh: MacBhreithiún was in a high-level diplomatic meeting, said the Leprechaun secretary, but was thrilled about the rescue of Jenny.

"Do we even know who wrote it?" Blond asked. She kept returning to the MEW, seemingly unable to forget about it, even to focus on the mission to get it back.

Before ǀXi!xuǂqe could snap at her, MacBhreithiún appeared. Completely unconcerned about making a liar of his secretary, he broke in: "Good point. If we could talk to the programmer, we could understand whether it can be hacked. Can we get someone in to find out from, Padraig?"

ÓCléirigh also seemed unfazed, either by being made a liar of by MacBhreithiún or the Taoiseach's proliferation of prepositions. He typed on his keyboard. "Sir, I've got Pyhare online, Sir. Says he has something…"

"What's it got to do with him? What does he know about anything?" MacBhreithiún was interrupted when a new tile with the Pombero tech's face materialised on the screen. Before the tech could speak, the GCPP Prime Minister brought him up to date. "Can it be altered?" he finished.

"Oh, it can be hacked," Pyhare confirmed. "There's no program yet written that can't be. If you had told me about it – maybe even let me see it? – while you were here…. That is, instead of warning me against going anywhere near it on pain of death…."

MacBhreithiún and |Xi!xu‡qe both looked chastened.

"Well, anyway. You weren't to know who was betraying you," the Pombero continued magnanimously, then, smugly, "As I understand it, you still don't!". And it was true, mistrust was rife in the Eastern Departments and accusations were flying in every direction. The GCPP was in a tailspin.

"Look, Pyhare, this isn't a joke." Recovering, MacBhreithiún drew himself up to his full height, a posture that is easier to achieve on a video call. Even for a Pygmy.

"That's not what I meant," said the tech. He seemed to be shaking with laughter. "Not what I meant at all. I can tell you, for one thing, that I am withholding some information from you..."

"What!" shouted MacBhreithiún, ÓCléirigh and |Xi!xu‡qe simultaneously.

"Calm down. It's good news: I know who wrote the MagDhuibhfinn Earth Worm."

There was silence as the Pygmies and the Giant digested this. "You remember that useless tech in the Trauco mission? His name is Ka'akupe. By the way, it means "behind the forest" in Guarani, and he certainly lost you in the forest!"

Again, ÓCléirigh cursed the "irresponsibility" of the playful Trauco. "Well? You would certainly not be suggesting *he* wrote it?"

"It's impossible!" |Xi!xu‡qe said, "he was scarcely able to work his equipment! I spent hours waiting for it to update!"

Pyhare looked smug: "They all work on the same base language, computers. You don't have to have the latest IBM with Windows 16 or Apple Mac with IOS Mt St. Helens. And you don't need to be online. In fact, he seldom goes online: claims it's too easy to be hacked. He leaves all that to his boss."

"Millalobo? Impossible! He's practically allergic to computers! I spoke to him," ǀXi!xuǂqe remembered the vehement disgust in the Trauco chief's voice.

"No. Not him. Fiura, his 'wife' and 2IC. She has a laptop and sets up all his meetings."

"But…" ǀXi!xuǂqe was lost for words.

"I told you, 'behind the forest'," giggled the Pombéro tech, enjoying himself now. "Anyway, that was the only version of the MEW that works. Ka'akupe told me. He couldn't check it online, obviously, so he doesn't know what is wrong with the other ones he's got. He says to write another one would mean starting from scratch." A look of sheer mischief crossed Pyhare's face, "He's quite miffed that you've lost it, you know."

"How does he even know?" interrupted ÓCléirigh, sounding very angry by now.

"It's got a built-in tracker. Traces every place in which it is plugged into a USB port. It's why he wanted you sent to him in the first place: to check that all his tracking records matched up so he could be sure the USB actually was the MEW. Simply a matter of plugging it into his computer. Oh, and by the way, he says we've got better mountains in South America if you wanted to lose it in the mountains, whatever that means."

ǀXi!xuǂqe, MacBhreithiún, Blond and ÓCléirigh looked each other.

So, the USB key had been accessed somewhere in the Trugberg facility.

Chapter 20 The Way of the Worm

"That's the trouble with you Western European and African Pygmies," Pyhare continued, "You think you're more sophisticated than us 'Far Eastern' types." He made a disgusted click like the one at the beginning of |Xi!xu‡qe's name, "Tch! Based on what? That you 'reached' us last? You're as bad as the Giants!" After a few more minutes of guilt-tripping them, the Far Eastern tech said, "Anyway, do you want to know what the MagDhuibhfinn Earth Worm does, or not?"

"Oh, spare me," groaned MacBhreithiún, rolling his eyes.

"ÓCléirigh? You know? But then why...?" |Xi!xu‡qe spluttered.

"Oh, yes!" exclaimed Blond, "Carry on, do..."

"'behind the forest'!" he tutted. "I will tell you anyway: the MEW is a worm. That is to say, it is a code that attaches itself to other code and installs itself on computers covertly. Once there, it can be used to make the host computer perform tasks – if the hacker likes – without the knowledge of the computer's operator. One of the first things the MEW does is replicate itself to every program on the computer, then it infiltrates all the other computers on the LAN, then it attaches itself to all outgoing traffic so as to reach all the other computers on the WAN and then the web. In that way, the MagDhuibhfinn Earth Worm will install itself in nearly every computer on earth in a matter of months, or weeks."

"So what's the point of it, then?" Blond was fascinated. This was what ǀXi!xuǂqe had avoided telling her.

"The MagDhuibhfinn Earth Worm is an 'Earth' program. It's function is to protect the Earth. It does that by turning things down and off."

"Meaning?"

"Most Giants on the planet – and most Pygmies – have been running smart household goods since the end of the rare earth crisis of 2028. In other words, the planet's most energy consuming homes are tied into the computer network. From remotely controlled lights to coffee machines, fridges, ovens, entertainment systems – television and gaming, mainly, huge! – water heating, home heating and cooling…just about everything is computer controlled. Even cars."

("Get on with it!" muttered MacBhreithiún.)

But Blond was outraged: "Surely you're not suggesting the MEW will turn it all off! There'll be chaos! Aircraft landing…"

"No. Not turn it off. Turn it DOWN. And vital services would be maintained… something about MAC addresses and IP addresses…. Imagine if every home heating system were turned down ½ a degree. Imagine if every air conditioner let it get ½ a degree warmer in every room. WORLDWIDE! The energy production savings would be enormous. How many of those old gas-fired power stations could be decommissioned? Now, imagine every fridge, oven, television set, games console was automatically forced to switch off its pilot lights and standby lights when they weren't necessary, if every machine turned its console lights down 5%, if all the lights in offices and shops and factories and airports and stations – if all of them dimmed by a couple of per cent…"

"People would just turn them up again!"

"Probably, if they could, but most likely they wouldn't even notice. The MagDhuibhfinn doesn't alter the temperature or energy usage on meters; it makes them lie. Eventually they'd just get used to it. And it's clever enough to know when it's being overridden and reduce its impact until it's not being overridden anymore. Then it can slowly increase its impact again: it's a process of education. I mean, all the cars are electric now: do you really need the headlights – or the running lights, or the indicators, or the dashboard lights to be as bright as they are? Would you notice a one per cent, or 3 per cent or even 5 percent dimming of them? And, of course, the more charge you use *in* your car, the more often you have to recharge it from the grid…. Do you see what its power is? The MagDhuibhfinn Earth Worm could reduce carbon emissions by truly Earth-saving amounts. And Giant governments couldn't opt out, back out or chicken out of the Cop agreements they make because the decision will have been made at local level, in every house, every device…"

Pyhare stopped. The Prime Minister had stopped complaining. In silence, he, his secretary, the Pygmy agent and the Giant agent went over what they had just heard. Then they burst out, listing benefits, dangers, chances of success, of disaster. The excited discussion felt unreal and stilted. And that feeling was only partially because of the unaddressed flaw in computer camera placement above the screen, which meant that, though they were all looking at each other, they had the eerie sense that they were standing beside themselves.

Mostly, though, it was because three of them were recalibrating their understanding of their mission, the bounds of what was possible and the future of the Earth.

Eventually, they all agreed that the MEW was probably the single most important object on the planet at that moment. And that it could not remain in the hands of GASP a moment longer. It was agreed that there was no option but to recover it.

At all costs.

"Just one thing, Pyhare," the Pygmy premiere sounded puzzled, "Why 'MagDhuibhfinn'? I mean who came up with that – surely not some South American hacker…"

"I am disappointed, Kiku, you are judging us again…but, no, you are right…"

"Erm. Um. I mean…" ÓCléirigh mumbled.

"What is it Padraig? Don't interrupt…. Or blow your nose or something…. I mean, who even knows how to pronounce the damned word?" Then MacBhreithiún noticed Pyhare laughing.

"I mean, Sir, as it was me that gave it the name, Sir…." ÓCléirigh stopped, blushing.

The Pygmy PM's eyes were huge. Blond was rocking with laughter and |Xi!xu‡qe – thinking back to MacBhreithiún's accusations that ÓCléirigh was a non-Irish pedant given to using Irish language that he did not understand – burst out laughing.

Eventually recovering some of his dignity, MacBhreithiún thanked Pyhare and locked him out of the call. To Blond, he said, "I have been in touch with your boss. She has sent plans of Trugberg. She says B.O.S.S. has been spying on GASP since the Cold War. Unsurprisingly. Giants…," he sneered, then bit his tongue and changed tack.

|Xi!xuⵊqe could see the embarrassment radiating lazily from the Clurichaun in ribbons of pink and green. "I will arrange a team to come to you immediately. They should reach you this evening. You know how important this is now and that it is vital to keep it secret...." He looked at the two agents, mumbled embarrassedly, wished them luck and ended the meeting.

Four minutes later, the plans of the GASP facility at Trugberg pinged into the in-box and they began planning.

That evening, Blond and |Xi!xuⵊqe were going over the plans when there was a knock on the door. There were running footsteps and they heard the key turning in the door. "Jenny! Don't. It could be..." Before |Xi!xuⵊqe could get to the little hallway, Jenny had turned the doorhandle. In the doorway stood, three dinky but distinctly malevolent-looking figures, "... anyone!"

"Wuttunee!" shouted Jenny, "You're safe!" she cried.

"Of course, Jenny Miler. It is hard to kill a Mannegishi. These here are Heorhiy, a Ukrainian Domovyk, and Torbjorn, Swedish Tomtenisse. They are here to..." But Jenny had leapt forward and grabbed Sequoyah in her arms.

Focussed on the delightedly scowling Mannegishi, she didn't seem particularly interested in the Domovyk or the Tomtenisse.

That evening, after they'd all eaten, Jenny was told to go off to the spa and relax again while plans were made for the Trugberg mission. She objected and, to the surprise of |Xi!xuⵊqe and Blond, Wuttunee argued that she should stay for the planning since she would be with them.

Blond nudged |Xi!xuⵊqe, "Looks like you've got competition!" she hissed in his ear.

"Nonsense!" scowled the Sān, "He's just pleased to see her! Natural reaction. Nothing more. At all."

But they agreed on condition that she stayed with them at all times. For her own safety, they said: what if GASP realised she knew something this valuable to them? On the other hand, they still weren't sure she could be trusted, though no one said anything in front of her.

For the rest of the evening and into the early hours, the four Pygmies, the Giant and the Canadian runaway pawed over maps on the computer and the blueprints of the facility. Around midnight, they received a set of satellite photographs, courtesy of someone in B.O.S.S. Finally, they could identify a route into the guard points covering the vehicle entrance. Reaching there, though, involved climbing down from the south ridge of the Trugberg onto the 250-metre-wide shelf above it, then abseiling almost a hundred metres onto the ice shelf that supported the runway to which snow vehicles and equipment were delivered. They watched two clips of an IL-76 heavy lifting craft landing and taking off and an Antonov releasing heavy loads on ski-pallets. Ant-like vehicles issued from the cliff base below a radar dome and dragged their booty into the mountain.

The pedestrian entrance was inset to the right, beside the vehicle entrance. While the vehicle entrance was usually closed with a snow-camouflaged roller door, the pedestrian entrance was usually unlocked. Its security relied on a guard room. From that entrance, they planned a route to the central computer room, identifying points to be neutralised or held, entrances to be hacked.

Amazingly the designs showed little in the way of high-level security.

"Logical," concluded Heorhiy in his Domovyk way, "Base location is almost impregnable and is supposed only for routine communications and storage. That is their story. But tell me: how do you know key is there?"

Blond leaned back. "We have a mole or, rather, an eagle. F.R.S.T. Freitag is a Major in the Combined Security Defence Directorate – GASP in German. Code named Golden Eagle. Also a tracker beacon puts it there."

Heorhiy humphed but looked impressed. "So," he said, "Down off saddle, across leedle snow plateau, down to guard post, into data room, get the USB key. Route out down mountain."

"Ah, yes. The route out…"

It took another hour to figure out a route down the mountain, and it involved taking – or stealing – skis.

Then it took Jenny ten minutes to reassure |Xi!xuǂqe that she would help him with his skis.

"Piece of cake," said Jemima Blond, eventually. "Now: tea!"

"The most completely hare-brained idea I have ever had the misfortune to be involved in," said |Xi!xuǂqe. Wuttunee, looking miserable, nodded. Torbjorn smiled. He liked snow.

Chapter 21 The Impossible Operation

It was a strange procession that left the Bellevue Palace a few minutes before midnight. As was usual when more than two Pygmies were together, they moved in the shadows, using the service entrances of buildings. Waiting for them was an MPV with darkened windows. The electric vehicle purred onto the A6. An hour later, they pulled into a darkened warehouse in Interlaken. Inside was a hive of activity. From two large delivery vehicles they unloaded equipment and weapons. They all changed into snow suits, checked the weapons: Heckler and Koch MP7s with ROTEX-III Silencers, and a brace of assault grenades, both smooth-shelled, designed to stun defenders without endangering attackers, and fragmentation for maximum kill. ǀXi!xuǂqe relished explaining the details to Jenny by way of revenge for the 'skiing lesson'.

Torbjorn watched Jemima strap a holster to her hip. "What's that, cowboy?" he asked, smirking.

"Colt M1911."

"As I said: cowboy. My God, the thing's an antique!"

"Oh, I don't know," she smiled drawing and aiming at his head, ".45 calibre. With a laser site." A red dot appeared on Torbjorn's forehead.

"Whoa! That's you done for, Tor," squealed Sequoyah delightedly.

"Besides, it's nice and slim. Doesn't ruin my figure," Jemima smiled teasingly and holstered the weapon.

Jenny made a show of looking uncomfortable but accepted a submachine gun and strict instructions to keep the muzzle pointed at the ground at all times. She proved surprisingly adept at learning how it worked but was ordered very firmly to keep the safety on and stay out of the way. Torbjorn wasn't exactly keen on having her behind him. Even though he was the least experienced mountaineer, |Xi!xu‡qe would be leading them off the mountain saddle: it would be dark and his synesthetic training would allow him to identify threats that the others would be unable to see or hear.

The MPVs drove them to an airfield: Skydive Interlaken, said a sign at the entrance. All five were relieved when the driver drew up beside an electric helicopter.

A helicopter taking off at 2 am would have seemed unusual to anyone who saw it, but the field was half a kilometre from the nearest houses, which were all dark. Soon they were skimming down a valley, surrounded by hills of increasing height, then a lake and the climb into the snowcaps. The pilot pointed out the looming presence of the Jungfrau to the south then the Trugberg peak to their north. Soon, they were dropping out of the machine, into the snow of the ridge. It was dark. A storm had moved in and the wind whipped snow in flurries around them. The helicopter hovered a moment, turbojets whining, then swung away to the east and was gone.

|Xi!xu‡qe motioned them forward into the darkness. Blinded, but his other senses fully alert, he nevertheless recognised the varying depths of the snow in colours: white where it was shallow, yellow when deeper and orange where crevasses might lurk. Around him, the high-pitched whine of

the mountain faces faded in and out depending on their distance. Ahead, he heard only a dull thrum where the saddle dropped away onto the ice shelf above their target. At his back was the comforting weight of his knobkierrie and he focused on it for a moment, settling his mind. He motioned the little group forward.

Torbjorn was efficient and quick in setting up the dropline for the descent of the steeply sloping ice field and the drop beyond. Soon they were crossing the 250 meters to the cliff above the laboratory. At the edge, all was blackness. But ǀXi!xuǂqe could sense the guard hut beneath them as a burnt amber presence. The Tomtenisse and the Sān established an anchor point and they began the abseil down to it.

One by one, they fell into the snow near the entrance.

The first guard to see Torbjorn, Jenny and Sequoyah stopped dead. He rubbed his eyes and peered through the glass of the guard post. "Jurgen," he said to the man at the console behind him, "there are some children outside. Come and look!"

Jurgen guffawed and stood up. Nonsense. But it was best to humour his superior.

"They've got toy guns! Ha! Ha! They must be lost. Open the door. They'll freeze. Look! Their mother is with them!"

The moment Jurgen swung the door open, a dark whirlwind of fury burst through. Neither man had time to think before the kierrie laid them out. There was no noise. In the hut, the blue of the CCTV screens flickered. It took a moment to redirect the remote cameras so that there would be a clear, unrecorded passage to the door of the motor bay. There was no indication that anyone else was watching the feed but it was better not to take the chance. And a recording could be embarrassing later.

Such was the confidence of whoever ran the facility, that the vehicle access door was up even though the pedestrian gate was locked. Torbjorn, Heorhiy and Wuttunee crossed the driveway to the left side; |Xi!xu‡qe, Blond and Jenny moved down the right. Torbjorn, Wuttunee and Blond held their rifles at the ready. Heorhiy wielded a short club, gleefully; more grimly, |Xi!xu‡qe held his kierrie before him. There was no need for the Pygmies to keep low but Blond was hunched over and Jenny copied her. She still carried her MP7 a little awkwardly but seemed to be watching Blond carefully.

The two guards in the garage were smoking and chatting. Heorhiy and |Xi!xu‡qe took care of them quickly. At the end of the vehicle bay was a cargo lift and, beside it, a solid steel door. They lined up on either side of the door. Blond stepped forward and swung the door open. Almost simultaneously |Xi!xu‡qe and Heorhiy slipped through, sideways on.

Nothing happened. To their left was a wide concrete staircase leading up. At the top a walkway doubled back 180 degrees right so the top passage would be looking down into the stairwell they were in. It was almost dark and difficult to be sure what was there.

The Pygmies, even |Xi!xu‡qe, could not sense anything clearly because of the complex mix of building materials: rock, steel, glass, reinforced concrete, electrical conduiting.

Torbjorn and Heorhiy went first. Both held their machine pistols, significantly lengthened by the silencers, at the ready. Leading, Heorhiy swivelled to check the landing above the staircase; Torbjorn swept the walkway. They crouched at the top of the stairs and waited for the others to join them. There was another steel door.

"What do you think, Tor?" whispered ǀXi!xuǂqe.

"I don't like these tin doors," said Wuttunee, "They make a noise."

"I suspect there will be resistance at the end of the lefthand corridor. That leads to the main communications area, remember? It is along the passage behind a blast proof door, in the left wall. Judging by the relaxed security, the doors will be open. But there will be guards to the right and the whole corridor has four windows, in the wall opposite that tin door, that look into offices and work areas. We can expect people there."

Blond shifted forward, "The key will be to the left somewhere, because that complex also houses the computer suite at the end of the corridor, next to the mess. To the right as we go through the tin door the passage leads to another door. Straight ahead beyond it are the guards' quarters and to the left of them is a security-coded door. Past the guardroom is the storeroom entrance where the cargo lift opens. The security-coded door is of some interest. Eagle only got into there once but he says there are offices and laboratories. I would love to see what's in there. It's a biometric pad, though: tough to breach. We'll be in trouble if the key is in there."

"No. Logic says it's in the computer suite. Besides," growled Wuttunee, "that is not our plan! We should stick to the task."

"I agree with Sequoyah," said Torbjorn, "It is likely to be heavily defended, the guards are concentrated there and getting in is too hard. And holding the one narrow door is easier for us than holding two or three rooms."

"Agreed." |Xi!xuǂqe assigned each of them a task. The team formed up on the door, and went through, Torbjorn and Blond covering the corridor to the right, |Xi!xuǂqe, Wuttunee, Heorhiy and formed a triangle that fanned to the left. Jenny was behind Tor. All of them were crouched below the level of the two windows that were now to the right of their direction of motion.

The rear-guard pair would remain facing the entrance to the barracks, storeroom and laboratory complex. They would hold the door to the stairs that was their main escape route. The other two windows, which were to their left, had hanging metal blinds. Impossible to look in without moving them, though Jemima tried.

The other two windows had no blinds. Heorhiy raised his head above the sill of the fourth window. "Room is about 10 metres wide. Same deep. Dim lighting but four islands each with four workstations. Sixteen operators, most with headphones. Not military. Not armed. Opposite solid sliding panel door at the left is large, oval conference table, right of windows. Three officers in military uniform, high ranking. Overseeing computer operators? Closed. If we don't alert them, they won't be a problem."

"That's different from what Golden Eagle said. There should be a big canteen there. Blond?" |Xi!xuǂqe looked at the British agent.

"He was here only a month ago. This is all new. What's changed?"

"The MagDhuibhfinn Earth Worm," Heorhiy mouthed.

"This is about hacking the coding! That's why there are so many computers!" said Wuttunee.

"Good. So, the communications arrays are still to the left in the corridor ahead. That means there's an area at the end of the facility on the right we know nothing about."

Wuttunee's hand flew to his mouth. "They would never keep the key in the same room as the hackers. It's too easy to steal – a lunch break, sleeping period.... And it's worth a living fortune! The World!"

ǀXi!xuǂqe and Jenny looked at him. "Since when do you know so much about computers?" said ǀXi!xuǂqe. "And why didn't you help me at the Trauco HQ?"

"Would that be after you," he looked pointedly at Jenny, "hacked my phone and then had all those secret meetings with Piyêsîs? You didn't tell me what you were doing, did you, Kiku? If you had, I could have got you into Millalobo's system without any trouble."

ǀXi!xuǂqe looked crestfallen. He knew what those wasted four hours had cost.

"And we wouldn't have been at Bosque Mbaracayú when Kleynmans came and there wouldn't have been the battle and..." The Mannegishi fell silent.

"Pisamboro forgive me! Sequoyah, I swear by all my forefathers' gods, if I had known...! But you were so mysterious. And Kleynmans kept showing up..."

"Of course I was mysterious!" spluttered Wuttunee indignantly, "I had been detailed with keeping MacBhreithiún aware of where you were. I was calling them. But I wasn't allowed to tell you, obviously. Mainly because he was afraid of the opposition in the Council. He was right. But not about..."

Jenny's eyes had filled with tears. She reached out to Sequoyah but he was too far away to touch. "Poor Pi!"

The sudden clatter of a door opening and a shout of laughter brought them back to their situation.

"Guards!" spat Heorhiy, "You'll have to finish your confession another time!"

Just then, the door at the end of the corridor opened and a man in a dishevelled uniform came through looking over his shoulder. The door shut behind him. He turned. The cigarette fell from his lips as he clutched frantically at his holster. And fell.

Bouncing off his head, ǀXi!xuǂqe's kierrie turned a lazy circle in the air and fell.

If it hit the floor the noise would alert the other guards.

The heavy head of the weapon thudded into the plump stomach of the prone guard and rolled almost noiselessly onto the floor.

"They'll know soon. Quick!" Heorhiy pushed the connecting blast door open.

For a split second, they all expected a shout, shots.

Nothing came. either from ahead of them or behind, from the direction of the guardroom. Through the door was a short corridor. The wall on the left was punctured by a double sliding door, three metres along it. It was wide open: the communications room, as expected, and there were sounds of voices. Six metres along the right-hand wall was a length of wall with a closed sliding door. It had not been in the blueprints or Freitag's plan.

Clearly, the facility had been re-tasked after the taking of the USB key. The newly built section – where the mess had been on Golden Eagle's map – was obviously there for the task of cracking the MagDhuibhfinn Earth Worm.

But to get to it they would have to cross the open door of the Comms room.

Jenny moved up to the interleading door. She was clearly preparing to take up position behind Wuttunee.

Focused ahead, Heorhiy slithered along the left-hand wall and |Xi!xu‡qe and Wuttunee moved along the right. There were no windows.

Wuttunee looked at Heorhiy. He was watching the Comms room doorway. He nodded.

Heorhiy crossed the open door.

Then |Xi!xu‡qe and Wuttunee.

Jenny was stuck, alone at the interleading door and between the two groups.

Noticing, |Xi!xu‡qe made to cross back to her.

"There's no time, Kiku!" hissed Wuttunee, "Someone will find the guard soon. Without your kierrie, it will be a firefight. Tor and Blond won't cope alone at close quarters."

|Xi!xu‡qe looked at the Mannegishi. This was a surprisingly competent man. Not the whining child of the Pryor Mountains. For the second time, he was re-evaluating the other Pygmy. But he was wrong. |Xi!xu‡qe signalled Jenny across to them. Wuttunee did not object: his leader must have a reason.

|Xi!xu‡qe made eye-contact with each of the team. Using his hands, he detailed Blond, and Torbjorn to secure the corridor should anything break out.

He pointed at Wuttunee first, then Jenny, and tapped his shoulder once: With me. Jenny may have seen the key; she obviously knew more than she had let on. She might be able to look for it if he couldn't.

Wuttunee…Wuttunee…he owed Wuttunee. Besides, a computer technician would be useful.

The sliding-door into the mystery suite was closed but its upper half had a glass insert. He couldn't see through it, though. He looked at Blond down the corridor, who was smiling. "Jump!" she mouthed. Feeling a fool, he launched himself vertically, like an excited chimp, he thought. They wouldn't forget this.

There was nothing in what he now saw was a wide-ish corridor constructed of prefabricated panels. The door to the computer room, on the right, was shut. Opposite, there were two doors, the first a sliding door. He caught a brief glimpse of a nameplate:

```
Generaloberst

Bernt Brücke

Direktor
```

A Lieutenant general? But who on earth still used NVA ranks? Not the Bundeswehr. Still, a three-star general. This must be an important posting. Certainly not a quartermaster's store.

The immediate question was who was in the other office.

|Xi!xuǂqe had to see the further door.

He jumped again.

Whether it was that he had not jumped high enough or because the sensor was faulty, he did not really expect the sliding door to open.

But open it did.

Trusting Wuttunee and Heorhiy to cover him, he landed and rolled like a ball to the far end of the ten metre long corridor. He fetched up, rifle levelled, outside an ordinary door. It was closed and on it was a sign saying

> Eingeschränkt! Zugang
> nur mit Genehmigung –
> Restricted! Access
> strictly by Permission

There was a keypad set into the wall beside it. He smiled.

Across the corridor, Wuttunee was signing to Heorhiy and Jenny to join him. They crawled to where he was.

"What do you think?"

"Absolutely! No doubt. It will be in here," whispered Sequoyah. "And that's a very simple keypad." He fished in a side-pouch and came out with a decoder. Levering off the screw covers – "They use the screws as ports to arm them once they're screwed on." – he slid a probe into the exposed ports. The screen on the decoder flashed through numbers and letters then stopped on a four-digit code.

Wuttunee disconnected the machine and pressed the buttons. The door clicked open.

Inside, the three found a computer. Just one. But it was surrounded by banks of screens. A nest of wires connected it to the screens and four other boxes. Each box had six ports. Each port a wire leading into the floor.

"Standard switches. Almost certainly to the hackers over the corridor."

"And there's the key!" Jenny reached out. So fast there was an audible slap, Heorhiy grabbed her wrist.

"They're working on it. If you remove it, all their machines will go down. The whole place will be alerted and they'll know exactly where to come!"

Jenny was wide-eyed, her mouth an O of shock.

"What can you do, Sequoyah?" asked ǀXi!xuǂqe.

"There's another USB port on this machine. I have a blank key in my kit – never travel without one!" He wagged his finger playfully. "My father once told me about a time when he went to a dance with the most beautiful – and playful – girl in his village. Alas! He realised too late that he had gone without a –"

"Wuttunee! We don't have time!"

"Erm, sorry, Kiku. Maybe another time." He plugged the spare key into the port and a window opened. There were four files on it. One was called 'Mirror' and he chose it. "It'll pretend to be whatever I tell it to." A dialogue box opened, asking what he wanted to mirror. He selected 'All'. The screen went black and a new one identified itself as MEW security. It offered him two options:

1. an ceann ceart
2. na n-amadán amháin

"Uh oh!" he said.

Chapter 22 Overcoming the Impossible

ǀXi!xuǂqe looked at Wuttunee. Jenny looked at ǀXi!xuǂqe. Wuttunee looked at both of them.

"Bloody heck, ÓCléirigh put in a firewall!"

"What does it mean?" said ǀXi!xuǂqe.

"Obviously we have to choose one. Any suggestions?" Sequoyah said.

"Red wire. Blue wire," said ǀXi!xuǂqe.

"We can't risk the natural world on a guess!" said Jenny.

"Why not, they're always doing it in James Bond. And Mission Impossible. And Scorpion."

"Those are movies, Kiku! This is real. How many times have you told me how vital this is? And think of the people who have died getting us to this point? And me – they even kidnapped me! You were worried. You were. You said!"

Sequoyah was looking serious. He stuck his finger in his ear. "Worrying makes my ears itch! Anyway, I don't see what option there is. Even if we dared to phone ÓCléirigh or MacBhreithiún, if we can't risk them picking up our signal – that's a huge communications array across the passage – there's not much hope of a signal inside a Swiss mountain in the middle of the Alps."

"Red wire. Blue wire," ǀXi!xuǂqe reached out.

"Wait!" said Jenny. "ÓCléirigh said something to me on the phone before we left: he said a 'áilleacht cheart like me' should be careful to come home safe. He said it meant I was a real beauty."

"ÓCléirigh said that? The old devil!" said |Xi!xuⱡqe.

"I thought it was rather sweet, actually!" she teased.

"And how exactly does that help us?" sneered Wuttunee.

"He said the noun and adjective were backward in Irish...Oh, it doesn't matter. Except it does. It really does! If 'áilleacht' is 'beauty' then 'cheart' must be 'real'. And it sounds like 'ceart'"

Wuttunee looked at her.

"He must be a hundred years older than you, the old...wait till I..."

"Who's lost the plot now, Kiku?" Sequoyah was smiling. "She has a very good point. It definitely improves the chances from 50/50, anyway."

He leaned forward, positioned his finger of the '1' on the keyboard. And drew back.

"Nope," he said, "there's no other way."

And he leaned forward and pressed the key.

Nothing happened.

"Yes!" he almost shouted, pumping the air, "Get in there, Sexy! Done it!"

"How do you know?" said Jenny.

"Well, do you hear any angry voices? Sirens? Gunfire?"

Just then, a dull burst of suppressed automatic fire came from outside the room. Instantly, |Xi!xuⱡqe and Jenny were in the short passage, weapons levelled.

"Damn!" Wuttunee said to the empty room as he snatched the USB key with the original MagDhuibhfinn Earth Worm on it from the machine.

The door of the computer room slid open and an officer appeared, looking to his left. Jenny fired twice from his right. He looked at her, Wuttunee and |Xi!xu‡qe in horror as he crumpled.

But |Xi!xu‡qe was over his body, firing short bursts into the computer room. He picked off the two remaining officers who had rushed to the window to look out. "Stay where you are!" he shouted at the hackers cowering at their stations. Methodically, he destroyed each computer with a burst of gunfire. One of the hackers had been playing Minecraft, he noticed wryly.

At the same time, Jenny, her back to the computer room wall, aimed her weapon into the office of 'Generaloberst Bernt Brûcke <u>Direktor</u>' and held the trigger till it stopped firing. Along with most of the door, the lock smashed. What was left swung open to reveal a black office chair, the leather shredded. From behind the desk a motionless hand protruded, its finger looped through the trigger guard of a pistol.

Wuttunee moved to the door of the connecting corridor. From there, he could see into the Comms room. A couple of guards had engaged Heorhiy and were firing from behind the four arrays. The Mannegishi emptied a magazine into the room and the guards took cover. Heorhiy pulled the pin on a fragmentation grenade – risky with these thin walls – and lobbed it to the very back of the suite, shouting, "Frag!"

The Domovyk, the Mannegishi and the Canadian hit the floor, arms over their heads. The explosion was followed by screams. A few fragments of shrapnel punched holes in the wall above Heorhiy's head.

In the main corridor, Tor was first to recover. A guard appeared in the door at the end of the passage. Before Tor had even properly raised the MP7, he fired a burst. The man's ankles were chopped from beneath him in an explosion of blood and bone. He fell beside the dead guard and someone inside dragged him back in.

Blond was up and moving forward on the left wall of the main corridor, firing down its length.

|Xi!xu‡qe was now outside the computer room, firing through the windows. The corridor had become a kill zone. The only entrance for the remaining GASP personnel was the door blocked by the inert body of the guard, with |Xi!xu‡qe's kierrie beside him.

By now, the floor was slick with blood halfway up to the door that led from the main corridor into the stairwell.

As expected, their way in was the only way out.

Jenny was now at the connecting door into the main corridor with Jemima directly in front of her so she had no line of fire. But the Giant was holding her own and the gunfire was becoming more sporadic. Either the GASP defenders had worked out that there was little they could do or there weren't many of them left.

Or they had another plan.

"Ammunition?" |Xi!xu‡qe asked.

"Nearly out. Two grenades. Concussion." Torbjorn.

"One mag. Concussion grenade." Heorhiy.

"One and a bit mags. Two grenades. One of each." Jemima.

"Two rounds left. Two grenades." Wuttunee.

"Two full magazines, and..." Jenny tapped the machine pistol.

"I'll have one of those, Jen," shouted Sequoyah, "I'm all out. I'm reserving my grenades for the electronics."

A burst of heavier fire came down the corridor and slammed into the rock wall at the end of the service corridor.

"That's it. They'll be making a bid to cover the exit soon. And it sounds like they're finding heavier ordinance. It's only a matter of time. Now or never. Tor, on the 'go' get a conc. as far down the passage to that door as possible. Heorhiy, nail anything that comes through the door until the grenade goes off. Jemma, get ready to hold the position beyond the second window. Then try to get your grenades into the mystery room: conc. first, frag as far to the back left corner as possible. Sequoyah, follow up on Jemma to cover her against the stairway door – you never know. I'm getting the door open and secure. I'll take Jenny with me. Jen, you'll cover the staircase ahead of us while we secure our retreat."

Each nodded, preparing grenades and magazines. Jemima loosened the flap on the pistol.

ǀXi!xuǂqe nodded at Tor. Heorhiy pumped two and three-round bursts into the far door. The grenade bounced then rolled past the kierrie into the half open door and stopped just beyond the fallen guard in front of the door to the mystery room.

There was a split second of complete silence.

Then a sheet of flame blew both doors off their hinges. Blond and Wuttunee were moving instantly. ǀXi!xuǂqe, pushing Jenny ahead of him, was first through the door.

Before Jenny and ǀXi!xuǂqe reached the head of the stairs, the quick rip of Heorhiy's bursts signalled a counterattack. But Jemima was at the broken window. She lobbed in the smooth-shelled grenade and ducked, firing at the door. Guards were crossing into the mystery room. Soon, they would have a window from there onto the corridor. The crash of the conc. stopped them for ten seconds. That was enough for her to bowl the frag. grenade, left-handed, along the inside wall. There was a frantic scuffling, lost in the vicious smack of the explosion and the roar of metal fragments ripping through wood, plastic and flesh.

ǀXi!xuǂqe was still at the stairwell door. "Jen, I don't think there are too many. We'll be a minute. Hold the stairs." To his surprise, she was at the head of the stairs, rifle at the ready before he had finished speaking.

He turned back to the door. "Heorhiy! Sub Tor and Sequoyah! Jemima, out!" He swapped places with her at the door. "Sequoyah, I'm covering. Out! Heorhiy, Wuttunee, Tor, out. Get the stairs. Help Jenny. Secure an exit."

All three went through the door. Now they were all in the stairwell. ǀXi!xuǂqe was at the open door, covering the main passage as the others started making their way down the stairs.

Then, he stepped into the main corridor, firing intermittently and disappeared. The door slammed closed behind him.

Jenny looked up. "Kiku? Let's go! NO!" she screamed as he disappeared. She turned to run after him, the machine pistol ready.

Sequoyah flung an arm round her waist as she ran past him: "He knows what he's doing. Leave him. You can do nothing now but give him another problem to worry about."

The others were beginning their cautious descent of the stairs. The Mannegishi waited with Jenny. Both watched the door.

"It's time, Jenny. We must go. There must be a garrison with more guards and they will have got an alarm out. The helos will be on their way already."

"No! A few more minutes!"

"No time, Jen," his tone was gentle, "We must go. There is no reason to put us all at risk for the thing he went in there to save."

"What can have been important enough to die for in there?"

"Not in there, Jenny Miler. Out here."

Then, when he looked at her, she understood.

Just then the door crashed open and the stringy figure of ǀXi!xuǂqe appeared. He laughed and raised his arm in triumph.

In his clenched fist was his knobkierrie.

But Wuttunee had been right. When he opened the garage door, they saw a detachment moving into the garage through the vehicle entrance. He, Jemima and Heorhiy were losing the battle to keep them back as the uniforms weaved among the vehicles.

"They are going for the lift, Kiku," shouted the Tomtenisse, "If they can get up, they can come through above us, down the stairs."

"Can we put that lift out of action?" said Wuttunee.

"Not possible unless someone gets a grenade in the works," said Jemima.

"I've got two. Cover me!" shouted Wuttunee.

Just then, an ear-splitting roar blew the steel door back. Torbjorn rammed it back into place with is shoulder. "Here's an interesting problem!"

"Not a problem. Open the door enough for me to see out," Jemima had her pistol in her hand. When the door opened slightly, she scanned the space in front of her.

"There! Left, just inside the pedestrian entrance!"

Sure enough, a guard had just loosened a grenade from his belt and was pulling the pin.

A red dot appeared on his forehead. It became a black hole. He crumpled. The grenade dropped. The four men around him looked horrified. Then it went off.

"And that," said Wuttunee, "is why you don't throw frags in attack."

In the momentary shock of the grenade's devastation, |Xi!xu‡qe stepped through the door and launched his remaining grenade at the vehicle entrance. When this assault had driven the guards into cover, Torbjorn tore the door open. He had a grenade in each hand, the pins already out.

"What?" shouted Sequoyah, clutching at his belt, "the little bastard picked my pockets!"

But Tor was already in front of the lift door. He had to get the lift floor up to drop the grenades into the hydraulic engine in the well. Holding the detonator safety levers, his hands were fully occupied with the grenades. It was all he could do to punch the call button.

Suddenly, chips of rock flew off the rock near his head.

Gunfire, both MP7 and Jemima's blessed Colt, was returned from the door, careful, measured: as it always is when a unit is running out of ammunition.

The green 'summon' light started blinking. The doors were opening.

Tor fell to the floor, rolled behind the body of one of the guards they had encountered on entering. The cover wouldn't last for long but it was all there was.

The doors were open.

The body beside Tor moved as rounds slammed into it. They had guessed his plan.

The floor of the compartment lifted, two centimetres, five centimetres. It needed ten to make sure the grenade's mechanism wouldn't catch.

Six centimetres.

With a jerk the lift floor stopped. Someone, something had stopped it.

There was nothing for it, Tor realised, "It's stuck," he shouted, "I'll have to post them through by hand!"

Immediately, the gunfire from both sides intensified.

Tor flexed his arms. This was going to be the greatest push-up in history. Something stung his leg. He launched himself horizontally, a foot off the ground, towards the narrow gap beneath the lift compartment.

His body bounced towards the gap. His eyes saw nothing else. He neither felt nor cared about the punches he felt in his legs. When he came to stop a yard from his target, he was only dimly aware of the muzzle flashes of his friends, from the door two metres away. The breath was punched out of his lungs. He felt the floor growing slippery beneath him. It would help him reach the gap! he thought. But it was getting a little dark now. He could only see the light in the lift well. That's strange! he thought, why have a light there. Better put it out.

He slid the first grenade through the letterbox opening. Struggled to get the second from his left hand. It didn't seem to be working so well. Slid the second through. Then all went black.

Except in the garage. The blast beneath the lift pushed Tor's body away from the door.

The door from the stairwell opened. ǀXi!xuǂqe, Wuttunee and Jenny poured through, firing the last of Jenny's rounds. Jemima and Heorhiy dashed to Tor, grabbed his epaulettes and pulled him back into the stairwell.

Jemima and Heorhiy frantically loosed his uniform, applying field dressings. "Jesus!" the English agent whispered, "he can't possibly…"

"Yes, he can! He must! Stop that one inside his thigh. It might have hit an artery."

As they worked, a strange silence fell in the garage. Then there was the sound of engines, distant, faint but unmistakeable.

"Why have they stopped attacking?" said Jenny.

It was ǀXi!xuǂqe who replied: "Because those aren't their forces. They're ours."

Soon, Tor was on a stretcher. The others were trooping, shell-shocked and surrounded by disarmed GASP personnel, from the vehicle entrance.

Jenny, Jemima and the Pygmies were ushered into a Humvee by Giants. No one joked about their having to be lifted into the vehicle.

And then they were on a Leonardo AW171E in Swiss colours, cutting through the early morning light back to the base in Interlaken.

The next morning, they met for breakfast. At first the meeting was sombre, then a medical officer came in with news about Torbjorn.

"He has sustained severe injuries – gunshot wounds and shrapnel in his legs and left torso. Most have been sutured but there are some internal injuries that still represent a threat. However, he is stable and we expect a recovery…"

The table did not hear the rest of the sentence. It didn't matter. They drank to him, in orange juice, and soon started going over the battle. Before long, they were taking the good-natured piss out of their leader.

"Ha! Ha! And when you jumped up to see through the window!"

"You looked like an excited chimp!"

"And then that roll thing when the door opened, what was that? You looked like an armadillo!"

ǀXiǃxuǂqe looked hurt. "Well, it worked. Just like Jenny's logic and your USB mirror... SEXY!" he laughed.

Heorhiy scowled then laughed with them all.

And Lieutenant Commander Jemima Blond sat beside them feeling that she had grown precisely as tall as them.

Chapter 23 A Delicate Negotiation

Jemma Blond, ǀXiǃxuǂqe, Jenny and Sequoyah had met for lunch in the Rossli Hotel. It was a sunny day and they were waiting in the rattan chairs on the veranda on the corner of Hauptstrasse.

"There's another person in one of those green hats with feathers," said ǀXiǃxuǂqe, tensing up. He remembered the feather the girl in London had mentioned, and the feather with Artyom's body.

"Take it easy, Kiku. This is Switzerland. The Alps. It's the national dress." Jemma was trying to reassure him, he knew, but he couldn't shake the unease.

"Ridiculous!" he snorted, testily. "If I were to wear my 'national' dress…" He broke off as a wave of nostalgia engulfed him. Memories of the hot sands of the Kalahari, the pale sky, the children in their beads. He touched the bag beside him, remembering the buck-leather skirt that had been clothing enough in the sun. Into his mind drifted his mother's voice, singing,

…Take my face and give me yours!
Take my face, my unhappy face -

"You'd stick out like a sore thumb!" Wuttunee broke into his dream.

"And freeze to death," |Xi!xu‡qe added, returning to the present and its problems. "Jemma, what are the instructions about getting the key to B.O.S.S.?" he asked Blond, feeling the leather bag, knowing its contents beneath his hand.

"I've had the orders. I'm to take the key to meet with our mole – Golden Eagle, who gave us the Trugberg plan –"

"– the one that was out of date and wrong," butted in the Mannegishi.

"– that we used to get the key back –"

"– from GASP, who stole it in the first place!". Sequoyah wasn't letting it go.

"Shut up, Sexy!" Jemma hissed, "These are my orders."

Listening, Jenny had grown more and more thoughtful. "But he's got a point, Jemma. Golden Eagle, Friday, or whatever his name is –"

"– F.R.S.T. Freitag," Jemma corrected, a little pompously.

"– betrayed GASP, apparently. But his information wasn't very good: we nearly lost Tor. We got in so easily: all the doors were open. And it was a close-run thing. Who's to say that wasn't deliberate? That we weren't expected to fail, to die there And even if we had got out, if Sequoyah," she emphasised the name to restore some of the Mannegishi's wounded pride, "hadn't taken the key, we would have concluded that it was destroyed, that we had failed. And all the time B.O.S.S. would have had it…and not *your* faction of B.O.S.S., either: the GASP-allied faction who apparently want it to control the world or something."

"True," interjected |Xi!xu‡qe, "being able to boost world energy consumption would be worth a fortune to the energy companies."

Jenny summed up: "So First Friday – yes, yes, I know, Freitag – might really have meant to throw us off the trail. Giving the key back to him just makes no sense at all!"

Blond looked thoughtful. "It's true that the mission was touch and go. And I suppose the one thing we do know is that we have the MEW in our possession. And that we are probably the most trustworthy people to carry it…"

"Jem, with all due respect," Jenny continued, "Kiku had carried that thing all round the world. He could have surrendered it to B.O.S.S. at any time. In fact that was his mission, in essence: get the key to Europe and hand it over to B.O.S.S."

"That's true," added |Xi!xuǂqe, "and I couldn't understand why MacBhreithiún gave it to me to take to America, of all places. It seems obvious now: I was the hare in a dog-and-hare race. The further I travelled and the faster I moved, the more B.O.S.S. showed their hand as they became increasingly desperate."

There was a silence. Wuttunee broke it: "The only rational course of action is for the four of us to get the key directly to Jemima's boss."

"Can we trust *her*, though?" Jenny said.

"Of course! I've known Edam Ward-Back for years. Besides, she was the one who arranged the materiel for the Trugberg raid."

" – "

" – And the relief forces that saved our skins."

"That's it then," said |Xi!xuǂqe as the waiter sidled up to their table. "The four of us, for security and to make certain it gets there. And for Tor." He raised his glass.

"Excuse me, ladies, sirs, your table is ready now," the waiter wheedled. They stood.

And as they did so, |Xi!xu‡qe had a clear view through the window of the Arcobaleno cafe across the street. Taking a bite of a large pizza was Arsenei. The unmistakably Goblin face, furrowed low brow, paused in mid-bite, and the Zlydzen looked up. For a nanosecond, his cruel, glittering eyes locked with |Xi!xu‡qe's.

"Come on, Kiku," called Jenny, "I'm starving!"

"You're always starving. I've never seen so much food disappear into so small a person...," he mocked, absentmindedly, starting towards the street. But she grabbed his hand and tugged him away.

Another time, |Xi!xu‡qe swore to himself. And what would he do now, anyway? There would be another time.

Back in Blond's hotel room, Blond, Wuttunee and |Xi!xu‡qe were on a Wavel call with B.O.S.S. HQ in the UK's NSA.

"No, ma'am, I've swept it, this morning and since we returned, and again before initiating this call. And I'm on the NSA VPN." Her boss had demanded Blond's assurance of the security of their conference. For day-to-day communications, most agencies had originally used WhatsApp because it was public and widely used but since that had been taken over by Meta in the 2020s, the promise of end-to-end encryption had been open to doubt. Calls like this were made on Wavel, routinely, and over a VPN whose servers were run by the NSA.

"Who else is in the room with you, Commander Blond?"

"Sequoyah Wuttunee, Mannegishi of the GCPP, Ma'am. He travelled with Kiku, erm, er, Kiku from Canada and was at the battle of the Jogahoh in Bosque Mbaracayú. And also at Trugberg –"

"Strong credentials! Tānse, Agent Wuttunee. Tawow."

Sequoyah's eyebrows rose and a broad smile broke out on his face.

Blond went on, "And Kiku, of course!"

"Your courage and resourcefulness precede you, |Xi!xuǂqe."

"Thank you, Lady Edam. I am glad to meet a Giant who is not my enemy. Finally."

Blond looked troubled, then amused: acceptance indeed!

"Ouch!" said Ward-Back, wincing ironically, "But I'm not surprised. Blond, is the woman Jenny Miler with you?"

"No, Ma'am, as a civilian she is felt to be vulnerable."

"I think you should call her in, don't you?" There was a moment of hesitation - as though she was considering explaining something, thought |Xi!xuǂqe. "From what I hear of her actions at Trugberg, she deserves a seat at the top table, don't you think?" the NSA Head's voice was sweet but there was no doubting the command.

When Jenny had joined them, Ward-Back confirmed that there was no one else in the room – again – and began.

"Just to be clear: you have the USB key with you? Is that correct?"

"Yes, Ma'am. We have it," Blond assured her.

"And how do you know that the MagDhuibhfinn Earth Worm is on the key?"

|Xi!xuǂqe leaned down till he was in PIP. "I have seen the files on the key several times, er, Ma'am? And they are the same as the first time I saw them. Wuttunee confirms that the data on the relevant file has not been corrupted or altered

since the key was handed to me by Taoiseach MacBhreithiún in…at the GCPP meeting place. And it was confirmed by Trauco HQ."

"Just Lady Ward-Back will do, |Xi!xu‡qe. We know where the Seanad Leprechaun is. How is the red-headed sot?" the NSA Chief was almost laughing.

"He's fine. Or was when I saw him. A little worried now, I think; we haven't told him about the MEW, yet." |Xi!xu‡qe was just managing to hide his astonishment. The NSA knew about the GCPP? It's officers? How much? Personally? Sounded like it.

"Don't worry. He'll know by now, although he'll claim he did not: to protect our, um, relationship. Not everyone in the NSA or other agencies knows about it – the relationship. Or, come to think of it, the Pygmies. Most still think the 'Little People' are a myth invented to frighten children and spies. It is knowledge held only at the very top of most governments, in fact."

"That is welcome news," said |Xi!xu‡qe, "In the past…"

"Yes. We have not been kind. But you see the treatment of the First Nations and the other First Peoples – yes, I know, that is the entitlement of the Sān, and rightly so – though improving is still dogged by suspicion. The Rhodes Must Fall movement and what followed, Black Lives Matter and lately Reify Indigenes have had some effect on the majority of world populations. There is widespread guilt about slavery and land rights."

"With respect, Lady Back-Ward, it would have been much easier for me if someone had told Magnus Kleynmans about all this…"

"Wheels within wheels, Agent |Xi!xu‡qe. Wheels within wheels. I'm sure you've worked some of it out already. Now," she said, her tone made it amply clear that the subject was closed, "we need to get that key installed on a B.O.S.S. computer. You understand that –"

"– launching it from a Pygmy machine would raise immediate suspicion and retaliation. Yes, I have been briefed." ǀXi!xuǂqe had never liked being lectured, an irony he was blissfully unaware of. And his experiences with Giants in the past few weeks had been nothing like the Fairy Wonderland that Ward-Back seemed to be concocting.

"So I need it here. Cop, bless them, was another resounding failure so the MagDhuibhfinn Earth Worm is our best hope, we think."

'WE' thought ǀXi!xuǂqe, who is 'WE' exactly? But he said nothing.

"Therefore I have sent a delegation, shall we call it? – of a Pygmy and a normal, er, Giant…you know I really don't care for that term…to collect it and deliver it to our suite at GCHQ."

"In Cheltenham?" Hah! thought ǀXi!xuǂqe, you're not the only one who knows their enemy! Aloud he said, "We don't think that's a viable option."

"What!" Ward-Back started visibly, losing her calm assurance of authority. "What are you talking about? It must be mounted on a B.O.S.S. central computer. Otherwise it will instantly be labelled enemy action and stopped before it spreads. It will take –"

"Three weeks, give or take, to go online worldwide and become completely effective. I know. I was briefed." ǀXi!xuǂqe was feeling bad for the NSA Giant, now. He knew that she had not expected opposition. She had probably never encountered a direct challenge from a subordinate. But he was not a subordinate. Not of hers. Or her people. It was not the Pygmies who had screwed up the climate, melted the ice-caps, destroyed habitats, decimated biodiversity. "The MEW will stay with me and the people *I* trust until the time *I* choose."

"Agent |Xi!xuǂqe, your cover is comprehensively compromised. Blown, as they say. You are a target and will be, all the way to London!"

"London? Why London?"

"That's where we are. That's where the meeting must take place."

"Unsound logic, Lady Ward-Back. Are all your personnel on your side? Can you trust them? All of them?"

"Where to then?" Ward-Back was looking pouty, now. Like a child who has been scolded, thought |Xi!xuǂqe. Blond, he noticed, had worked her way to the back of the group. Jenny's chin was jutting out determinedly. Bless her! thought |Xi!xuǂqe. Wuttunee had grim satisfaction written all over his face.

"Blond! Your assessment." The NSA Chief practically barked.

"Ma'am, we've discussed this very carefully. There is no doubt that we – the Shadow Faction – have been betrayed at several levels. We understand much of the machinery of |Xi!xuǂqe's mission but there are elements we do not. Freitag's role is one of them. The informant of Bootha at B.O.S.S. Sub-Saharan branch we don't know either. There are other unanswered questions that point to a breach of security in B.O.S.S. Artyom may have been assassinated by a PPSS agent, Arsenei. That casts doubt on PPSS security. You know that there are factions whose loyalty is, er, questionable in the Pygmy establishment."

"I see," Ward-Back's expression was thoughtful, "I wondered about how the MEW got into GASP. We never cleared that up here. Arsenei is a possibility…"

"Therefore," finished Blond, "the only people we feel can actually be trusted are the four of us. And Torbjorn, the Tomtenisse. But he.... Anyway, no one else. We'll deliver it."

"In conclusion, Lady Ward-Back, if London is where it must go, then so be it," the Sān was decisive, "but we will be the ones to arrange its delivery."

"All right. I see your reasoning, though I have serious reservations. How, exactly will you go about it?"

ǀXi!xuǂqe leaned forward so his face occupied most of the little screen: "Wheels within wheels, Ma'am."

The Giant chief smiled and the screen went black.

Chapter 24 A Nasty Surprise

The first order of business was to find a USB key that looked enough like the MEW key to pass as a double.

Then they spent hours planning routes, booking air tickets, cancelling them, double booking others, booking hotel rooms in cities as far apart as Vladivostok and Jakarta, as obscure as Kohtla-Järve in Estonia and Madang in Papua New Guinea. Their imminent arrival was leaked to the Eastern agencies: the Taotao Mo'na of the Mariana Islands were alerted. The Hawaiian Menehune promised to throw a party. On Hokkaido, the Koro-pok-kuru, offered hospitality in Toyotomi but they didn't speak Japanese or English and no one understood Ainu so they didn't know what that entailed.

It didn't matter. They had no intention of going to any of these places.

By the end of the week, every counter-espionage agency of every government, world-wide, had people in place either to welcome them or to capture them. Communications had become so tied up that personnel limitations created enormous holes in security coverage. Especially in major centres: there were fewer spies in Washington than at any time since the British occupation of Boston; residents of Moscow enjoyed a noticeable depletion of traffic on the streets; in Beijing, the vast block that was the Ministry of State Security building echoed emptily for the first time since it was built.

Every minor port known to be in use by agencies was watched, often by several agencies simultaneously. More secret identities were blown than had ever been before, changing subsequent efforts at espionage completely.

Carrying a fake MEW, Blond and Wuttunee flew into Manchester airport as mother and child. They were watched by operatives of four separate agencies.

Jenny wheeled a glowering |Xi!xu‡qe out of Heathrow in a wheelchair.

So incredibly obvious was their actual port of entry that there was only one NSA operative to watch them. They were met in the Terminal 2 carpark, ushered into an Uber and driven to St Ermin's Hotel.

Within the day, the plans had been laid for the installation of the MagDhuibhfinn Earth Worm.

A long, grey Mercedes with blacked out windows fetched the two at the back of the St Ermin and they were driven towards the Embankment. On the way, they were handed thick black blindfolds and told to put them on. No amount of objecting made the slightest impression on the two Giant minders who sat opposite them in the limousine.

Eventually, the car slowed and they felt it turn and nose downwards.

When the car stopped and they were led out, |Xi!xu‡qe refused to move. He drew the kierrie from its resting place at his back: "Where are we? If you don't give me some information I can work with, I will go no further and your masters will never learn the whereabouts of the device."

He could not see the look of alarm on the faces of the minders. It was a bluff: he guessed that he was expected to have the USB key on him. But not that there had been official discussion about taking it from him by force in the vehicle.

"The garage of SIS," said the one, "We are ordered to maintain security until you are in the Director's office. Now, please, Sir, we must go. We know nothing more and Lady Ward-Back is expecting you." He hesitated, clearly embarrassed, "and not at midnight."

Recognising the phrase, and thus reassured, ǀXi!xuǂqe relaxed his grip on his kierrie slightly. It seemed safer to go along with them. But he kept a careful note of each turn they made, every lift, counting every floor by the coming and going of noise and voices outside on the landings. No PPSS operative – perhaps no Pygmy – had ever been inside the SIS HQ. From the outside the great sandstone and bottle-green edifice seemed lifeless. It had supposedly been abandoned in the first decade of the century but the PPSS had long suspected that that was not the whole truth. The information he was gathering about how many floors were operational and the density of personnel on each could be invaluable.

Somewhere on the way, ǀXi!xuǂqe touched Jenny's elbow and she grasped his hand. She did not seem nervous, though. Her palms were dry, her grip untrembling. Brave girl! he thought. Blindfolded in a lift, on foreign soil, with Giants she had no reason to trust, she seemed steady. Even after the traumatic events she had seen. He thought back to the Marriott Fairfield Inn in Toronto. Her courage in helping him – the mission would have ended there without her. And then the thugs in Toronto. And in Billings. And then the battle when only the intervention of the Jogahoh had saved them. Not to mention being kidnapped and transported to Berne. Or the Trugberg affair. She constantly surprised him with her courage.

Truly, she was a woman worthy of a !Kung warrior. Suddenly he realised that *his* palm was sweaty and released her hand.

Finally, they were marched along a carpeted corridor high in the building, a door was opened and they were seated side by side on chairs. |Xi!xu‡qe sensed the presence of others in the room. Many others. The minders left and the doors closed. He tensed as he felt someone loosen the blindfold.

He was seated in front of a large desk. Behind it sat a woman with a face like the ice cliff they'd descended in the Alps. Her eyes were set deep, below a smooth but formidable forehead that was unlike the wrinkled face below it in which was set a wide mouth with a cruelly thin upper lip but surprisingly full lower one. The mouth was half smiling but that did little to lessen the startling impact of a cloud of grey – no, silver – hair swirling around the long face in sweeping prominences, interlaced protrusions and arches …the image of a sterling silver tea set popped into |Xi!xu‡qe's mind. Or the frieze on a Greek temple. He was mesmerised despite himself.

"Good morning, |Xi!xu‡qe," she said, pronouncing his name fully, "I am Lady Ward-Back. I've followed your progress with interest. You have certainly provided employment for the world's intelligence agencies this last week. I'm sure they're grateful; life is so dull these days."

|Xi!xu‡qe fought off the urge to stand up. "I'm glad to meet you, Lady Ward-Back. I believe I have you to thank for Trugberg." At the same time, he thought 'following your progress'? 'this week'? How could she? Could someone have told her? Was she bluffing?

"Oh, that!" the older woman waved a navy blue-sleeved arm. "Nothing by comparison with what you have done. But let me introduce you."

Only then did ǀXi!xuǂqe tear his eyes from her face.

Kleynmans! He was on his feet, reaching behind his head for his kierrie, "You!..."

"Stop, ǀXi!xuǂqe!" the woman at the desk ordered. "Kleynmans – codename MiniMan – had his mission. You will understand."

ǀXi!xuǂqe took some consolation in the fact that he and Jenny had been right about 'MiniMan' on Wuttunee's phone. But why had the Mannegishi…?

The aristocratic woman was still speaking: "Now, this is F.R.S.T. Freitag, of GASP, code named Golden Eagle, as you know. He provided the blueprints of the Trugberg lab."

"Incomplete!" ǀXi!xuǂqe snarled.

"Best possible," replied Freitag with a slight German accent, "The facility was closed for 'refurbishing'. As you saw, they have changed its function. I was not permitted entrance."

Ward-Back cut in, "You know an Taoiseach MacBhreithiún, of course."

The Clurichaun stepped from the dark corner of the room, where he had been almost invisible. "Kiku, my friend!" he shouted, rushing forward with his arms open, "It's greatly relieved I am to see you again. There were so many times…"

But ǀXi!xuǂqe, wrapped in his embrace, interrupted: "Mac, not you? Surely? You're not working for them?" As he said it and the implications occurred to him, the Sān agent's lined features crumpled into a dark cloud of fury.

219

"No! No! Never for a single moment, Kiku," protested the Pygmy, a look of horror on his face, "The reverse actually....This is so much more complex than you know. We all work together. The enemy are not...well, they're not..." Shaggy locks shaking, as the GCPP First Minister gave up. "Look, Thebault is with us, too! And others..." he looked towards Ward-Back.

"We have a meeting," she said approaching him, "in the boardroom next door. It's about to start. Many people are waiting to meet you. Shall we?" she gestured gracefully towards a plain, double wooden door.

He did not like the way things were going. Too many enemies in one room. And MacBhreithiún – what was he? It was he who had told the PPSS agent that there were 'elements' in the GCPP who were trying to stop his mission. But he had given him the MEW, so...? And where were Blond and Wuttunee?

For the first time, |Xi!xu‡qe looked at Jenny. He meant to apologise for getting her into another mess but she seemed calm. Calculating, he thought. Tsodilo! She is brave, this one. Or else she too...

But he did not have time to finish the thought. To his astonishment, Jenny stood and started towards the door. Freitag was next, with Kleynmans behind, MacBhreithiún followed him and Lady Ward-Back stood beside her desk looking at |Xi!xu‡qe, head tilted, waiting to follow him.

It seemed rude not to follow them.

Unable to see past the Giant who had stalked him since the Botswana border, his body clenched like a fist, aware of the weight, lightness, heft of the kierrie at his back, |Xi!xu‡qe followed.

As they entered the room and Kleynmans moved to the left, |Xi!xu‡qe saw past Jenny and MacBhreithiún.

The room was dimly lit, presumably the better to see the enormous features of the man on the screen. So!

And yet.

In confusion, |Xi!xu‡qe looked around the seats at a huge horseshoe of a table in front of the screen.

"Thebault! Jessica! And Wuttunee!" he all but shouted, "ÓCléirigh! I…I don't understand!"

"|Xi!xu‡qe," came a voice from the screen on the wall. It was Bootha, his greatest adversary. "Ag, welcome, man! This must be difficult for you but there is a reason, an explanation for it all: first, you must understand that your whole operation was a multi-agency collaboration. Its purpose was simple: get the MagDhuibhfinn Earth Worm to an SIS quantum computer such as the one in the building in which you now stand. This is a nexus of the main communications and cyber capability of the Giant intelligence agencies. Cheltenham, too, but you…well….

"Involved in the planning and execution of your mission were both Pygmies and elements of Giant governments and their intelligence agencies. It is an informal alliance – we often go by the melodramatic name of The Shadow Faction." Bootha seemed to shudder with embarrassment. There were titters around the room. "And I am their designated coordinator. The…er…Shadow Faction…have allied to help counter those influences that were deliberately undermining planetary efforts to limit global warming and climate change. We have found ourselves pitted against giants of the fossil fuel, agricultural and manufacturing industries – them and the politicians and civil servants who they recruited.

"You will be aware that all attempts to wring agreement from the agencies with interests in limiting climate change – and who hasn't got an interest? – every conference of those parties, Cop – has been undermined at government executive level. The Shadow Faction – ag, yissus! Can't we think of a better name! – have been working to counteract those who have undermined the Cop agreements. There has been little success. The failure of the Pygmy Peoples' conference was the last straw. It was decided to take more direct action. But how do you get round the combined determination of fossil fuel businesses, the greed of manufacturing cartels and inertia of governments?

"So, it was not until the MagDhuibhfinn Earth Worm was finished that there was a way. It is a program capable of tipping the balance of human influence. The programmer was a true genius by the name of, er –" Bootha looked down at some notes on the desk in front of him, "Ka'akupe…"

"What!" exclaimed |Xi!xuǂqe, "Ka'akupe! that clown Trauco in Chile! Not possible. I don't…." But words deserted the noble !Kung warrior. Suddenly, he began to get an inkling of the distinctly minor role he had played in the operation in which he had believed himself the 'umkhonto', the spearhead. He looked at Jenny, hoping not to see mockery on her face.

"Ja, exactly," Bootha continued, "he caused you some trouble, of which more in a moment. To continue: unfortunately, not all the Shadow Faction people were entirely on board with the functioning and aims of the MagDhuibhfinn Earth Worm. They thought that whoever gained control of it would effectively run the world. Of course, their reasoning rested on a misunderstanding: once deployed on billions of devices, the MagDhuibhfinn Earth Worm cannot be controlled; it can only be stopped. Some Pygmies became, well, effectively traitors."

At the table there was some uncomfortable shifting and looking around.

"A conference was organised to try and get agreement across the Pygmy world but...well, that was sabotaged. And then they began making efforts to capture the USB key with the MagDhuibhfinn Earth Worm on it. Some were being paid by Giant agencies on behalf of governments who also thought they would be able to repurpose the program to allow them to manipulate energy use. Needless to say, the petrochemical and manufacturing industries bankrolled their covert efforts," bitterness crossed Bootha's face.

"Anyway it was clear that we had to put the MEW plan into action," he continued, "Several attempts were made to steal the key. We evaded all of them but another problem confronted us: all the major computing arrays were guarded in depth; thanks to a senior Pygmy officer, our enemies knew we needed one for the MEW. At any point, a betrayal could lead to.... Well, in any case, it was decided that a decoy had to be run. That's where you came in |Xi!xu‡qe. It was clear that most Giant agents in Europe and the Far East would be tracked and might be hard to trust. We considered Lieutenant Commander Blond but, well, she's quite high profile and, er, forgive me Jemima, easy to follow. We needed someone from a 'clean' agency. That left the Americas, your Far East, and Africa. But because the Pygmy communications system had been penetrated by the anti-Cop agencies, we couldn't be sure of the 'Far East' – the Korpokkur, Taotao Mo'na, Menehune, Mannegishi and Memegwaans, the Nimerigar, Pombéro, or Trauco. Not until you restored communications in the Pryor Mountain facility..."

"Erm...," |Xi!xu‡qe's head was spinning, "I'm sorry. I...I...don't know who I'm talking to here but, well, how on earth does a Giant know so much about Pygmy security? I thought Giants were all sworn to keep the First Peoples – the

First Nations and the Forest Tribes and the Nature People – all us 'Little People' as you call us, in darkness, in servitude. That you had taken and meant to hold onto our lands, that you destroyed our cultures and our tribes and had stolen our children's futures, rendered us invisible as the frightening whisps of Giant children's nightmares, to be hunted and destroyed or, better, simply denied. I thought..."

"You are right, Kiku," came MacBhreithiún's voice from elsewhere in the chamber, "that is how Giant governments work: to make us invisible so that they can deny us, even our existence. It was ever thus, since ancient times, and it became accepted as fact. But not all Giants believe the old lies. The efforts of your own people, the First People, and the work of those who fight for justice for all 'others', the 'concealed' people of humankind – Black people, First Nations people, Aboriginals, Māori, Travellers, even Giant women, the differently abled, the LGBTQIA2S+ – have convinced a powerful cabal of Giants that it is time to bring humanity together again..."

"Ja. This is all true," Bootha interrupted, "And the time for hope is here, Eoin, but we must move on now. So, the decision was taken to have you, ǀXi!xuǂqe, protect the key. You would take it away from danger to the vastness of north America, er, the Far East..." Abruptly, he turned to someone off screen, "Van Der Merwe, make a note to recentre the world around the IDL!" Then, apparently unaware of the bemusement this command had caused in the SIS conference room, he continued, "Your mission was supposedly to restore GCPP communications. Then, when we had effective, secure control of this SIS facility, you could return with it." He paused, momentously, "Now we have."

"Not so fast! Stop. Wait! What about the kidnapping? Artyom? Was that Arsenei?" |Xi!xuǂqe interrupted.

"Yes, you were right about that. He engineered the snatching of Jenny. And also the placing of the Goliath tarantula in the Pryor Mountain HQ. Perhaps they thought that harming Jenny might stop you, somehow. We don't know who he was working with yet. Mind you, according to General Danny that room was originally designated for you – until you turned up with a guest. So we're not sure…but we will find out."

"But he can't have been acting on his own! And where is he now? I'd like to get my hands on him…" He stopped, clenching his fists.

This time MacBhreithiún spoke. "Again, you are right. We think he might be in contact with this man: Jeffry Heinzforth." On the screen appeared a square, pink face, loose about the jowls and with an ill-suited, flat-bridged nose and pale blue eyes.

"CIA. Europe Bureau chief," said |Xi!xuǂqe, "Jemma Blond told me about him. Involved with GASP."

MacBhreithiún nodded. "We eventually identified a group within the Grand Council. Mrs Donoghue seems to have been against the MagDhuibhfinn plan from the start. She recruited others on the Council. Arsenei was one. Hugh, Afallon and Locryn. Peyton, too, I'm afraid. They conspired with her but they were not acting alone. They contacted GASP sympathisers in B.O.S.S. through GASP, whose leadership are still very right wing, to evade more 'enlightened' elements of the Western agencies. You see, they knew that some B.O.S.S. elements were pro LP and might get wind of what they were doing. If the Shadow Faction had been aware, we would have fielded and nullified the threat they posed. As it is, it went all the way to the top. Peregrine Falcon, the European Security director for Western Europe, got hold of their communications and took over the operation. It's true, he was acting in the interests of Giant security, but his policies – philosophy, approach, whatever you want to call it – are obsolete now." The Clurichaun sighed and his rosy, lined face was sorrowful, "Well, the Scottish and Cornish Pygmies have been arrested and will be tried. Arsenei disappeared in Europe. Mrs Donoghue was the key traitor. Worst of all, she wasn't just against the MagDhuibhfinn Earth Worm plan, she saw an opportunity advance herself. Of course, she has been stripped of her titles and a Pygmy case is being prepared against her. Treason against the Earth. Even though there is no such Giant law in existence – yet – the penalty will be severe. Falcon will probably face similar charges. He has been replaced. Actually, by the man who orchestrated your mission."

"Is she why he, Kleynmans, was trying to stop me! I thought he was one of yours!" He looked back at the screen and Bootha.

"No. Ja, he is. I sent him after you to make the other Giant agencies think that you were carrying the key."

"But I was!"

"Ag, but they didn't know that. While you were charging around North America, we were running an operation to convince GASP and other B.O.S.S. offices that the MagDhuibhfinn Earth Worm was here, in Europe."

"So you effectively undermined your own operation – and me! As it turns out, by the way – for what? They could have just given up on me – I was in America, after all, and they didn't know where. As far as they were concerned, the FBI and CIA – the two biggest and best funded secret agencies in the world, mind you! – could easily capture one !Kung Pygmy." He stopped. "Hang on!" He turned to MacBhreithiún, "You said the ES Western Europe Director had been replaced by…"

"The man who orchestrated your mission. Yes."

"You mean…"

"Mr Bootha. Yes."

ǀXiǃxuǂqe's jaw tightened.

"Congratulations, Sir," Kleynmans called out.

"Ag, thanks, man…" To his credit, the former Head of the Sub-Sahara (Southern Africa) branch of the Bureau of States' Security blushed and bowed his head modestly.

Lady Ward-Back broke in, sounding impatient, "Absolutely, ǀXiǃxuǂqe. So to keep them…er…focused, we needed someone tracking you. Kleinmans. That way, they would think you must be important enough to pursue. Unfortunately, you were too good: you kept bloody disappearing. Even from us! The episode on the ferry from England to Ireland showed that. We had to find a way of keeping track of you. Quickly. We couldn't just ask: that would have to be done through the Grand Council and we strongly suspected that there were Pygmies in the Council who could really betray you. Eventually, we had a kind of relay. Fortunately, because you stopped trusting one of them – Sparrow."

"So, Kleynmans was guided? Fine. I suspected that by the time we reached Billings and was positive after Trauco," ǀXiǃxuǂqe paused, remembering Piyêsîs and the others, "but *how* did he know? I thought Wuttunee was telling him…was a traitor – sorry, Sequoyah …"

"Yes. Sparrow. A double agent working for us who Magnus trusted. Sorry, Magnus, but you seemed to be on to him and we thought Kiku was, too. Eventually, he couldn't tell us much. Fortunately, we had someone else to take over who could also replace your contact in Toronto."

"Right. Jenny and I worked that out…" Suddenly, ǀXi!xuǂqe stopped and turned, horror etched across his face. Then his mild features collapsed in pain. He stared at Jenny. "In Toronto, she said! Before Sequoyah and Pie! YOU! YOU!"

And he felt like his world had collapsed. His face slowly turning hard, cold, he stared at her, remembering all the late-night chats, the confidences, the memories. He remembered how she had shown up just when he needed her. And how she had insisted on helping him and her courage at the hotel, in the alley. Why would she even *know* a sympathetic Cree travel agent? Why drop her whole life to run away with him – and all the time he had thought…Fool! Fool!

"That's right," Bootha's voice boomed from the screen, "her job was to keep Kleynmans – who really did think he was trying to stop you – one step behind you so you were never there when he reached the place he'd been told. But Magnus is a bloody good agent. Eventually, he realised and contacted the FBI. They had tracked your plane across the Canadian border and were far too close for comfort. With his help they would have got you at Billings. Easily. Her plan with the two airports was brilliant! She threw them off for long enough. Wuttunee did the rest."

"Yes," Sequoyah cut in, "he nearly caught us up at Billings. I had to think fast!"

"And so the Trauco base…?" The Pygmy's head was spinning.

"Ag, ja, that was a real pity. You wouldn't leave without updating that bliksemse computer."

"And Jenny was begging me…but I wouldn't listen. So, it WAS my fault…Piyêsîs, all those Giants, the Trauco, and the Jogahoh, the others…"

"Kiku, don't," came Jenny's voice from beside him. He almost brushed her aside but realized the weight of the guilt she must feel for her loyalty. It takes real courage to stick to a path that you know is right when it leads you to betray the one you serve. And when you know the cost of it. She had stayed with him all the way through, knowing that he would find out that she was betraying him, knowing what his reaction would be, expecting rejection, anger, even retribution. She had stayed at his side: his bodyguard.

He turned to her, "I see you now, Jenny Miler. You are a gentle and true friend, I knew that. And now I see too that you were brave and selfless. And I have not properly valued you." He took her in her arms – she was as tall as he – and she stooped to lay her head on his shoulder. "Yet."

Chapter 25 How to Change the World

|Xi!xu‡qe and Jenny accompanied MacBhreithiún, Lady Ward-Back and ÓCléirigh to the Giant HECTlc suite in the bowels of the SIS building. The glow of LEDs lit their way. Hundreds of screens, attended by scores of technicians and analysts, cast their light on the floor at their feet as they walked. Hundreds of fans whirred in accompaniment to the deep hum emanating from the air-conditioner ducts above their heads. In the centre of the suite stood a square glass tube about 5m on a side, reaching from ceiling to floor. In its centre was a black, hexagonal central column made up of computer screens and peripherals. The glass room had one sliding door with a palm pad beside it. The glass walls were heavy, solid.

"Bulletproof, sealed and climate controlled," murmured the NSA Director, "The only other access is through the two metre thick base and ceiling – titanium reinforced corundum concrete."

The heavy glass door hissed open and they were ushered into the presence of the most powerful computer ever built.

Ward-Back spoke softly: "Clear the room, please." The four analysts signed off their screens and left, nodding to their Director. She was obviously liked and respected. The door hissed shut behind them and the sound of the main suite with all its personnel and electronics ceased. They might have been the only people in the world. "This is probably the most secure room on the planet. When it was installed, they had to blow a hole through the core of the building to install the concrete housing – well, anyway, it was impossible to do it without making a lot of noise and smoke. You probably saw it in that film, 'Skyfall'."

"What?" they all exclaimed together.

"Oh, yes. That was a bit of camouflage. Of course the huge explosion you saw was just added pyrotechnics for the film. What was really happening was a controlled detonation that broke through several reinforced concrete floors into this room. It was great fun and I got to meet Daniel Craig and Dame Judy Dench. Amazing! They even used the building site to film in. Though I think that surfaced in 'Spectre'. Sometimes the best place to hide is out in plain sight." She glanced sideways at |Xi!xu‡qe and Jenny. "Anyway, Mr ÓCléirigh. Your terminal," she finished casually waving at an office chair in front of one of the screens.

It took ÓCléirigh a moment to get over his shock. When he had gathered his equilibrium, ÓCléirigh mumbled, "Erm, Padraig, your Ladyship," and stepped forward.

"Poorig, exactly," Lady Ward-Back repeated as if she was reassuring the Leprechaun of his own name. He winced. "You do know how to install the application, I take it?"

"Oh, it's right certain I am. To tell the truth, I was with Ka'akupe during the design and did some of the modules myself. Not that I'd be wanting to blow my own trumpet, y'know, like, but…"

"Padraig, get on with it, will you already?" came an irritated growl from MacBhreithiún, "He always goes all

Irish when he gets flustered. Perfectly reasonable otherwise, mind you."

Above the head of the two Pygmies, Lady Ward-Back smiled, her eyes twinkling.

"Erm...Kiku? If you would...I mean..."

ǀXi!xuǂqe dug in his worn leather bag and handed the USB key to ÓCléirigh.

The Clerk inserted it into one of the ports in front of him. Instantly, the light in the room switched to a deep red and a deep bell tolled. The screen flashed 'Intrusion – System Lock: 30 seconds' and the timer started to count down.

"Oh. That's me," said the Director. She leaned over the head of ÓCléirigh, who looked embarrassed to be so close to the woman, and typed in a string of characters, then held her forefinger to a small oval pad. The alarms stopped but the countdown continued. As it reached '10', an arm swung out of the column at head height – Giant head height – and a camera unfolded from it. Lady Ward-Back looked directly into the camera.

Suddenly, the countdown stopped, the clock disappeared and the two choices appeared.

1. LPSMTP/LPIP
9. MDEW

"1," said ÓCléirigh pressing the key. He sat back but, before his back – or head, since the chair was set for the Giant operator – hit the backrest, the screen was filled with screeds of symbols that scrolled past almost too fast to see.

"That doesn't look like any coding language I've ever seen," exclaimed Lady Ward-Back.

"Well, to tell you the truth, it's a bit of a thing that Ka'akupe and me came up with. Based on the Khuzdul[i] language, that was the one –"

"Padraig," growled MacBhreithiún.

"Sorry, I'm sure," said the Leprechaun, "Sorry. But begorrah I've never seen a computer like this. This code has the decoding key built into subroutines embedded in the main code and the machine has to decode the code into ordinary code before it can recode the instructions to –"

MacBhreithiún was tearing at his hair and hopping from foot to foot. Jenny was giggling and ǀXi!xuǂqe was looking in frank amusement at the bobbing head of the Taoiseach. Coolly, and with infinite grace – and a mischievous grin on her face – the Director said, "It is a quantum array that uses edge computing to help with time-sensitive data. It helps with machines that have limited connectivity. I'm told it has trawled the whole world of data. Apparently that's measured in queccabytes, now, though –"

"A queccabyte is 10^{30} bytes," interrupted ÓCléirigh, "Sorry, ma'am. But that's impossible! A gigabyte is 10^9 bytes! It's estimated there are over 11 queccabytes of information! That's incredible. Oh, if Ka'akupe and me had had a computer like this..." Apparently, the thought overwhelmed him: ÓCléirigh's eyes misted over as he embarked on a dream of what he could do.

"I'm sure the two of you will be invited back, if this works," announced Ward-Back, "I'm sure there's a lot you can do that will help re-balance the new world..."

"New world?" MacBhreithiún and ǀXi!xuǂqe repeated together.

---

[i] The secret Dwarf language invented by J. R. Tolkien.

"I should think so," continued the Giant Director, "If this works – *if this works* – the United Nations will almost certainly credit the true inventors of the MagDhuibhfinn Earth Worm. That means the Pygmy peoples may finally be recognised. I know that at least half the world's governments, Giant governments, have every intention of appointing Pygmies – especially the most nature-enabled among you – to advise on rewilding, farming and fishing control, and all the other Giant mistakes that have got us into this mess. If the MagDhuibhfinn Earth Worm works, the world will be on the way to healing itself, anyway..."

"Is there a way, Lady Ward-Back, that we can read the energy use in Britain now?" ÓCléirigh was looking mischievous.

"Yes, of course, we've been monitoring it for decades. You can access the data for London through the GLA Carbon Offset Directorate. It's quite accurate now; it was upgraded to include all incoming energy sources in –"

While she talked, ÓCléirigh was busy negotiating City Hall's labyrinthine electronic web. Eventually, he said, "There you are. This graph shows the total energy usage for the last week in real time. Look here," he pointed at the line. "See? It's gone down a bit. I'll zoom in to the last 24 hours."

The dip at the end of the graph was even more pronounced.

"Here. For the last hour."

It was immediately obvious that the line was dipping as they watched it.

"The same will be happening in all British cities. And it's probably started across the channel. In about two weeks – probably less, given the edge system – it will be worldwide.

Jenny, |Xi!xuǂqe, MacBhreithiún, ÓCléirigh and, towering over them, Lady Ward-Back, watched spellbound as the thin green line gradually wormed its way down.

They didn't even notice the slightly puzzled looks of the technicians outside the cubicle, long accustomed to an ambient temperature of 20°C, as their world became a little cooler – even as the thermometers on the wall stayed steady. They hadn't even noticed the minuscule dimming of the ambient lighting.

Chapter 26 The Greatest Show on Earth

They were back in the County Wicklow meeting room of the Grand Council. ǀXi!xuǂqe looked up with fondness at the ancient and matted tree roots that formed the ceiling, blackened with the smoke of past fires – now replaced with infra-red heating panels and LED lighting. All new. The funding from the European Council and the UN had changed a few things in the lives of the Pygmy peoples of the world. "It will just increase the energy use of Pygmies," grumbled MacBhreithiún to ÓCléirigh, "We'll be as bad as the Giants!"

"You can't use that word anymore," scolded ÓCléirigh, "and besides, the energy savings produced by the MagDhuibhfinn Earth Worm were so much greater than expected that we are still easily within the targets identified at the Paris Climate Agreement. The latest projections are for a .2° increase. And the sea ice is reforming in the Antarctic. The Thwaites glacier – or what's left of it – seems to be stabilising. All in two months, Eoin! Two months! It's a miracle, so it is! And we've added solar panels, into the bargain!"

MacBhreithiún rolled his eyes. "Solar panels!" he snorted, "This is Ireland, Paddy. If you can't see the hills, it's raining. If you can, it's going to rain."

An Taoiseach had taken to calling his clerk 'Paddy' ever since he had become *Sir* Padraig in recognition of his contribution to the MEW. The response of ÓCléirigh had been to become more irrepressibly Irish than before. Mind you, who could blame him? thought *Lord* Eoin MacBhreithiún, not a little smugly, considering his own elevation to the peerage: Earl Eoin MacBhreithiún, Duke of Dubh Linn. But, he thought, fine sounding as it was, the comparison to Máel Sechnaill mac Domnaill[9] referred to in the entitlement ceremony had really stirred his blood. High King of Ireland! A fine ring, that had! Catching himself, he mentally slapped his wrist: all this mediaeval nonsense! And look how it turns your head! Roisin, plump, pink-cheeked Roisin, who had made his bread since their marriage, was forever referring to herself: Duchess this, duchess that! He smiled. Sméagol, plain and pure.

He looked around the chamber. Tonight, this momentous night, they would be joined by a Giant for the first time ever: Jemima Blond had been invited as an honorary guest and observer.

"Where is Kiku? I thought…."

"It's tawny now. He can't be far."

MacBhreithiún was used to ÓCléirigh's peculiar confusion of his senses and he, himself, could taste the golden iridescence that he associated with |Xi!xuǂqe.

The guests of honour entered the hall, |Xi!xuǂqe with Jenny Miler and Jemima Blond flanked by Sequoyah Wuttunee. The excited assembly stood.

With some satisfaction and a little guilt |Xi!xuǂqe noted the gaps where the Bwca, Brunaidh and Bucca customarily sat: Peyton, Afallon, Hugh and Locryn were 'away'. Mrs Donoghue was also missing, in jail under a heavy sentence.

On a giant screen at the back of the Chamber, the image of a much bigger, more modern council chamber swam into view.

"I've been there!" shouted MacBhreithiún, "That's Room XX, the Human Rights and Alliance of Civilisations Chamber!"

"Twenty. Room twenty, I think you'll find that is," muttered Sir Padraig.

"You've been to Geneva?" the Duchess Roisin, Countess of Dublin, whispered suspiciously.

"What's that thing on the ceiling? Look at the ceiling!"

"My God!"

"Beautiful!"

"Shut up, everyone!"

The cameras swung round the Chamber, taking in representatives from every nation and people on Earth. For the first time, the world saw twenty-four places arranged within the sweeping inner arcs of seats. And at them, the representatives of the Pygmy peoples of the world sat. A huge cheer went up from the Grand Council and Council members started pointing and calling out the names of the representatives of their peoples:

"Look: Amista!" shouted, Inina the member for the Taotao Mo'na. Her animosity forgotten, she was pointing excitedly at a face on the screen, "She's my cousin!".

"And Monashinouku! She's from the Rebun in the Floating Islands where my mum lives!"

"Stop! Everyone. A Pygmy is speaking!"

And indeed, the camera had come to a stop on a short person standing on a step behind the lectern, speaking up into the microphone.

"Who is that? I surely do not recognise her," said MacBhreithiún, who had chaired the hastily convened selection committee the week before.

"That's no Pygmy," laughed Roisin, embarrassing her husband yet again, "That's Greta Thunberg! She's grown!"

With difficulty, ÓCléirigh and |Xi!xu‡qe shushed the excited Pygmies.

"…and so it is the for the **first time** that we can see a United Nations where **all** the people of the world are **represented**…"

"She is Swedish but her English is excellent," replied ÓCléirigh, awed.

"She sounds like an American!" whispered Roisin.

"…and the **blah! blah!** of previous Cops can maybe be **consigned to history**. Even **without** a formal agreement of any kind, or the action of the **'old'** world governments, the Pygmy peoples have brought about an **enormous** change in the rate of planet warming and climate change. And we – **Giants**! Yes! Giants who **persecuted** them **mercilessly** – are **shamed** by their **wisdom and commitment** to **our** planet.

"**Think**! Just think for a moment: **without** them, we would have had to face the likelihood that there would have been **no** planet to bequeath our children – **you** had **stolen** it from your **own** children! What chance would **ours** have had? **My** generation, which I have often said is more mature than you **'world leaders'**, would have been left with the **impossible** task of sucking hundreds of billions of tons of **your** CO_2 out of the air. **You** were doing **nothing**. We had **no** hope. **Until** the arrival of the Pygmy peoples and their nature wisdom. **Now**, it looks as though there may be a **chance**, thanks to them…"

"She hasn't even referred to the Pygmy delegates yet! Typical Giant politics…" hissed the Greek delegate's husband.

"Oh, shut up, Socrates," she hissed back. "I knew I shouldn't have brought you!"

"Please be quiet, both of you, this is important," said lXi!xuɬqe.

"…so, if our available CO_2 budget is greater now than it was at Cop30, it is thanks to **them**. They have achieved in a month what you – **adults!** …"

"Hang on! We're adults, too!" shouted someone, but he was quickly hushed.

"…even **accepted**, let alone addressed, for the **past 45 years**. Ever since the science first **conclusively** confirmed that the health of planet was deteriorating at a **lethally** dangerous rate! Perhaps it is time to admit it: **big** people have been a **liability** for much of history and it is time for us, the **Little People**, to take the lead!"

The applause in the Geneva hall was drowned out by the raucous delight of the chamber of the Grand Council of Pygmy Peoples. When order of some sort was finally re-established, the proceedings had moved onto a vote for the formal adoption of permanent representation of the Pygmy Peoples' on the Security Council. The Secretary General, Arora Akanksha – the youngest in history – formally proposed the vote, recommending the adoption of the motion.

And the voting began.

"Afghanistan."

"In favour."

"Albania."

"In favour."

With every 'in favour' the Grand Council erupted excitedly. But only until the next announcement. And it was not until Angola that the mood was dampened.

'Abstain." Came the answer. And there was a groan as the Pygmies realised that their acceptance might not be universal.

Belarus was the first sign of opposition.

By the time the voting reached Kirabati, who voted in favour to no one's surprise, the fervour had been dampened somewhat. All of the smaller, seaboard nations were in favour. As were those with very long coastlines. Most of those who had suppressed Pygmies were against, fearing reprisals, no doubt: Angola, Burundi, the DRC, Gabon being among the traditional first homes of the Pygmy people voted against. Eswatini came as a shock and raised doubts about Lesotho, Moçambique, South Africa, Zambia and Zimbabwe. Malawi and South Africa voted in favour, in the event, but Lesotho voted against.

Still the voice of the secretary droned through the rollcall of nations. Still the results came in.

By the time there were thirteen countries left to vote, the vote was poised so that only six votes were needed for victory. Already, MacBhreithiún had broken out a bottle of poitín.

"Uganda."

"Oppose."

Not unexpected but a groan, nevertheless.

"Ukraine."

"In favour."

No surprise but a heartfelt cheer. Pygmies still felt a fraternal tie to the brave nation.

"United Kingdom of Great Britain."

"In favour."

A cheer.

"United Republic of Tanzania"

"Abstain."

"What! Why?"

"United States of America."

An enormous cheer!

"In favour."

"Uruguay."

"Abstain."

"Huh! Oil!"

"Uzbekistan."

"In favour."

A cheer. There had been some concerns about Silk Route countries.

"Vanuatu."

"In favour."

Another small island nation. Of course.

"Bolivarian Republic of Venezuela."

An oil economy. No chance.

"Opposed."

"Vietnam."

"In favour."

"Yemen."

"Opposed."

Some of the Pygmies sat up. What was that? What was the count now.

"We need one more!"

"How many countries left?"

"Two."

Shocked silence followed.

"Zambia."

"Opposed."

The Great Chamber of the Grand Council of Pygmy Peoples groaned in unison.

"And finally, Zimbabwe."

"That's it. We've lost!" ÓCléirigh had tears in his eyes. MacBhreithiún, the unopened bottle in his hand, was grim faced.

"In favour."

There was a moment's stunned silence in the Great Chamber.

Then the Grand Council of Pygmy Peoples exploded.

In both chambers, one thousand, one hundred and eight-four kilometres apart, Pygmies were erupting in joyous celebration. By the time the Secretary General stood to formalise the vote, |Xi!xu‡qe had to shout at the top of his voice to keep the Grand Council in order enough to hear.

"I can declare that Resolution 2611 of this united Assembly of the Nations is adopted."

But ÓCléirigh had abandoned his glass and was drinking from MacBhreithiún's bottle. Roisin was hugging Eoin MacBhreithiún in a way not fully befitting a countess in public. Sequoyah was dancing with Jemima Blond. No one noticed the considerable height difference at all and both, heads thrown back, were cheering and laughing fit to burst. Indeed, Elves and Leprechauns, Brownies, Gnomes, Pyxies, much maligned Goblins and Trolls were dancing deliriously together. And the joy of the Pygmies was punctuated by the popping of champagne corks from bottles that looked like, but were not, magnums.

Somehow, it seemed as though a whole new world had suddenly materialised.

In the ornate Room XX, the UN Secretary General was being interviewed. She shivered and put on her jumper, apologising to the reporter that it was a little colder than usual.

|Xi!xuǂqe turned to Jenny and smiled.

"That'll be our contribution," he commented drily. "It seems as though not even the Secretary General has been told. Someone should tell the world leaders at least. Don't you think?"

"I suppose people are still afraid of the backlash if the Giants realise that they are being manipulated by Pygmy technology. It wasn't exactly a runaway vote of acceptance, was it?"

"True. When do you think they will be mature enough to know the truth?"

"Perhaps when they can spell 'MagDhuibhfinn Earth Worm'," Jenny laughed.

"That long?" he cocked his head ironically, his eyes disappearing into the deep well of wrinkles.

Chapter 27 Restitution...

The aftermath of the vote was interesting.

All the permanent members of the Security Council had supported the Resolution.

However, there were some curious closures of facilities that few had even known existed as soon as governments realised that these were not as covert as they believed, being in the middle of what turned out to be Pygmy lands. Many Russian closures were situated in places that were their traditional preserves of the Domovoj; they did not seem surprised. Near Guanjia, in east-central China, a vast network of tunnels was abruptly evacuated. Several thousand personnel were quietly moved from sites in the US. Britain abandoned SAS training grounds in the Highlands. Deep in the world's rainforests, complexes were suddenly abandoned to nature – or quietly annexed and repurposed by the Pygmies and First Nations peoples the land had been stolen from. Against a background of Pygmy protests leading to embarrassing revelations, mining and logging machinery was mothballed or abandoned to rust. Australia gained a new wetland sanctuary after the on-off-on-again Central Queensland Coal Project was definitively declared off again. In New Zealand, Stockton became an international water sports venue called the Happy Valley Olympic Centre when the mine was flooded.

There were some conflicts. The Japanese, Micronesian and southern European Pygmies had to embarrass their governments in various ways until their Giant populations came to realise the extent of their Pygmy populations. The 'old world' governments, especially, tried to backtrack on their promises in terms of Resolution 2611.

There were demonstrations on the streets of most cities.

In London, a huge protest was mounted in Parliament Square because the government, citing 'lack of geographical definition' (whatever that meant) tried to block the creation of extra seats for Pygmy constituencies in the Commons. "I can absolutely assure you," the British Prime Minister announced, her voice oozing with commitment, "that my government is fully committed to righting the historic wrongs done to the Pygmy peoples. We are actively looking at setting up a commission to determine how best to advance the status of our Pygmy population in the entirety of Great Britain. A number of initiatives are already in the planning stages. Within a matter of a few years, Little People will take their place among us as full citizens, represented in this mother of parliaments. That is the right thing to do! And this Government will get it done!" The shadowy Pygmy Research Group, heir to the defunct ERG, fought tooth and nail to stop a suffrage bill based on proportional representation of population groups rather than areas.

When it became clear that 'looking at' meant 'thinking about' a commission merely to *talk about* inclusion, an estimated two and three-quarter million people around Great Britain took to the streets. Giants and Pygmies waved placards, shouted slogans and flew a huge balloon of the Interior Minister in the guise of a unicorn "because his promises were about as real".

Placards were good-humoured:

slightly threatening:

challenging:

Troll
your MP!

abstruse:

> **Goblins demand rights!**
>
> **Governments are**
>
> **Goebbels**

and strident:

> # Piggies out!
>
> # Pygmies in!

The PRG failed and were disgraced and dissolved.

Worldwide, no fewer than 63,317 suits were filed against Governments for their crimes against Pygmies.

However, it was when the children of the world led by Greta Thunberg – now old enough to be their mother – refused en masse to go to school, wear jumpers or eat their dinner, that the slothful Giant governments finally caved in.

Alongside these, and other, often secret events, whole swathes of various countries were turned over to traditional control. Often, these regions cut across national borders.

Councils of First Nations, Māori and the aboriginal peoples of several countries – cautiously, at first: there had been centuries of disinformation about their magical properties and imagined malice – welcomed Pygmies onto their governing bodies.

The Trauco had a difficult time convincing the Chileans and Argentinians that their women would be safe.

In the United States, millions of red baseball caps were brought out of storage: on them was the legend 'MAGA' – which some factions claimed stood for 'Make America Giant Again' and always had. "Always knowed there was a conspiracy!" screamed the internet.

In Ireland, Giants were thrilled and excited to discover that they had always been right. However, Leprechauns and Clurichauns spent hours trying to explain the difference between them, and convincing Giants that there was no pot of gold.

Retail businesses were thrilled at gaining a huge new, never-before-contemplated customer base. Worldwide, outdoor adventure holiday companies made a killing selling 'Pygmy familiarization experiences'.

Giant manufacturers, on the other hand, were of much greater concern. (Although the terms 'Giant' and 'Little People' had been increasingly deemed politically unacceptable, there seemed to be no alternative to 'Giant'.) Companies were not geared up for sudden changes to their 'mission statements' that excluded the carbon-producing activities from which they had made their money. It was hardly a surprise. Clothing manufacturers had a particularly torrid time of it, what with bans on denim manufacturer, radically new sizes and the swiftly changing climate demands.

Sometime later, MacBhreithiún was talking to Jenny Miler and ǀXi!xuǂqe.

"Well, the Giants will be able to stop using so much energy but what about the big energy companies? Texaco and Shell and Gulf, for example. And what about all the countries that only exist on oil revenues? OPEC as a whole.

And Norway? And the Russians have only had Nordstream 2 online for 8 years after that stupid Ukraine business; they're not going to stop it. Especially after they fixed that hole they blew in it; talk about cutting off your nose to spite your face! None of those countries are going to sit back and watch their precious reserves become meaningless."

|Xi!xuǂqe winked at Jenny: "That's Phase Two."

* * * * *

Then suddenly, |Xi!xuǂqe disappeared.

One morning, Jenny waited at the breakfast table of MacBhreithiún's house, where she was lodging. The Clurichauns had turned out to be conservative about certain things and insisted that Jenny sleep at an Taoiseach's house. Consequently, every morning |Xi!xuǂqe had to come from the Council complex to have breakfast with her.

That morning, Roisin put a plate of eggs and bacon with fresh woodland mushrooms in front of her. Jenny was expecting the Sān to join her, as usual. She started eating but stopped after five minutes. Turning to Roisin, she asked, "I wonder where Kiku is."

"Only pray it's not as it is with that lazy oaf, Eoin, of mine!" she replied, impatiently, "Still in bed and it's gone half of six. Sure, he's getting' worse, and everything. But I'm sure Kiku's a different kettle of fish," her voice became reassuring, "It's a strong fear óg[i] he is, by my soul!"

"It's very unlike him, though," Jenny said, realising that she was worried, "I think I'll go and look in his room."

"Though ye'll be finishing yer mushrooms first, will yer not...?"

---

[i] young man

But Jenny was gone. Roisin looked after her but the look on her face was not angry or disapproving. Instead, her features were smoothed and softened by the memory of her first knowing Eoin. Lazy oaf that he is, she thought, fondly.

The path to the Council meeting house through the fields and down the hill seemed to pass quickly. Indeed, Jenny was almost running. She slithered down the last hill, stopping at the newly installed gate that led onto the road. She didn't notice the profusion of blood-red fuchsias, in late bloom now. Looking the wrong way, she saw that here were no cars coming and she hurried on.

"Is Kiku here? Only he's missed his breakfast…"

"Well, I must say, we were just wondering the same and thinking he must be with you until Caoimhe came to tell us his bed was not slept in."

It took Jenny a moment to work out that 'until' meant 'when'.

"Cweevah? Where is he?"

"Sure Caoimhe is a girl, so she is, though sometimes…"

"Where is she, then?" Sometimes Jenny wondered how the Leprechauns ever managed to get anything finished, they were so easily distracted.

"Well, here she is now! Caoimhe, lass, put down yer axe and come here. Jenny Miler wants to ask you a question, so she does."

The plump Leprechaun blushed and curtsied before Jenny.

"Oh, you don't have to…. Never mind. Do you have any idea when Kiku left. Or where he went?"

Nothing useful, however, could be gleaned from her or any of the staff of the teach cruinnithe.

She went to the guards at the main gate.

Unsurprisingly, they had not seen him leave: after all, there was no fence around the 'compound'. The gates simply spanned the track. The loss of Pygmies' anonymity had resulted in a new need for security. It was one of the aspects of Giant recognition that did not fill the Leprechauns and Clurichauns with delight. So they were in no hurry to build a fence.

* * * * *

IXi!xuǂqe looked towards the new-risen sun, back down the road he'd come. After four hours, he had still not forgiven himself for leaving Jenny and the Pygmies without any indication of his intentions. However, it was certain that they would have tried to stop him had he told them. And they would have succeeded.

He did not want to do what he knew he had to.

He had made his way down the hill towards the stream, thinking to reach the coast somewhere near Dun Laoghaire, where he had landed...when?...a long time ago.

However, striking a farm road, he had seen a wagon of hay coming his way. Delighted to see what he took to be a Leprechaun in his way, the driver had creaked to a halt and jumped down, marched over and rung IXi!xuǂqe's hand.

"Well sure oi didn't t'ink oi'd be meetin' oop wit de loiks o you on such a foin morning with the sun just peeping tru da clouds and all and look at you, all little and...and...a Leprechaun! By God, me mam would tell me of your loiks but we never listened, you know, like? Just laffed! Screw loose, we were tinkin' but, well, look at you loik, standing there. And how are you this green morning, would ye say? Sure it's a beautiful day, is it not?"

"Sure...erm...yes, it is a lovely day. From what I've seen they're all lovely in Ireland...." |Xi!xu‡qe was about to go on but the man was irrepressible.

"Sure they are. But you speak loik ye're not from Ireland herself. Is that so?"

"No. I'm from..." thinking better of saying 'Botswana', the Sān opted for something altogether less demanding, "...Africa. I am a Sān Bushman," Something must strike home, he thought, and you never know.

"Sure! I never would have believed it! Here in me own backyard, so to speak, a Bushman! Would ye be hailin' from the Kalahari, then? And was yer family moved on by the Government there? It was a truly terrible ting they did to you, so it was! Loik de Brits.... But ye'll be getting' yer homelands back again, no doubt, now that the Little People – oh! Sorry, sir, the Pygmies. Yer know we've been so long accustomed to myths of 'De Little People' that changin' comes hard so it does, even dough such names were used as ways to cruelly sideline and demean your folk over the centuries. Anyway, I was saying about that brave fellow, the Sān like yerself, what the newspapers is full of telling the courage of him in travellin' all over the world to fox the wicked, the t'ievin', the ...."

Seeing that the man had lost his stream of thought in his indignation, |Xi!xu‡qe broke in, "That's very kind of you, sir. My name is Kiku and I need to get to a ferry. I have, er, business to attend to on the mainland. In Europe. I mean." Hoping he had not insulted Ireland, he was about to go on....

"Kiku! Sure it's not you yourself, is it, God save me? In the flesh! Oh the bravery of you! It will never be forgotten!"

Although he was a little flustered by this outburst, |Xi!xu‡qe gathered his thoughts. "I wonder whether you could show me the way to Dun Laoghaire…"

"Sure Oi can, and no trouble at all. If you go along on dis road ye'll come to a junction with a road called de Gap Road on account of it goes t'rough a gap, don't ye know. Now if ye keep going along dere till de T junction, ye can go left or right. Now, if ye take de left turn ye'll come to Ballysmuttan Upper, a beautiful little town, though it's not really, ye know," he winked conspiratorially, "but it is true that if you take a sharp left and travel up de track ye'll come to Seefin Passage Tomb, a most fascinating burial place and well wort' visitin'. However, if yer get there, ye've gone de wrong way. Ye should have taken de roight turn at de T junction…" The man stopped and seemed to think for a while. "Look, I'll tell ye what. To do ye a favour, seein' as it's yer brave self and sure it's the least oi could do, now, I'm on me way to De Lamb, for de market, yer see, dat's on the Blessington Road and dere's a bus comes down dat road, you know, and it'll take you to straight on up to Dublin, where you can get a ferry, no trouble. And it'll be a better way to go since getting to Dun Laoghaire is a fearful journey unless you start from Dun Laoghaire itself." And with this the wagon driver collapsed in laughter and made to mount the wagon. Understanding little more than that he was expected to get on, too, the secret agent – no longer secret – clambered up the wheel and, seeing no seat for a passenger, shuffled over the pile of hay and sat facing backward. The driver clucked his horse on and they started moving.

Beneath the great, blue Irish sky and the emerald fields, in the golden scent of the hay |Xi!xu‡qe felt the sweet taste of air that was finally free for his people. But he could not imagine a world in which he returned to his home and family while the cabal of Pygmy traitors, and the vicious Arsenei, were free. There must be some price for them to pay for Piyêsîs, for Torbjorn, for the Jogahoh warriors, for the forgotten and lost Pygmies of the ages. And the GCPP seemed to have been distracted from the sabotage that had disrupted Pygmy communications in the first place. Why should the saboteurs not try again? He could not find peace in such a world. Vengeance was not in his nature but, somehow, he felt the call of his ancestors from distant Tsodilo Hills, of Pisamboro, and the great spirit, Kaggen. There would be no peace, no safety for the world while the Zlydzen assassin and the other traitors were free to do the work of those who would destroy the Earth itself.

No. That wasn't it.

His motives were not grand. They were altogether shabbier, meaner: he wanted Arsenei to feel the fear of Jenny Miler, drugged, kidnapped and alone. He wanted him to suffer the fate of poor, betrayed Artyom.

That was all.

At the ferry terminal, there were no questions although there was still some curiosity. Giants were not yet used to seeing Pygmies. Children, especially, struggled to contain their excitement. And ǀXi!xuǂqe, bronze of face, wiry and armed with his knobkierrie, was no ordinary Pygmy. Though he could travel freely now, there were still some who found that accepting a whole species of humans was a challenge their imaginations were not quite up to. ǀXi!xuǂqe used his kierrie as a kind of walking-stick or staff in such situations. It reassured some people. And discouraged others.

Crossing to Great Britain posed no problems. Within days of the vote, the post-Brexit Northern Ireland protocol had finally resulted in the acceptance of the inevitability of the unification of Ireland. Brexit itself had been revoked after a none-too-valiant effort at 'getting it done' and the United Kingdom had re-joined the European Union, which had accepted that, in the new world order, the idea of greater federalisation was a nonsense: Pygmies who had innumerable ways of travelling across land masses, simply refused to accept any of the 'Giant' borders as a cost of 'belonging'. It was rapidly becoming clear that there was precisely nothing Giant governments could do about it: in fact, the world was federated and there was nothing they could do about that, either.

He changed his name, becoming a skiing holidaymaker on his way to the Alps. He concealed his knobkierrie in an Evoc Ski Cover he bought in Dublin. From Holyhead, he travelled to London. And started his hunt.

His first port of call was St Ermin's hotel. They remembered him there but it couldn't be helped; it was the only place he wouldn't arouse undue curiosity. Then he contacted Jemima Blond.

Chapter 28 ...and Retribution

"Kiku! What are you doing in London?"

"Some unfinished business, Jemma. Can we meet somewhere?"

Eventually, she came to St Ermin's. He would rather not have told her he was travelling under an assumed name but he needed a passport, or identity document at least. Though few bothered in the EU anymore, his appearance might raise questions. And the Swiss would probably demand something.

"I can get ID for you. Passport offices all over the world are swamped and have taken to issuing quite simple documents. It'll take a day. But what is this unfinished business?"

He told her about the original plot to disrupt Pygmy communications, "That's what I was originally told I was coming to Europe to fix: the communications break down. And there was one. The MagDhuibhfinn Earth Worm was the real mission, obviously, and was substituted for the original mission, at least as I understood it. It took over everything and, well, events since then have distracted the GCPP from the traitors. But they won't just go away. Relations are still delicate, er febrile, enough between Giants – beg your pardon – and Pygmies that, if someone wanted to, they could set everything back. Imagine a bomb exploding in a crowded Giant place and Pygmies being 'identified' as having planted it..."

"My God, yes," replied Blond, "it could become the whole West versus Jihadists thing again. *That* was constantly stoked by false flag ops – Western agencies planting bombs and blaming Muslim Jihadis – which kept the feud running even when Muslim leaders were desperate for conciliation and Western governments were trying to meet them halfway. A lot of that was the work of the CIA, by the way. We were sometimes used, too," Blond looked down guiltily, "Our leaders don't come out of it well. The UK, Britain, then, sold all those arms to both sides..."

"Yes. I have to do something about it. We must get them out in the open. Warn our governments." It was a misdirection. ǀXi!xuǂqe said nothing about revenge. Better not to muddy the water. For the same reason, he didn't tell her when he visited an illegal arms dealer in a posh house on Richmond Hill.

So, armed with an identity document in the name of Gerhardus van Biljon and a Sig P365 SAS, ǀXi!xuǂqe crossed the channel.

As he had suspected, the Border Force officer at Harwich took one look at him and demanded his passport. Some things never change. But, stumped by the soft uvular 'g' of 'Gerhardus' and the unfamiliar surname, smiled and hastened him board: "Have a good trip, Mr Fumblejohn," he said, smirking. ǀXi!xuǂqe entered Europe unchallenged, comforted to know that his name would fit in perfectly at The Hague, where he disembarked. Many other Europeans would struggle to get their tongues around it. That would help distract them from the bulge at the top of the Evoc Ski Cover.

It was, of course, impossible to hire a car for someone of his stature – all the very few suitably adapted cars were booked up for months as Pygmies caught up with thousands of years of missed tourism, but the railways were punctual, comfortable and plentiful, if not as discreet. |Xi!xuǂqe was soon on his way to Zürich, where Jemima Bond's contact in the French Sureté had last placed Arsenei. He arrived at the Hauptbahnhof and caught a taxi to a residential block in Aemtlerstrasse, opposite the Sihlfeld cemetery, where Bond had arranged a 'diplomatic' flat for him.

He spent an hour learning to dismantle and operate the Sig. The tritium bullseye sighting system was useful: such a small weapon could be difficult to aim quickly but the sight helped. He practised drawing it. With no protrusions, it slid in and out of his jeans pocket smoothly. It was heavy with the 15-round magazine fully loaded so he took 5 rounds out.

Then he waited.

In the early evening, a Wavel came through on his phone.

"Secure?" it read.

"VPN," |Xi!xuǂqe replied.

"Crowne Plaza. 21:45. Heinzforth. Await Arsenei. End."

So much for information, thought |Xi!xuǂqe, but it was enough. At quarter to nine, he changed into navy corduroy chinos, a black polo shirt and a dark blue jacket. The Sig slipped neatly into his trousers' front pocket. At the door of the flat, he pulled a thread from his jacket lining, moistened it and stuck it across the door and the door frame. Next he pulled a hair from his head and stuck it to the bottom of the doorknob. Then he went to the café down the road for a meal.

Afterwards he walked down Badenstrasse until he reached the Crowne Plaza hotel. Across the road was a street vender called Créperie Luzius. It had plastic chairs off the street. He bought a crêpe and chose a chair that was partially hidden by two grey wheelie bins and a chain-link fence with some sparse creeper growing up it. His position allowed him a good view of the cars drawing up at the entrance to the hotel.

At exactly 9:45, a silver Mercedes saloon glided silently up. It was unremarkable except for the fact that the passenger who emerged from the back wore dark glasses despite the near darkness.

|Xi!xu‡qe rose and moved closer. He was still covered by the bins and sparse vegetation. An unusual figure he might be, but he was unlikely to be seen in the fast-failing light. Unfortunately, the central reservation between him and the hotel was marked by blocks of grass around the tram tracks. It provided no cover. Between the right carriageway and the hotel slip road there was a hedge. In late autumn, it looked full enough to provide a little cover.

|Xi!xu‡qe weighed his options. Was crossing the dual carriageway worth the risk?

Then the man, reaching the portico, turned round, took off his dark glasses and looked up and down the road.

It was Jeff Heinzforth. Even at a distance, he recognised the square face, loose jowls, thinning blond hair and slight shoulders from the NSA HECTIc meeting in London. And the sunglasses. Almost certainly an American.

But he seemed to be waiting for someone. The information that he had been given in the text suggested that it might be Arsenei. Had the text meant that? Or was he to take Heinzforth – he had told Jenny the man was 'of interest' – and await information about Arsenei? Was he playing someone else's hand again? ǀXi!xuǂqe cursed. He did not want Heinzforth. If he killed the CIA man, would Arsenei disappear? He certainly would if Heinzforth was waiting for him now. ǀXi!xuǂqe wanted Arsenei. Arsenei had betrayed them, betrayed the Pygmy Grand Council. Betrayed Artyom. Kidnapped Jenny. He had given the key to GASP, leading to the Trugberg operation, so the injuries to Torbjorn had really been his fault as well.

It was Arsenei he was looking for, he reminded himself, but Heinzforth and the traitorous PPSS agent were working together. Blond and Ward-Back had linked the two.

ǀXi!xuǂqe was not entirely ready for what happened next. An old, black, petrol driven Zil pulled up and a diminutive figure got out. It wasn't Arsenei, though.

The two set out down Badenerstrasse, the Pygmy almost running beside the Giant. He was talking animatedly.

At least Arsenei was not out of the picture yet. These two clearly had a destination, perhaps a rendezvous with his target. Setting out in pursuit, ǀXi!xuǂqe nearly lost them behind the tram station at a big traffic circle: 'Letzigrund' said the sign and beyond it was a huge sports stadium. In huge silver letters on the side was the legend 'STADION LETZIGRUND'. The lights were off, he saw through the open clerestory beneath the roof. Crossing the roundabout at a trot, ǀXi!xuǂqe was just in time to see the Giant and the Pygmy meet another Pygmy at a gate in the South entrance.

There was plenty of cover afforded by the tram terminus and the trees. Beyond that, he had to trust to the wide bases of the power poles. In his favour, 15 minutes had elapsed and it was nearly dark now; the shadows cast by the streetlights were very deep.

When the three went into the stadium through an open turnstile, ǀXi!xuǂqe followed. He was hidden by the artfully rusted steel wall that held the stadium name. If the ground had not been in darkness, they might have been a father and his two sons going to watch a football match. It was clear that his quarry had no fear of being seen...much less followed.

Inside were raw concrete walls, shoulder height to a Pygmy. He could hear their voices as they went up a ramp of polished grey concrete.

"It could stop UN's plens to endink vossil fuel production for next decade, anyvay," a morose Pygmy voice was saying in a Central European accent.

It was Arsenei!

ǀXi!xuǂqe's mind went back to the Domovoj's droning speech in the Grand Council meeting. It was he who had advocated 'neutralising' the traitor. It was he who the other delegates had eagerly selected to do the deed.

"Don't underestimate them," This was the deeper voice of a Giant: Heinzforth, "Don't underestimate them," This was the deeper voice of a Giant: Heinzforth, "The you pack chemists are close to finishing it." ('you pack'? ǀXi!xuǂqe was puzzled.)

"Look," came another accented Pygmy voice, indignant, "Arsenei tells me nothing. If I riskink my life plantink bomb..."

"Oh, shut up, Uglúk! You have not stopped vinink since Berne: 'But I don't vant to kill her!'" Arsenei imitated a whiny child, "'iss only a child', you sayink. Vot kind of Troll are you? Huh! And look vot heppened."

"He's a Troll?" said Heinzforth, "I always thought..."

"Believink your own propaganda, Giant?" sneered Uglúk. To Arsenei he said, "Is not my fault. Anyvay, who organizink rrelief force at lab!"

So, the troll had been at Trugberg. Where, though? The concealed rooms with the biometric lock? Was the Zlydzen there, too?

"Organised? Organized? All you had to do vos get message to Jeff!" Arsenei's voice was scornful.

"Yeah, well, he vos not next door. I had to phone to Basel to find him. And hurry! And benk! Benk! Benk! All the shootink! Oy!"

"You are vinink again, Uglúk! You always complainink. Is time you better stop," warned Arsenei.

"Guys. Stop," came the voice of Heinzforth. Then, in a conciliatory tone, "Listen, Uglúk, you pack: IUPAC, the International Union of Pure and Applied Chemistry – in North Carolina are near perfecting a chemical system for enhancing degradation of methane in the permafrost..."

"Who cares from permafrost?" piped Uglúk.

"That's not the point. It will also degrade gas, even if it's trapped in rock – no more fracking. And also, in the research they've developed an organism that eats petroleum, or something, I don't really understand the science. Anyway, it reduces crude oil to an inert compound. They plan to use it to plug existing and new oil wells by turning the top layer into a sort of stopper, trapping the oil deep underground."

"But vy vould they do that?" Uglúk.

There was a silence.

"They're trying to 'save the planet', you dimwit," came Heinzforth's voice eventually.

"I know this. I mean they can have not doink all this in so few months..."

"Oh. They've been working on ways of dealing with oil spills for decades. Obviously, priorities have changed, thanks to your Little People buddies!" The CIA agent's voice was dripping with sarcasm. "So now it's up to us to sort it out. Destroying the research is how we're going to do it."

"Vot I not understandink is vy ve are in Zürich. Is not this laboratory in America?" asked Arsenei.

"I'm European Station Head, Arsenei. Of the CIA. I think someone might ask questions if I suddenly turned up in Durham, North Carolina. Or anywhere in the States, for that matter. And anyway, no one will think anything of me meeting two Little People in Europe..."

"Pygmies," interrupted Uglúk.

"...seeing as the EU was so quick to accept your people."

"That's not exactly accurate, Heinzforth," said |Xi!xu‡qe stepping from behind the wall, the Sig levelled at his chest.

Uglúk screamed, splattering a wave of green terror into the air.

Arsenei stared. "Kiku! What the hell... How, I mean..."

Heinzforth was tugging at the zip of his windcheater.

"Don't," warned |Xi!xu‡qe.

Uglúk shrieked and flung himself at the Sān, who tasted the acrid fury even before he heard the scream. The troll covered about half the distance before two 9mm rounds from the Sig slammed into his chest. A look of disbelief covered his face as he stopped and slowly fell to his knees.

But |Xi!xu‡qe didn't have time for him. Heinzforth had managed to get the zip down and was drawing massive pistol from his shoulder holster. There was no doubt that being shot with that would put paid to the little Sān.

His first round hit Heinzforth's left shoulder but the Giant hardly seemed to notice. Thanking Sig for the negligible kickback of the little weapon and the rapid aiming of the bullseye sight, |Xi!xu‡qe fired another two rounds to the left of his first. One hit the American's cheek, shattering bone. The second left a neat hole in his throat. The CIA man's weapon clattered to the floor as his hands flew to his throat.

Arsenei made to go for the fallen gun but then turned and fled through a gap in the concrete wall labelled D31. At first, he seemed to consider running down the steps onto the pitch. |Xi!xu‡qe raised his weapon. Before him was Arsenei's back. The Sān hesitated.

Not in the back.

Then the Zlydzen turned right.

As soon as he stepped through the gate, |Xi!xu‡qe saw where Arsenei was heading. Twenty metres beyond him was another exit. Beyond that was an enclosed area marked 'Restaurant'. Either choice would disadvantage |Xi!xu‡qe. Would the Zlydzen go for the exit or the restaurant?

Expecting Arsenei to duck right, he fired. The bullet ricocheted off the concrete balustrade. Instinctively, the Zlydzen ducked his head and plunged through the gate. |Xi!xu‡qe ran back through D31 and turned left.

Arsenei's head was just disappearing down the exit ramp.

Reaching the bottom of the ramp, |Xi!xu‡qe saw the Zlydzen slip through the main gate onto the road. He was heading towards the Crowne Plaza. Across the street in the tram terminus, a few shocked white faces stared from the shelters, their attention drawn by the shots in the stadium and the two Pygmies running.

Halfway to the hotel, Arsenei looked back at the Sān, 40 metres behind him. From the look on his face in the unforgiving glare of the LED light, |Xi!xu‡qe could see that the Zlydzen had realised his mistake: he was in the open. An easy target. But Arsenei couldn't know that the Sig was hopelessly inaccurate at that range.

Panicking, Arsenei swerved right, diagonally towards the side street next to where |Xi!xu‡qe had waited. If Arsenei made it to the right-hand side of the street, messy with street furniture and obstacles, he would be able to get off the open street and among the residential buildings.

He reached the créperie and plunged down the side street.

By the time |Xi!xu‡qe arrived, the other Pygmy was nowhere to be seen. |Xi!xu‡qe ran twenty metres down the street and stopped. A few metres further on was an area of open ground.

Nowhere to hide there.

Suddenly, the Sān picked up the unmistakable dot-dot-dot dash of footsteps, to his heightened senses, a yellow pulse. Light steps, judging by the colour. They floated down from the building to his left: Schlotterbeck Areal. A great barrel of a building, it was clearly being refurbished. A temporary door in the surrounding fence swung very slightly on its hinges.

Inside, |Xi!xu‡qe found himself at the base of what looked like the bottom of a huge spinning top. A ramp circled up it. There were footprints in the dust that covered the ramp. Many. He stepped forward and looked at the confusion of tracks carefully.

His father's voice came to him from long ago: 'See the differences'. One set of footprints sprang out at him: alone among the rest, their outlines were unbroken. They lay on top of the rest.

Listening carefully, he followed them. There was no hurry now, he knew. The urge to seek height was nearly always a fatal one: you could only go so high and the higher you went the fewer ways there were to get down again.

Occasionally, he caught grey-green, sour whiffs of the Zlydzen's fear. As he climbed, all the floors became either open-plan or glass-walled.

Nowhere to hide in them. A kind of bitter pity for the fleeing traitor flicked crossed his mind.

When the trail eventually issued onto the roof of the great cylinder of the building, it was fairly obvious that Arsenei's options had run out. Apart from the two central structures that housed the head of the stairwell and the lift machinery, there were five glass islands. Each looked down into the offices below. The whole area offered practically nowhere to hide. It was unlit but the light-spill from the rest of the city cast a muted glow. Besides, |Xi!xu‡qe had other senses to follow.

The roof of the oblong, south-west wing of the building was five floors below and seventy metres away.

"Arsenei! Come out. You can't hide. I can see the sound of your fear from here. There's nowhere to run."

But the Zlydzen did not answer. |Xi!xu‡qe started forward, following the high-pitched vermillion whistle of the other Pygmy's fear and panic. It got darker and more high-pitched the closer he got. It's sheer intensity filled him with disgust...and anger.

"What was that you were saying to your Troll friend, Uglúk about killing Jenny in Bern? Did you actually order that?"

"No! Yes! No, it wasn't me. Heinzforth said you would..."

"Would what, Arsenei? Follow you and destroy you if you hurt her?"

"Yes! No! I didn't want to. It was.... We are fighting a war, here, Kiku! You don't know it but the Giants will turn on us again."

"So you thought you would kill an innocent girl..."

"No!" the terror was almost inaudibly shrill now. It was beginning to change through purple into a deep blue fan that radiated from behind the grey, concrete structure to ǀXi!xuǂqe's left. He angled left, keeping it on his right, weapon side.

"The problem with people like you, Arsenei – oh, yes, and Hugh, and Locryn and Afallon – is that you confuse what is good for others with your own ambitions. You delude yourselves into believing that what they tell you is good for you must be good for everyone. And maybe it is sometimes. Maybe what you identify as being of benefit for everyone else is real, but your ambition makes you easy meat for the Heinzforths, the cynical politicians of the world. People like him, and the super-rich and the powerful who control them, see in you empty vessels who can be filled with their poisonous conspiracy theories and greed, and you accept willingly – as long as they make you think it's *your* poison."

The Sān was only metres from the low roof of the featureless structure, his senses heightened by the moment.

The Zlydzen was sobbing now, great, blue and brown, oily globs of misery and terror that lolloped, bubbles in the polluted lava lamp of his fear, then escaped to float lazily around the curved roof, dissolving into the air.

"And then when they no longer need you, they're gone. And you're left. Alone: nothing more than a traitor to the people who gave you life and fed you on the dreams of your ancestors. Can you feel your father's gods looking down on you now? Can you feel the disappointment of your mother and her ancestors, who lived their lives under the heavy yoke of Giants? Giants who have now become our friends and protectors? Does she look down and wish the world had been the garden of hope for her people that it now is for us? And what does she think of you, now?"

There was a sob that rose as a great deep note and a filthy brown globe, reeking of burning wood.

From behind the smooth curve of the grey walls, there came a shriek and the patter of running feet. |Xi!xuǂqe levelled the weapon, waiting for the Zlydzen's desperate charge.

But the sound moved away instead and then plunged suddenly into violent purple, all-enveloping cloud of damp despair that enclosed the Sān like mist.

Cautiously approaching the edge of the building, he looked over. Just visible in the gloom below him was a building site, a forest of steel rods awaiting the concrete they would reinforce. Amongst the steel was a ragged shape, jerking brokenly.

|Xi!xuǂqe watched as a black puddle spread from the figure and surrounded it.

Arsenei stopped moving.

Chapter 29 The Birds and the Bees

The light was beginning to dilute the deep blue African dawn, sending the night animals scurrying for the cover of their burrows. The bush babies that |Xi!xu‡qe and Jenny were looking for would be making for their nests in the acacias.

"We will sit by those trees. One will come. You will see," he said.

"They're thorn trees. Will it be alright?" asked Jenny.

"There is nothing to fear. Look. The tree is bare. It is too dry. If there were mambas, we would see them easily."

"Mambas! What are they?" In truth, she was only half interested to know. What she wanted was to listen to his accent, which had taken on the sway and cadence of his own language. She had noticed it the moment he had first spoken to them, in introducing her to his people. Well, not at first. At first, she had been hypnotised by the maze of clicks, trills and long, deep vowels of the language he spoke to them. One day, she hoped, she might learn to speak like that!

"The mamba is a snake. Like a cobra he has a hood. But he also lives in trees." |Xi!xu‡qe carefully scanned the branch of the tree they were about to sit under. "Very aggressive. And big!" He spread his arms as wide as they would go. "Yes, and very poisonous. The worst in Africa. If he bites you, you will die after 10 minutes."

"What! And you've only told me now!" she shrieked, jumping up and looking up into the tree.

"But he hunts on the ground. Very fast. Fast like a child running."

Jenny was in paroxysms of fear, too frantic to see the smile spreading across |Xi!xuǂqe's face.

"Jenny Miler, why would I bring you to this place, my land, and put you in danger? My home, this desert, is like your home in Toronto: there are many dangers. There, you know the dangers and how to avoid them or deal with them. Here, I know how to avoid harm. I would not bring you near harm." He touched her arm as if to assure her that she was under his protection.

She relaxed. "Of course, I know *that*," she murmured, draping his arm around her shoulders and pressing her cheek to his chest. Her mind went to the joy with which his people had greeted her. Such openness, friendship. And they weren't even his family, all of them. It was like she had been welcomed into the whole community. Different from Toronto.

There was a rustle in the tree above them. Her body stiffened.

"Look!" whispered the Bushman, "Look, Jenny. Bushbaby."

Slowly she tilted her head up. Peering down at them over a fat branch were six huge, orange-brown eyes set in three furry faces surmounted by pairs of enormous ears. The impression they gave was of utter astonishment.

"Oh! They're beautiful! So cute!" Slowly, she held her hand out towards the nearest. The eyes followed her hand with interest that changed into suspicion and, suddenly, alarm. The three heads disappeared.

"They are timid. Many animals hunt them. But they would not be here if there was danger, a mamba, about. We can sit."

As they sat, their backs to the grey-brown trunk, she rested her head on his shoulder. "This is a beautiful place. I would never have thought that a desert could be so sparse, so empty, but so beautiful."

"Ah," murmured |Xi!xu‡qe, "but it is not empty. It is full of life. In the day you can see gemsbok with their great horns, meerkats, and springbok, weaver birds in thousands, wildebeest, hyenas, leopards and warthog, steenbok, robins, falcons, grouse, vultures…. Many, many animals and, beneath our feet, insects and tubers that can be dug up and eaten. My people learned to live well in this place long before your Giant ancestors were starting to cross from Africa to become the people of Asia and Europe."

In front of them, the plain and its grasses, scrappy in the early summer, were slowly turning mauve as the horizon deepened its grey into pink, vermilion and then yellow.

Then a great orange arc of the sun broke over a low line of distant hills.

"Do you see those hills?" asked |Xi!xu‡qe, pointing. She followed his pointed finger to where a rounded outcrop rose above the plane. To its left, lay more such outcrops, looking from her perspective like a figure leaning against the larger hill. "The big one is Male Hill, the smaller ones are Female Hill and her children, then Child Hill. Those are the Tsodilo Hills, where we are going to meet my ancestors. My people have been painting their life on them for 40,000 years. Our history is there. There, we have left the offerings to the gods of that place and our families who have died in this place," he waved his free arm to indicate the wide expanse of the veld, which turned from blazing goldenrod, cadmium and chrome yellow in the distance to scarlet, carmine and maroon nearer. A silhouette detached itself from the outline of a camelthorn to become a gemsbok, the sweep of its horns a lyre against the searing yellow ball that was the risen sun.

For a time that they did not measure, the two sat motionless as the animal grazed before them.

"This is right, Kiku," whispered Jenny.

"How is it right, Jenny Miler?"

"This is a place that my mind, soul, oh, I don't know, that I *should* know. It feels like it knows me already. It feels as though I am looking into myself not out across the veld."

"Did you not say that your mother spoke of her ancestors? That they were Twa of Itenge?"

"That is what she said, I think, but I have looked it up and.... Well, it's just a story."

"Itenge," he said, "is 60 kilometres, 35 miles north of here. You are near the home of your mother's people. When we get to Tsodilo, we can look in the Female Hill where people lived 30, 000 years ago: some of them were !Kung, my people, and probably Twa from the Kavango, too: your people."

"Maybe my people knew your people!" murmured Jenny. The gemsbok looked up and moved away slowly.

ǀXi!xuǂqe smiled. "Maybe they did, Jenny. Who could ever say that they did not? But what is sure is that, when we step onto the ground of the Tsodilo, we will be at the resting place of both your ancestors and mine."

"Together again," she smiled and kissed his cheek, "after all this time."

"Maybe that is the stars talking."

Afterword

Of course, the story told in this book is fiction. As far as I know, there is no Sān called |Xi!xu⧧qe and, if there is, I apologise humbly and unreservedly. I doubt it though, since I made it up just for the sounds – and the problem it would represent for you, Reader! Nothing is simple, after all. First, I have to confess that I can make no claim to be an expert on the people I write about. But I do have a great sympathy for them.

Because the Sān, like the First Nations, are real peoples. For 40,000 years before the Bantu peoples and the Europeans arrived in Southern Africa, the many peoples who came to be known as the Sān roamed the land. The Khoi roamed the rich grasslands of the savanna with their cattle while the Sān lived off its natural bounty. Together, they learned its ways and rhythms so that they became a part of the land.

Many tribes of Sān inhabited South Africa though they are now more likely to be found in the northern parts: Namibia, Botswana, southern Angola and up into Zambia and the Democratic Republic of the Congo. They speak a large range of languages, most of which use the five clicks described in the 'Notes on pronunciation'. These languages have been divided into four main branches[i]. They are by no means all mutually intelligible. It is most likely that Jenny Miler's Twa ancestors, who were probably taken from the Congo, would not have been able to speak to |Xi!xu⧧qe's Gwi ancestors. These Peoples, harried now almost to extinction (there are estimated to be only 100,000 still

---

[i] Citation from intro to Gall. (Gall, 2001)

living[ii]), are the remnant of the birth of humankind; if the suffix 'kind' is not too cruel an irony, considering what has been done to them by *our* ancestors.

They are indeed small in stature but are fearsome hunters and their knowledge of poisons and the accuracy of their arrows and spears – which they developed primarily for hunting – earned them a reputation as warriors to be respected. Sadly, they were often forced into conflict by the depredations of various groups of migrating people.

Even though his mother and father are not both Sān, then, |Xi!xu∤qe is a child of his people who, in my fictional story, has taken his place in the world of international intrigue and espionage.

Their story is a tragic one. The genocide visited upon them – a destruction that continues to this day through the theft of their ancestral lands – is one of the great untold stories of history. To our shame. Even as you read this book, they are struggling to maintain a foothold in the few lands they still inhabit, alongside the wild animals they share it with, in places like the Kalahari National Park in Botswana.

If you want to learn more about them, Sandy Gall has described what was done to them in his book, 'The Bushmen of Southern Africa' (Gall, 2001)[10] or you could read Laurens van der Post's 'A Story Like the Wind' (Van der Post, 1972)[11]

I have borrowed from these books because my own knowledge of the Bushmen, though greater now, was so pathetically inadequate when I started writing this story. All I knew was that the world lacked a Sān hero as it lacks awareness of these wonderful Peoples. I hope I have not done any injustice to Sandy Gall's intensive research. But,

---

[ii] From Survival International.
https://www.survivalinternational.org/tribes/bushmen

most of all, I hope I have brought the Sān, the Khoekhoe and all the other Bushman Peoples to the attention of a younger, more sympathetic generation than mine has been.

On the theme

A central theme of 'The Little People and the MagDhuibhfinn Earth Worm' is that of 'othering'.

It seems that a major way of denying the rights of other groups is to emphasize their differences from us and then claim that those differences make them less worthy of our regard than those who are 'like' us. Of course, othering can be used against any species, race, group, or individual. It is as old as the hills.

It has been used – is still used – to deny the rights of Africans, Asians, Jews, the Romani people, travellers of any ilk (banded together as Gypsies for ease of discrimination), First Nations peoples of North, Central and South America, Australian Aboriginals, Māori.... Any people who were not 'white'. Of course, so were 'white' Irish people in the 17th Century (and then some) by the English. Also Welsh people in the 12th Century by the Norman invaders, as well as Cornish people by the people of Devon, Dorset, Somerset, Hampshire, Wiltshire and Sussex. Not to mention the Scots. American separatists were othered by the ruling English in the 17th Century. Then the 'rebels' of the Southern Confederacy othered the 'Yankees' of the north, who returned the favour, and they killed each other with equal fervour.

Nor is othering a new phenomenon. In Africa, the birthplace of man, othering was also birthed. Zulus under Shaka othered other Nguni peoples and drove the Ndebele and Ngoni northwards, as well as subjugating the Sotho and

Swazi peoples. They othered the Xhosa tribes, too, who in turn othered each other. All of these peoples othered the Sān hunter gatherers. The very name 'Sān' is an insult that identifies them as 'those who own nothing' or 'those who do not herd cattle'. (And how well accumulating and herding cattle have worked for the planet!) The Twa of the lakes and swamps of central Africa are thought by some to be among the ancestors of modern 'bushmen' or Sān peoples. In pre-history, it is (perhaps fancifully!) thought they migrated south from Lakes Malawi and into the desert south west of Africa to escape the othering of expanding Bantu peoples. They were comprehensively othered by Nguni of all stripes, and by the British and the Boer settlers. They were hunted for sport, enslaved and forced to conform to the cultures of others. Eventually, driven south then west and then north, they settled in the Karoo, the Kalahari, the Namib, and the Caprivi. Then they were othered by the Tswana tribes who established themselves in what is now Botswana, and they have been fighting to maintain their old relationship with the desert and its animals ever since, while authorities of one sort or another forced them to integrate, to live 'like us'.

In short, anyone can be othered and then treated as less valuable or deserving, as alien or threating…and every race probably has been.

Language

A major tool of othering is language. It both facilitates it and overrides it. In Africa, the beleaguered and much-othered ancestors of ǀXi!xuǂqe (called Bushmen – perhaps a tool of othering by implying savagery and technical backwardness) were named 'Hottentots' by the Dutch Boers, a word to emulate and mock the meaningless (to the Dutch speakers!) sounds of the Bushman's language, with its clicks.[iii]

The reduction of their language ignores the fact that the little people (they are on average 1.5 metres, or 4'6" tall) speak at least four, distinct major language branches. It also brushes over the fact that the clicks that exist in modern Nguni languages like Zulu and Xhosa are borrowed from Sān languages.

That is why, when |Xi!xu‡qe encounters the Pygmies who mockingly proclaim their inability to pronounce his name, he begins by pointing out that our languages are all different: that we are all different. Further, that dealing with difference is difficult but that ways have to be found to do it. Further still, that to make judgments about difference (including language) is an inherent act of othering and, therefore, rejection and discrimination.

However, he offers a solution: he understands that not every language is made up of the same set of sounds (called 'phonemes'). Phonemes that exist in his language may not exist in others. We must understand that the speakers of one language are bound to experience difficulty uttering phonemes that do not occur in their own language. The solution is that the speakers of any language have to make allowances for the speakers of other languages.

There are innumerable examples of his first point: think of the 'r' phoneme in Japanese being reproduced as 'l' because the English 'r' and 'l' do not really exist as separate phonemes in Japanese.

The Welsh phoneme 'll' does not exist in English. In Scots, the 'ch' in 'loch' is often realised as /k/ by English

---

[iii] As a matter of interest, the Greek word 'barbarian' uses the same, emulative technique to other the language of non-Greeks: foreigners.

people: 'lock' rather than the soft rasping at the back of the throat that produces the sound of both the first 'l' in Welsh 'll' and the 'ch' in Scots 'loch'.

The 'oo' phoneme in French, made by vigorous rounding of the lips and keeping the tongue almost flat on floor of the mouth while saying 'i', defeats English speaking learners of French because the sound only really occurs in English after the 'y' insert, as in 'beautiful'.

There are 107+ sounds represented on the International Phonetic Alphabet (the chart used to show how speech sounds are said). That is supposed to cover the sounds used in all the (known) languages of the world.

But it doesn't. For one thing, languages combine sounds to make others: the vowel in 'sound' is a combination of the 'a' in 'car' and the 'u' in 'flu', for example.

Furthermore, there are 5 consonant clicks on the IPA chart but they can be combined in many ways in different Bushman languages. One such can be said to have over 120 consonants. English has around 20, depending on accent.

All in all, Standard English spoken using Received Pronunciation (arguably a rather old-fashioned accent like educated/smart/ upper middle-class London/Oxbridge) uses about 44 phonemes in total.

So, this book is a kind of allegory. The difficult names are a touchstone. Allowing them to ignite prejudice and discrimination is wrong-minded. I have made some effort to represent the different ways of speaking English. No disrespect is meant to those speakers in this – even when the effect is comic, as it may be. Beware. In fact, I did it to try and create a sense of the complex linguistic world in which we live and how, for the most part, we simply accept it and carry on. Dealing with these differences can be difficult, though. Most of the time we find ways, or manage to curb our desire to giggle or mock.

Occasionally, however, speakers of one English (French? Arabic? Russian? Igbo?) dialect will pick on the speech of other speakers; the intention is almost always to 'other', to diminish, them.

'The Little People and the MagDhuibhfinn Earth Worm' urges you to resist that temptation.

That is the final point IXi!xuꞀqe is making when he meets the Grand Council of Pygmy Peoples. It leads to the kind of mindset that allows one group to minimize and abuse another in the same way as biased history does: would Homer have told the 'Iliad' in the same way if the Trojans had *really* been a Pygmy people? I bet he would: it's not much of a victory if you take "10,000" ships jammed with six-foot warriors to destroy a little city manned by a few thousand five-foot-tall defenders, is it?

Naming

A note on the name 'Pygmy'. The word has been used variously as standard nomenclature and profound insult at different times. I have chosen to use it because it is at least a 'neutral sounding' name for people who are not the size that we regard people as being, i.e. 'normal'. To call them 'Little People' seems insulting and othering in itself since it implies that we (who are othered as Giants in the novel) are 'ordinary' People: what people *should* be. The word 'Pygmy' seems to come from the Greek measurement from elbow to knuckles" (according to the Oxford English Dictionary) so it feels like it could carry some of the dignity that 'dwarf' (a seriously loaded word) or 'Little People' do not.

I also thought of the many re-inventions of the word 'gay' and how it has been reclaimed by Gay people from being an insulting term for 'homosexual' to a proud identifier. In the world of the novel, 'pygmy' has undergone a similar journey.

By contrast, the term used for those symbols of imperial othering, Giants, is meant as an insult. I thought of the giants in the Jack series of folktales, which, I believe are quite common in many cultures. In particular, the giant in Jack and the Beanstalk is particularly wicked – and savage: "...I smell the blood of an Englishman' he says in the English version, threatening to "grind his bones to make my bread"! Others that spring to mind are Polyphemus and Goliath. Giants have been objects of derision, too: in Jack the Giant Killer, they foolishly attack each other at the slightest provocation! But giants have been reclaimed. Roald Dahl's 'BFG' is an example. Female giants seem much more amenable: the wife of the giant in 'Jack and the Beanstalk', is often represented as gentler: she hides him from her husband in some versions. As in Western culture, though, powerful giantesses are often simply written out of stories. I have tried to reinstate them through Jemima Blond and Lady Ward-Back!

Names

Obviously, I had enormous fun thinking up the names for my cast of characters. Equally obviously, most people (and certainly English speakers like me) will have difficulty pronouncing them.

Don't bother. Suit yourself or just bleep over them. If you are reading the story aloud to others, make something up.

- The title is explained on the first page. A note on 'McGuffin': a McGuffin is a device in a film or book that is used merely as a driving force for the plot. Everyone wants it, or to destroy it, or stop others from getting it but it is not the real story itself. It is the actions of the characters in pursuing it that makes the story. I believe it was coined by Alfred Hitchcock.

- ǀXi!xuǂqe: the spelling is phonetic, from the IPA. I invented this name specifically for its impossible appearance. I advise sticking to 'Kiku'. But, for the intrepid, there is a guide in the Notes, below.

- !Kung: the '!' represents a click – the same as the second in ǀXi!xuǂqe but followed by a little purr made with the tongue at the back of the mouth (like 'ch' in 'loch'). It is very difficult; you are doing well if you get the click.

- There is a website that will be of help at (https://www.internationalphoneticalphabet.org/ipa-charts/ipa-symbols-chart-complete/)

- Magnus Kleynmans: 'kleyn' is pronounced /claine/. It is a variant of the word 'klein', which means 'small' in Afrikaans. The 'a' in 'mans' is like the 'u' in 'up' and the 's' unvoiced, as in 'so'. I leave the joke to you.

- Balthazar Bartholomeus Bootha: the surname, as 'Botha', is quite a common Afrikaans one. The Christian names are taken from the Old Testament.

This is how the other names are said, or sound in my mind:

- Afallon: in Welsh, the 'll' is said /chl/ where the /ch/ is the sound in the Scots word 'loch', made as though clearing the back of the throat. The single 'f' is /v/ so: /avachlon/
- Mrs Donoghue: /donner-hew/
- Eoin MacBhreithiún: Irish orthography (how sounds are written down) is different from English. He is Owen /macbrown/, basically.
- Heorhiy: both 'h's sound like the /ch/ in the Welsh /ll/ above, though less vigorously pronounced. The middle vowels are separate: /chi-orchi/
- Ka'akupe: /kuh-uh-koo-pi/
- Marjatta: the 'j' is pronounced 'i-y' – Mari-yutta
- Нарбут is Cyryllic: 'Narbut', pronounced with a short /a/ and rolled /r/. The /u/ is short as in 'put'
- Padraig ÓCléirigh: /paw-rik o-clairy/
- Piyêsîs: /pie-ee-sis/
- Pyhare: /pea-har-i/
- Thebault: /teb-bolt/
- Sequoyah Wuttunee: /sek-wee-uh woo-tun-ee/

I enjoyed finding names that actually relate to the areas, peoples and languages in the book. I enjoyed building jokes into them even more.

It should be noted that the names and languages are those of the Giants local to each Pygmy culture. I don't know whether the Pygmy peoples originally had their own languages. Or, beyond the click in Nguni languages, whether the Giant languages were influenced or even taken from original Pygmy languages. Probably both, if the history of modern creoles is anything to go by. Unfortunately, such knowledge is lost in the mists of time.

I used some baby naming websites for names. If you like, you can look them up to see what they mean.

Bibliography and Textual Notes

I have used many Wikipedia links, in thanks for which I make a monthly donation to the platform. Here are some that may be interesting.

https://en.wikipedia.org/wiki/San_people
https://en.wikipedia.org/wiki/Domovoy
https://en.wikipedia.org/wiki/Nisse_(folklore)
https://en.wikipedia.org/wiki/Twa
https://en.wikipedia.org/wiki/Little_People_of_the_Pryor_Mountains
https://en.wikipedia.org/wiki/Iroquois
https://en.wikipedia.org/wiki/Cherokee_language
https://en.wikipedia.org/wiki/Languages_constructed_by_J._R._R._Tolkien

I am also grateful for the information provided by the other sites I have referenced or found information on, including the sites of commercial organisations such as Billings Logan International Airport, St Ermin's Hotel in London, websites dedicated to mythology and various manufacturers. I hope that these references are viewed as helpful signposting since there is no sense in which I seek to profit from them, per se.

Notes on the text

---

[1] This link offers IPA (International Phonetic Alphabet) renditions of the sounds in |Xi!xu‡qe's name but it is worth noting that the clicks change in different San languages and depending on other sounds they occur with. Obviously, his name would not be written in IPA symbols. I've used them to skip a step.

Here is a table of the clicks I have used.

	Laminal		Apical	
	dental	palatal	alveolar	lateral
Symbol	ǀ	ǂ	!	‖

Complicated as they may seem, the main difficulty with them is that we are unaccustomed to them. They are all made by sucking air in, for one thing, which we don't do in any English sounds, really. The first {ǀX} is made by sucking the tip of the tongue against the back of the top incisors, then pulling away suddenly. The second {!x} is made by sucking the middle of the tip of your tongue up against the ridges just behind your top, front teeth and releasing the suction quickly. The third is made by sucking the middle of your tongue against the roof of your mouth and then releasing the suction quickly. I haven't used the fourth.

If you are interested in a more complete table, try http://www.phonetics.ucla.edu/course/chapter1/clicks.html.

If you want to hear the sounds, you can type the symbols below into a web browser to download a sound file. Please note that the site is the property of Jenny Ladefoged: (http://www.phonetics.ucla.edu/index.html.)

I have relied on Peter Ladefoged's work out of loyalty: his 'A Course in Phonetics' was my first coursebook in the subject, so ǀXi!xuǂqe owes him a debt of gratitude, too!

The above table is simplified from Wikipedia.

[2] **Kaggen** is a shape shifting god who is a major creator in the San universe. His name means 'praying mantis' but he is many things. ǀXi!xuǂqe is not religious, per se, but he seems to like the mythological character Pisamboro, who is an equivalent of the Greek Prometheus. For more about the belief system of the Kalahari San people, go to www.krugerpark.co.za>Nature Guide>History & Culture>African Culture>San

[3] https://www.kellyinnbillings.com/ to see the Kelly Inn Hotel, chapter 11.

[4] https://whc.unesco.org/en/list/1021/ for information about Tsodilo Hills. Also https://africanrockart.britishmuseum.org/country/botswana/tsodilo/

[5] Rademaker, Laura, et al. "The Amazing Archive of First Nations Stories Written on Stone." *SAPIENS*, The Pathway Project, 22 Apr. 2022, https://www.sapiens.org/archaeology/first-nations-rock-art-archive/?utm_source=SAPIENS.org%2BSubscribers&utm_campaign=dc0a1e1575-EMAIL_CAMPAIGN_2022_7_21_COPY_03&utm_medium=email&utm_term=0_18b7e41cd8-dc0a1e1575-227468792&ct=t%28%29.

[6] From www.native-languages.org. See also: https://edmondlifeandleisure.com/the-cherokee-legend-of-the-little-people-p10901-76.htm

[7] https://www.britannica.com/topic/Cherokee-language

[8] The Trauco are children of the snake god Coi Coi-Vilu. They are able to attract young and middle-aged women. https://en.wikipedia.org/wiki/Trauco

[9] Máel Sechnaill mac Domnaill was High King of Ireland in the 10th Century. https://en.wikipedia.org/wiki/M%C3%A1el_Sechnaill_mac_Domnaill

[10] Gall, S., 2001. The Bushmen of Southern Africa. London: Pimlico.

[11] Van der Post, L., *A Story like the Wind*. 1972 ed. first published by: William Morrow.

Printed in Great Britain
by Amazon

23380136R00163